FINDING FINLEY

by
RILEY HART

Copyright © 2020 by Riley Hart
Print Edition

All rights reserved.

No part of this book may be used, reproduced or transmitted in any form or by any means, electronic or mechanical, including photocopying, recording, or by any information storage and retrieval systems, without prior written permission of the author, except where permitted by law.

Published by:
Riley Hart

This book is a work of fiction. Names, characters, places and incidents are products of the author's imagination or are used fictitiously. Any similarity to actual persons, living or dead is coincidental and not intended by the author.

All products/brand names/Trademarks mentioned are registered trademarks of their respective holders/companies.

Cover Design by Sleepy Fox Studios
Cover Photography by Carlton www.bycarlton.de
Edited by Keren Reed Editing
Proofread by Judy's Proofreading and One Love Editing

FINLEY

I may be young, but I know what I want.

I yearn to be submissive, both in and out of the bedroom. There's nothing I crave more than being under the control of another man. Handing over power would fulfill a need I feel down to the marrow of my bones.

What I don't know is how to get it. This kind of relationship requires complete trust—something I don't give to anyone except my only friend.

Then along comes Dr. Aidan Kingsley. For the third time in my life, he helps me, without even knowing it, and someone like that, I can't help but believe in. This is the man I'm meant to be on my knees for. Aidan is meant to be my *Sir*.

AIDAN

I've never had a full-time submissive.

I've certainly never had a houseboy, but when I meet Finley, I can't seem to turn him away.

Instead, I decide to keep things simple, showing Finley that he can take pride on his knees but also stand on his own. He takes care of my home, and he gives me control, in a strictly platonic way, even though he wants more. He's so beautiful, so naturally submissive, that I'm having a hard time sticking to my rules.

The more he flourishes and the more he craves from me, the tougher I find it to deny him. Before I know it, he's under my skin. In my bed and in my heart. It wasn't supposed to go this far. I was only supposed to give him the tools he needed to find his own strength, yet somehow, in the finding of Finley, I found myself too.

But my precious boy is only twenty; nineteen years my junior. And as I've told him, forever is a long time, and nothing in life is guaranteed.

Warning: Finding Finley contains various kinks, BDSM elements, domestic discipline and a nineteen-year age gap. Please take that into consideration before deciding if this book is for you.

Finding Finley is part of the Desires Unleashed collection—which is not a series, but a line of books with similar themes. Please be aware Desires Unleashed are not your typical Riley Hart romance. You can expect the mental and emotional journey to be led by the physical/s*xual moments—which will be intense, frequent, and kinky.

Special thanks to Kate Hawthorne.

PROLOGUE

Finley

"I'M TEN YEARS old. I should be able to stay at home by myself." I loved my mom but hated that sometimes she treated me like I was a baby. I was the man of the house. It was just her and me, and it always had been. There was no reason I couldn't take care of myself and the apartment.

"Not overnight, Finley."

"But, Mom—" *Boom. Boom. Boom.* I was interrupted by banging sounds from the party in the apartment above ours. Mom worked the graveyard shift at a local hospital. She was in housekeeping, which meant she had to clean up all the gross stuff all the time. She said she was thankful for the job, that it was a good one and I should appreciate it too, but all I knew was she was always tired, had to stay up all night, and that she worried about me. She even made a babysitter stay with me, but Karen had called at the last minute to say she was sick.

She sighed and pinched the bridge of her nose. "I don't know what to do. God, I don't know what to do. Why does everything have to be so hard?" Mom paced the small living room. It was super clean. Mom always said we might not live in the best places, but she'd damn sure make them a home.

She didn't have to keep speaking—I knew what she was thinking. There was a break-in three apartments down from us two weeks ago. Mom was worried about me. Mom was always worried about me. It was my fault she was alone and lost her family, which made guilt weigh down my bones, so I said, "I'll go get my stuff." I wasn't going to make this harder on her.

We came up with a plan. I was going to stay in the ER waiting room. She packed me snacks, a blanket, books, and a Game Boy she'd saved to buy. If anyone asked, I was supposed to say I was waiting for my mom, who was in with the doctor, but she hoped no one would notice. This was LA, and the waiting rooms were always crazy-busy.

I sat there for hours. I was bored and sleepy, but the lady sitting beside me kept saying she had bugs under her skin and sort of freaking out. I didn't want bugs under my skin, so I grabbed my stuff and left. I wasn't supposed to go out of the waiting room, but I'd be good, quiet. I'd still look like a patient waiting.

I wandered around the hallways a bit. They kept the doors locked to the main side of the hospital, so I couldn't go far. My eyes were getting heavy and scratchy, but I didn't want to go back and risk getting bugs under my skin.

There was this part of the hallway that dipped in, like someone had cut a rectangle out of the wall from floor to ceiling. I sat down on the ground in it and leaned my head against the wall, blanket over my legs, and played my game for a bit.

The next thing I knew, there was a hand on my shoulder. "Hey…are you okay?"

My eyes jerked open to see a guy kneeling beside me. He had on a white jacket that said *Dr. Kingsley* on it. He had black hair and big brown eyes, and he smiled at me. A nice kind of smile that made me feel like maybe he was a nice guy. Still, I froze. The story Mom had told me was there, sitting on my tongue, but I couldn't make the words leave my mouth.

"Are your parents here? Are you sick?" Dr. Kingsley asked.

My stupid words still wouldn't come out, and I just kept looking at him.

"Finley…oh my God. I was looking for you!" Mom pushed between me and the doctor and wrapped her arms around me. He stood, looking at us, at Mom in her uniform as I watched him over her shoulder. "Don't ever do that again. I thought I lost you. I don't know what I would do if I lost you!"

She was squeezing me so tight, I could hardly breathe. Then I felt her go stiff, like she just realized what had happened. She let go of me and turned to the doctor. "I'm sorry. Please…my sitter didn't show up, and I couldn't call in at the last moment. I need this job, and I didn't know what to do. He won't cause any problems, I promise."

He frowned. "You brought your son to work with you?"

"I don't…I don't have anyone, and I couldn't afford to miss. I know that's not your problem—it's mine. But I'm a great worker. I've never missed a day, and—"

"What's going on here?" Another doctor approached. He was older, with gray hair, and his smile wasn't as nice as Dr. Kingsley's.

"I…" Mom started and then dropped her head.

Stupid. I'd been so stupid. She was gonna get in trouble, and it was all my fault.

"Nothing," Dr. Kingsley said. "This little boy is here

with his aunt. They're waiting for his mom in the ER, and the housekeeper was just going to take him back to his family now."

Oh God. He'd lied...for us. He'd saved Mom her job, so we wouldn't have to move again and she wouldn't cry every night, trying to figure out what we were gonna do.

"Thank you for the help," Dr. Kingsley told Mom.

"No problem. I... Thank *you*," Mom said. She ushered me away, but I couldn't help looking over my shoulder at Dr. Kingsley as we went.

I HATED EVERYTHING.

I hated this stupid city and my stupid grandparents for not letting Mom live with them because she had me.

I hated school and teachers, who either looked at me like I was nothing or with nothing but pity in their eyes.

I hated social workers and foster families and Mom...I hated her for dying. For leaving me alone.

And missed her. I missed her so much, I couldn't breathe. So much that sometimes I wished I'd had a massive heart attack and died too. She was young, everyone said...so young, but I guess they'd never had a broken heart before. Age didn't matter. I knew that was what killed her—a broken heart and exhaustion, for being on her own for fourteen years with me.

Anger ripped through me, mixing my sadness with fury.

I didn't care, not about anything, and I never would. Not after losing her.

Eventually, I found myself in a grocery store. Was it weird that I didn't even know how I'd gotten there? I'd run away from the foster family. They weren't my family. I'd never have family. I didn't need them or anyone else.

I walked up and down the aisles, ending up in one full of candy. I had no idea what made me do it—maybe because I hated the world, or was angry I had no money, or what—but I grabbed a candy bar.

A tall guy with dark hair stood about ten feet away from me but didn't appear to be paying me any attention. My eyes found him, then looked the other way as I slipped the candy bar into my pocket.

"I wouldn't do that if I were you," the guy said.

"Fuck you," I gritted out, then felt itchy and weird. I lowered my eyes. "I'm sorry." I had no idea where *that* had come from.

"Are you hungry?"

"Yes," I replied, and suddenly I was embarrassed of my jeans with the holes in them and the dirt on my hands.

"Look at me," he said, and when I did, a gasp tore out of my throat and I stumbled backward. It was *him*, the doctor who'd saved Mom's job four years ago. My eyes filled with tears, and I hated those too. What the hell did crying do? It didn't help jack shit.

A worker came down the aisle, straightening product. I started to shake and wiped at the tears in my eyes, wondering if I was spreading dirt around.

"Can I help you guys find anything?" she asked with a smile, but I couldn't look at her because I had a candy bar in my pocket. I was a *thief*, and that made me hate myself because I didn't want to be a thief.

He should turn me in. Dr. Kingsley should tell her what I did because I deserved to get into trouble for it. I wanted him to say it, but he didn't. He told her we were fine, and when she walked away, he said, "Give me the candy bar."

My hands were still shaking when I handed it over.

"Come with me," he said, and I followed him to the deli. He didn't say anything as he ordered three sandwiches with three bags of chips, three apples, and bottles of water. He set the candy bar down and paid for it along with the rest of the food. They put it in a bag, and I followed him out of the store on shaky legs.

"Are you alone?" he asked.

"My mom's dead," I snapped.

His eyes softened, and something…I didn't know what it was…passed over them. He handed me the bag of food.

"Eat one of those sandwiches while I call someone, okay? You shouldn't be out here alone."

The second he pulled out his phone, I ran, ran as fast as my legs would carry me. Ran until I couldn't breathe. Ran until I was crying so hard, I couldn't see.

He had saved me…again.

And I wanted to go back to him. Wanted to tell him I was scared and didn't know what to do. It was lame and made no sense, but that was how I felt.

I also knew I didn't ever want him to look at me with the disappointment he had when he saw me stealing.

"Stupid," I told myself. Stupid, stupid, stupid. It wasn't as if I'd ever see Dr. Kingsley again.

But still, when they found me, when they brought me to a new foster family, and for every home I was in after that, I never forgot him.

CHAPTER ONE

Finley

Five Years Later
March

MY LAPTOP WAS old and took forever to load sites, but I was out of data on my phone, so I didn't have much choice. And I couldn't just close the website and walk away. I mean, I *could*, but I didn't want to. I never wanted to because it was the only access I had to what I wanted so badly. What I needed. What I'd longed for even before I'd understood it—hell, even now I didn't understand it. Not fully.

Why did I crave the things I did?

Why did I long to be on my knees?

What made me want to serve?

To have someone take care of me and protect me and to give those things in return?

The why of it didn't matter to me, though. I just knew it was…me. Knew it like I knew my name or that the sky was blue or that my mother had been the best person I'd ever known.

What I didn't know was how to get it. Not really.

I rolled over on the futon in my less than stellar studio apartment. It was also my bed and the couch. Against the other wall was a second one, belonging to Ian. We'd met in a foster home. He was my first kiss, my first jack-off session. My roommate and my very best friend.

We'd hit it off right away, like somehow we'd known we needed each other, and we'd taken care of each other. Our foster parents had been…I don't know that *abusive* was the right word, but they hadn't really wanted anything to do with us. We were free money, and they were better than most I'd been with. But when they caught Ian and me kissing, things had gone downhill fast, and we'd gotten out of there.

The web page was almost done loading, and I lay there, my pulse ticking faster with each second that went by—adrenaline and desire, excitement and curiosity, and the deep-seated hunger sewn into my DNA, amping up more and more until I was dizzy from it.

My head spun, which was ridiculous because I was lying down and I hadn't even done anything. All I was doing was waiting for porn to load like I'd done a thousand times before—only to get the slightest taste of what I thirsted for. But in a way that wasn't real, never real because I'd never had it. I didn't know if I ever would.

Finally, the screen came alive. A dark-haired boy, naked except for an apron, was carrying a plate toward a table where a man in a suit sat.

I'd seen this scene too many times to count, so when he set the plate on the table and said, "I made your favorite," I repeated the line along with him. And when the boy's Master told him, "Get yours and join me," I said, "Yes, sir," just as he did.

It went quickly from there. They ate together, and I grabbed my lube. Turning onto my side, I wet my fingers and waited, anticipation clawing at my insides. My cock ached, my balls tight. My hole felt empty, always empty, even though there had never been anything there other than my fingers. I could have used a dildo, but I didn't want that. I wanted the real thing, and that was always my problem because to have the very air that filled my lungs, to have these things I yearned for, I needed to trust. I couldn't give myself to anyone without trust. It was how I was built, another part of my genetic makeup I had no control over.

But I didn't trust. Not anyone. Not anyone who could give me *that*, at least. There was Ian, but even though he never gave a shit about these things I wanted, he didn't get it. He wasn't the same as me.

My eyes were riveted on the screen as they finished eating together, as the man pushed his plate away, then beckoned the boy over, who I so wished were me.

He removed his apron and went to his knees. He sucked his Master off as I worked a finger inside myself and jerked my cock with the other.

I cried out and came all over my hand when he was fed a load, my mouth watering for the same sustenance. I watched longingly as he stayed there afterward, nursing his Master's soft cock, his head on his thigh and the Master's hand gently rubbing his head. I rested my head similarly on the pillow, my cheek against the soft fabric I wished were warm skin.

And then…then I cried.

⁂

A COUPLE OF hours later, Ian came home from his job at the grocery store. I was sitting on my futon, dressed in a pair of jeans and a T-shirt. "I'm doing it," I told him. "People do this shit all the time without really knowing someone."

He sighed because we'd been through this before, but

this time I was different. God, I *ached* with need, felt detached from the world and my life. Like I wasn't solid. Like I wasn't real without it.

"Fin…" he said softly.

"I'm seriously gonna do it this time. I found a guy online." He wasn't the first guy I'd found, but he would be the first one I really went through with. How could I not? How could I keep running away from something I longed for so much?

"Where are you meeting him? The last guy wanted you to go to a club, but you're not old enough."

Being nineteen sucked. Lots of places were twenty-one and over. "His house."

Another sigh from Ian, then a sad, pitying smile. "Let me get changed, and I'll go with you. Same plan as always. I wait outside. You tell him you have to text me every few minutes to make sure you're okay. If you don't, I knock. If you don't answer, I call the police."

"What if he doesn't let me text?" We'd made this plan a thousand times, but I never asked that question because I thought a part of me knew I would never go through with it. This time, I *was*.

"If he's a real Dom…or Daddy or Master or Sir, whatever he is, he'll let you because it's your rule and will keep you safe."

I nodded. He was right; of course he was.

My leg bounced up and down as Ian grabbed clothes from the dresser we shared. We were comfortable around each other, so he changed right there.

We were quiet as we took the bus toward Silver Lake. From our stop, we walked. My heart was thudding against my chest, making it hurt. My hands fisted as my need to stay warred with my desire to run. I didn't understand it, how I could know I needed something to the marrow of my bones yet be too afraid to do what I needed to get it.

By the time we walked up to the house, everything looked fuzzy and I couldn't breathe. Ian wrapped his arms around me, and I let him.

"God, what's wrong with me? Why can't I do this?"

"Because you don't know him. Maybe because this is yours, so real and personal that it's like cutting your heart open, and you can't do that with just anyone. There's no shame in it, Fin."

"Other people do it with strangers. They do it all the time."

He shrugged. "They're not you."

For a moment, I hated myself. Wished I could be someone else. Not someone who didn't want these things, because I would never wish that, but someone who could give himself easily. But Ian was right. That wasn't me. "I'm sorry."

"Don't be." He twined his fingers with mine. "Let's go home."

CHAPTER TWO

Aidan

"WHY DO I put up with you? You're worthless! You can't do anything right, and you're raising Aidan to be weak just like you!"

My eyes jerked open at the familiar sound of my father's voice in my head—the things he'd said to my mother over and over my whole life, things he ended up saying to me.

Despite being on call earlier this week, I couldn't sleep. Between my scheduled patients, rounds in the ICU, and the trauma surgery after someone fell from a building, my brain had been buzzing. Some weeks were easier to come down from than others. Sleep was easier to find some days than others as well. This wasn't one of the good ones.

Giving up, I rolled out of bed, went to the sliding glass balcony door, and stepped out. The sun was just beginning to rise, peeking over the greenery that was so foreign in some areas of Los Angeles but more abundant in Laurel Canyon.

Bare-chested, in pajama bottoms, I sat on one of the chairs and watched the oranges and yellows rise until there was nothing but the sun there. It was hard sometimes, stepping away from the pain and death and traumas and returning to my life. To think that sometimes you could see the sun wake up and not know it was your last time. But I knew all too well about that, didn't I? I'd seen it too many times to count.

With a sigh, I rose and went back inside. I went downstairs and drank the one cup of coffee I allowed myself per morning. Afterward, I slipped into socks and running shoes and went to my home gym. My muscles ached and sweat stung my eyes as I pushed through a long workout.

Then I showered, dressed…wished I were in bed. There really was no point—I knew I wouldn't be able to fall asleep—and thankfully, I had the next few days off. I was only on call as a trauma surgeon six days a month, but those days were both brutal and needed. Strangely, they centered me, made me feel more human and gave me a connection to others, however brief, that I so rarely felt otherwise.

Even though I didn't need to, I went in to the hospital and did some paperwork. Before I knew it, the day had passed, and I sat back in my chair and groaned, knowing I still had to meet with David that night.

But I knew I would go because I had given my word, and when I said I would do something, I always did. I hated lies and people who spun them.

I guess there was also the fact that he was my friend.

I went home and changed into black slacks and a button-up shirt, then made the drive to a restaurant he wanted to try in downtown LA.

"Good evening, sir," the valet said when I pulled up in front of the building and got out.

I had to admit, the honorific sent a shiver down my spine. It had been too long since I'd played with anyone, and I was in desperate need of the kind of relief it brought me. It was likely why I was so edgy and had trouble sleeping.

"Good evening," I replied as he took the keys.

When I stepped into the restaurant, I saw David's dark hair at a round table in the corner. The lighting was dim, candles at each table. It was a bit pretentious for me, but I'd indulge him.

"Can I help you, sir?" the hostess asked.

"I see my party, thank you."

She smiled as I made my way toward David, who

rose to hug me. "You look tired."

"You know that's a way of telling someone they look like shit, right?"

David smiled, and we sat. "Would you rather I blow smoke up your ass?" he asked, and no, I wouldn't.

"Long week at work. That's all. How are you?"

"Fine. Hungry. You're late. That's not like you."

I frowned. "Five minutes."

"Still not like you."

He was right, but I shook him off. David and I met in med school, and we'd played together a few times over the years. He was primarily a Dom, but he very rarely switched for the right man. Apparently, that had been me, though we hadn't had a scene in a few years. David was easy in that I knew he would never want more from me, because I couldn't give him what he truly desired, which was submission.

"Good evening. Can I get you…" The waiter's voice trailed off, and I looked up at him. He was young, eighteen or so, and had these expressive blue eyes that were wide and intense as they held on to mine. He looked slightly pale, his brow peppered with sweat, but even though he was looking at me as if he'd seen a ghost, I didn't think that was what made him stare at me the way he did. "A, um…drink. Would you like a drink?"

He had this sort of button nose. His hair was blond, his jaw cut like a model, though he still had a baby face. He was…gorgeous. Very young, but gorgeous. "A glass of pinot noir, please," I replied but didn't turn away. I watched him, waited for his eyes to leave mine first, but they didn't. He just stood there as though he didn't know what to do, his plump lips parted slightly, and if we were in a different situation, I would wonder what it would be like to push my cock between them. To fuck his throat until tears ran from his eyes, then hold him and soothe him the only way I knew how.

"The same for me, please," David said, which seemed to snap—my eyes darted to his name tag—*Finley*—from his trance.

"Yes…yes, I'll be right back." And he scurried away.

"Jesus, what in the hell was that? Have you fucked him?" David asked, and I rolled my eyes.

"No. I would remember him."

"He's beautiful."

"Young," I added.

"But legal. He has to be eighteen if he's serving alcohol."

"Christ, David. Also, he looked like he might be ill."

"He looked at you like he wanted to jump your bones. And I hope he isn't sick. He shouldn't be here if he is."

He was right, of course, but that wasn't my concern. Worry worked its way through my veins. Did he have no one to care for him? It wouldn't be the first thought of most people. He was an adult, so he should be able to care for himself, and likely could. Yet that familiar instinct rose to the surface, to protect and cherish...after some delicious torture, of course. I wanted to fix and control the things I could. But really, how could I control a random boy at a restaurant?

Finley returned then with our wine. He didn't look at me as he set our glasses down, but his hands shook. I watched the liquid ripple as he pulled away. "Are you okay?" I asked, and his eyes snapped to mine, full of liquid silver.

"I...yes. Have you decided what you would like?"

I hadn't even looked at the menu. A quick glance at David told me he was ready, so I nodded at him before returning my eyes to the boy. His hand shook as he wrote what David rambled off, words I tuned out, instead watching the waiter.

When his eyes found me again, I held his stare. Watching. Waiting. And yes, he did look at me as though he knew me, but I couldn't for the life of me figure out where from. The hospital, maybe? But then, why look at me the way he did? I knew I hadn't played with him. I didn't typically scene with men as young as him.

"I'll have what he's having," I told Finley, even though I wasn't sure what it was David had ordered.

"Yes, okay. It will be out soon." Then he was gone again.

David and I spoke, but my mind stayed on the boy. He looked paler when he returned to bring us seared salmon, asparagus, and rice. He was still shaking, making me reach out in a way I shouldn't and touch his arm. "I think maybe you should sit down."

"I can't." He shook his head. "What? No."

But then our eyes met again, and I knew...*knew* he wanted to do as I said, that he longed for it, not just because he didn't feel well, but because I'd told him to. "Finley."

"I..." he began, then turned quickly. Multiple things happened at once—his hand caught my wineglass, spilling it; he stepped forward, running into another waiter and making him drop his plates, which clattered loudly to the floor. Somehow, along the way, Finley had tumbled down too.

I shot to my feet, not because of the wine dripping onto my lap, but to reach for him. He scrambled backward as though afraid of me, making me frown. I held my hands up to show I wasn't going to touch him.

"Finley! What are you doing?" Another man rushed forward, very obviously the manager. "Sir, I apologize for this. He's new and—"

"It's fine," I said without turning from Finley. "It's fine," I repeated.

"I..." he began, then shook his head, shoved to his feet, and ran for the kitchen.

"Please accept my apology," the manager told me. "We'll get you a new table, and your meal will be on the house, of course."

"We'll pay," I told him. "It was an accident."

From the heat in his face, I had a feeling this wasn't Finley's only accident.

The second waiter was cleaning up the mess, and the manager began speaking to David, who I knew would also assure him everything was okay. I couldn't keep my eyes from the kitchen, though. Was he okay? And why in the hell had he reacted to me the way he had?

When I felt a hand on my shoulder, I looked at David and realized the manager had gone. "What was that?"

"I don't know," I replied.

"I was going to ask you if you wanted to fuck me tonight. You look like you need it, but I have a feeling that's not going to happen, is it?"

I shook my head. No, it wasn't.

They changed our table, but I couldn't eat. It wasn't long before David said, "I haven't seen that waiter again."

No, I hadn't either. We likely wouldn't. "I can't... My head isn't in this. I'll get dinner, but I need to go."

David shook his head. "I'm eating my salmon. You know how rarely I'm willing to submit, and if I'm not going to get that, I at least want to have my dinner. You go. I'll get it this time."

I gave him a simple nod and went outside. My pants were still wet from the spilled wine, and the light ghost of a wind twisting around me sent chills running through me. I scanned the lot, wondering if Finley was there. He'd likely lost his job tonight. I'd seen it in the way the manager had looked at him.

I walked around the building but didn't see him. There was no way to find him, and really, it wasn't my business anyway. I sent David a text to let me know if he saw Finley again.

A couple of minutes later, the valet brought me my car. I'd made it halfway up the block, when I saw a small body kneeling beside the bench at a bus stop. Jerking my BMW to the side of the road, ignoring the honks as I did so, I parked at a red curb and jumped out.

His eyes snapped up to me, and the moment they did, I saw he'd been vomiting.

"Oh God, it's you again. What are you doing?" He pushed to his feet but then swayed slightly, grabbing on to the bench.

"You're sick. I knew you were." He hadn't hid it well and had no business being at work at all.

"I'm fine." Finley tried to take a step and swayed again. I reached out, held on to him, and touched his forehead.

"You're burning up."

"I'm *fine.*"

"You're not. Come."

He took a step with me…just that simply. As though obeying me was as easy as breathing, and I had to bite back a groan. Now wasn't the time for that.

Then he stopped, defiant, and oh, if he were mine, how I would have loved to punish him.

"I said I'm fine."

"No, you're not. Is there anyone to take care of you? Your mom—"

"Dead." His whole body tensed with a pain so sharp, I felt it.

Fighting to ignore the thoughts threatening to pull

me under, I added, "Anyone else?"

"I'm a grown-ass man. I don't need anyone to take care of me!"

My hand twitched with the need to put him in his place. "Other family? Siblings? Boyfriend?"

"Maybe I have a girlfriend," he said, and I cocked a brow at him. A touch of pink flooded his cheeks. That's what I thought.

"Finley…who can take care of you?"

"I…I have a roommate. He's working tonight." I let him go, but he was still unsteady.

"Let's go."

"No. I'm not going to the doctor. That shit's expensive. I can get myself home, thank you very much." He took a step…and went down. I was close enough to catch him before he fell.

I wrapped my arms around his small, too thin body, lifted him, and just stood there a second, unsure what to do with this precious boy.

Then I walked to my car, managed to get the door open, and set him in the passenger seat.

CHAPTER THREE

Finley

OH GOD. WHAT was wrong with me? I was pretty sure I was dying. I'd felt worse the longer the day had gone on but knew I had to go to work. I was already on thin ice because…well, because I was a shitty waiter. But I needed the money, so I went in, and with each second ticking by, I got sicker and sicker.

And now…now I was vaguely aware that I was with *him*, the steady motion of a car around me. How in the hell had this even happened? Out of all the people in Los Angeles, Dr. Kingsley had found and saved me twice, and now I was in a vehicle with him, fading in and out of consciousness.

He had lifted me…I remembered that. Held me. And now he was taking me who in the fuck knew where. "No hospitals…please…" I couldn't afford that, and frankly, they reminded me of my mom, of watching her work her ass off all her life and then watching her die there too.

I shouldn't have been going with him. I knew that. Regardless of how he'd helped me in the past, I didn't know this man. It wasn't safe...yet he felt safe. He felt familiar, and I was tired, so damn tired. I let myself be pulled under, lulled by the movement of the car and the scent of...the ocean twined with some kind of dark musk.

※

I WAS WARM...SO warm...nothing but softness around me. It felt like I was lying in the clouds...or maybe in my mom's arms. She had been so soft. I'd loved it when she'd held me.

My eyes fluttered, and the moment they did, nausea hit me, powerful and overwhelming. I turned to the side just as it surged up my esophagus and through my lips.

There was a trash can there...someone holding it for me...a strong hand rubbing my back.

"It's okay, boy. You're going to be okay. I've got you."

Calm washed through me, soothing. I felt it...like someone was taking care of me...then my world went black again.

THE NEXT TIME I woke up, I jolted to a sitting position. My head...fuck, that hurt. Oh God, I had gone home with someone I didn't know. My first thought was Ian. How long had I been there, and did my friend know?

My body was sluggish as I tried to climb out of the clouds...no, a bed. I was in a bed.

"I don't think so. You're not going anywhere." Despite my misgivings, I felt my lips pull into a smile. But then I remembered he wasn't who I wanted him to be, that I didn't belong to him, not really, and he wouldn't want me. I was only there because he didn't know what to do with me.

"I'm fine."

"Finley." Dr. Kingsley put his finger beneath my chin and tilted my head up. "Lie down."

Jesus, I was doing it—that simply, I was doing what he said. I *wanted* to do what he said, and I didn't want to leave.

"That's very good," he said. "Your fever isn't as high as it was, but you're still running a low grade. It's been a while since you vomited too, but you're nowhere near ready to leave yet."

My head shook...a no. Was I doing that? I must be,

otherwise it wouldn't have happened. "My friend…he'll be worried."

"Ian?" he asked, and that made my heavy eyes snap open again.

"How do you know his name?" Shit. He'd known mine too. "How do you know my name?"

"You were wearing a name tag. Ian was calling, and I answered. He was very worried about you. He's a good friend. You should have good people like that around you. He was determined to call the police on me, but I managed to prove to him you're okay."

I had no idea how long I'd been there. Hell, I didn't know how I'd gone to the bathroom, but as soon as I thought it, memories tickled at the edges of my subconscious, of Dr. Kingsley helping me into the restroom, his hand on me to keep me steady as I'd sat on the toilet and pissed like a girl. My cheeks flamed.

"Something just went through that head of yours." He brushed his finger against my cheek, and then there was a cup at my lips. I looked at him, watching him as he helped me drink, and somehow, I knew it wasn't the first time he had done so.

And he was…beautiful, with dark hair a couple of inches long and mussed. He had dark scruff along his jaw and a nose that was a little pointed, but not too pointed where he looked sharp. He was the most breathtaking man I had ever seen. He reminded me of a king—powerful and dominant in ways I felt in my soul.

I wanted to serve him.

I wanted him to control me.

It didn't make sense—obviously, it didn't, since I didn't know him. But it was what I wanted...and I did sort of know him, knew he helped people like me.

"Get some rest, precious boy."

As though he had control of my body, of my mind, I lay back and did as he said.

The next time my eyes opened, they weren't as heavy, my brain wasn't as foggy, and I thought maybe I was human again.

I sat up and looked at the room for the first time. I was in a queen-size bed with light-blue bedding and a white headboard and footboard. There was a nightstand on each side, an armoire, a dresser, and I could see a door open to a bathroom. Beside the bed was an armchair that had been pulled close but didn't seem to belong where it was.

It was where he'd sat...where Dr. Kingsley had

watched me and made sure I was okay.

My legs were weak as I climbed out of the bed, wearing clothes that weren't mine and were too big for me. A large T-shirt hung off me, and I had to hold up the pajama bottoms so they didn't fall down. His clothes. He had put his clothes on me.

I padded into the bathroom, and holy fuck, I had never been in a bathroom this size. There was a large claw-foot tub, a separate shower, and two sinks on a long counter. It was almost as big as the apartment I shared with Ian.

Fuck. Ian. I needed to call him. First, I took a leak and washed my hands. When I looked in the mirror, seeing his clothes hanging from me, I felt very, very small. Very young...and somehow protected.

The back of my neck pricked with curiosity. Where was Dr. Kingsley? And why had he taken care of me? But then, somehow, that second question felt obvious. It was what he did. He fixed people who were sick, and he took care of those who needed it. He had done it with me three times now, and he didn't even know me.

He was a protector.

A caretaker.

My cell phone sat on the nightstand, and I grabbed it, plopping into the middle of the bed and laughing.

The blankets were thick and fluffy and *God*, I never wanted to leave them.

I called Ian, who answered on the first ring. "Fin?"

"Yeah, it's me."

"Thank fucking God. I've been scared as shit that he was locking you up as some sex slave or chopping your body into tiny pieces. I didn't know what to do!"

It was likely naive of me, but I didn't think Dr. Kingsley would hurt me. "I'm fine," I replied, falling back onto the pillows. "He took care of me. I feel like I'm in that movie—you know, the really old one? My mom used to like it, with that redheaded chick who was a hooker and spent a week with a rich guy—*Pretty Woman*, I think it is. Only without the sex, and I was unconscious and puking for most of it."

Which wasn't sexy at all. I highly doubted Dr. Kingsley wanted to fuck me, though, even if I hadn't been puking.

"I'm so glad you're okay."

"I was really sick. How long has it been?"

"Three days."

"Holy fuck!" I shot to a sitting position. He had taken care of me for three days?

"Did he call work for you? Do you know?" Ian asked, and the reality of my situation slammed into me, crushed me like so many other things had done in my life.

"Fuck," I whispered. "I was fired…" Which wasn't just bad for me, but for Ian as well. He couldn't pay his bills without me.

"We'll figure it out. It's not your fault."

But it was my fault. It was always my fault. Jesus, why did I fuck everything up?

"When are you coming home?" he asked.

"Soon. I'm sure he won't want me here now that I'm better." Why would he? I was a dumb guy who couldn't hold down a job.

"Okay," Ian replied. "I'll see you soon, and don't freak out, okay?"

"Yeah, sure." But I was.

My clothes were folded on the dresser. I pulled off Dr. Kingsley's shirt and held it to my face, inhaling, hoping for his scent again. What had it been in the car? I couldn't even remember, but this shirt didn't smell like him; it smelled of sickness and me.

I took his clothes off and put mine back on, then slipped out of the room with his pajamas in my hands. Looking down the hallway, I saw multiple closed doors but no one else. I was at the door closest to the stairs.

"Hello?" I whispered as I made my way down. The house was…fuck, it was incredible. I'd never been in a house so beautiful, and I wondered if he shared it with anyone. If he had a wife, or if he could possibly like men like I did. Was the guy he'd been dining with his lover?

The living room was off to the right of the stairs. There was a hallway behind them, and the kitchen and dining room to my left. The first floor was all either hardwood or tile, but there was a runner rug around the couch.

I walked into the kitchen next but still didn't see him. As I stood there, though, all I could think of was what it would be like to live there…with him. To cook his meals and do his laundry and clean for him. To take care of him and have him do the same for me in other ways.

For him to order me to my knees and let me rest my head on his thigh like the boy in the video did.

It was then I realized that was what I could do for him. If I wanted to thank him for his help, I could give him that. Maybe not the kneeling part, but the other stuff.

So I took his clothes and found my way to the laundry room, which was off the kitchen. The damn room was large too, with a washer and dryer that likely cost what I made in six months.

After putting his clothes in, I added soap. There was

a basket there with a few other items in it, so I added those as well. It took me a moment to figure out how to start the machine, and when I did, a silly feeling of pride swelled in my chest.

There were a few dishes in the sink, so I emptied the dishwasher and cleaned the dirty ones as well. Those I hand-washed and dried before putting them away. He would probably think I was crazy. I had no business doing these things in someone else's house, but I wanted to.

It was so ordinary, such an everyday activity, but I liked the thought of doing it for him. For caring for him in this simple way.

I figured he had to be there somewhere. He wouldn't have left me in the house alone, and maybe he would be hungry? Maybe I could feed him or cook for him so he would at least have something for later.

The pantry was fucking huge, like oh-my-God-who-needed-that-much-food big. I searched it and the fridge to find something that kept well. I settled on spaghetti. His appliances were stainless steel, his cooking utensils top-notch. I got the ground beef going, then swapped the clothes into the dryer.

I was back at the stove, putting the bottled sauce on, when I heard, "What are you doing?" in that deep, baritone voice of his.

My body whipped around to face him. He stood there with his arms crossed, in a nice polo shirt and jeans. He wore socks but no shoes, and God, I *longed* to be at his feet. "I woke up and you weren't there. I...wanted to do something nice for you. I wanted to thank you." *And serve you, and please, please, please, can't you want that too?*

"You're sick. You don't need to be up."

"I feel better. And I washed my hands—shit. I'm still probably getting my germs everywhere. I'm sorry. I didn't think about that."

He frowned and moved closer. Had I disappointed him?

"It's fine." He waved his hands at me. "I'm not worried about your germs. I've been around them for three days now."

"I'm sorry." I looked down again.

"There's nothing to be sorry for. I'm the one who brought you here and chose to take care of you, yes?"

"Yes."

When I saw his socked feet, I sucked in a sharp breath, realizing he was close.

"You don't have to cook for me, or do my laundry and wash my dishes, by the looks of it."

Forcing myself to look up at him, I shrugged and said, "I know, but I want to."

CHAPTER FOUR

Aidan

OH, THIS PRECIOUS boy was beautiful…and exquisitely submissive. He wanted to submit to me—and he did, in many ways. The way he'd lowered his eyes, how he held his body, the way he looked at me. And when he murmured a soft, "Please," I knew there was a part of him that needed to cook this meal for me, to do something for me as a thank-you.

"Okay," I replied. "But if I allow it, you're going to have to answer some questions for me."

When he nodded, I walked over and sat at the small kitchen table, the bigger one being in the dining room. Finley continued cooking as I asked, "How old are you?" I knew the answer to that, of course. I'd looked at his ID.

"Twenty," he replied without looking at me.

"If there's one thing I won't accept, it's lying."

His eyes darted to mine, and I could see it there, the apology, but then he pushed it aside. "How do you know

I'm lying, huh?"

"Because I looked."

"You looked through my things?" he snapped.

"I looked at your driver's license, yes. You're in my home, and I know nothing about you."

That seemed to hit home because he nodded. "If you knew I'm nineteen, why did you ask?"

"To see if you would try to lie to me. Please, don't do it again."

"I won't. I'm sorry."

I shook it off. "It's fine. How do you know me?"

His eyes went wide. It was there, his desire to make something up, but he wouldn't. He didn't want to lie to me, not really. He wanted to obey me. It was in his body, in how he moved and spoke, and in his eyes.

"I don't have to do this, you know? Like, I could leave right now."

"You could," I replied, but I didn't think he would. "How do you know me?"

Finley sighed. He didn't look at me as he opened the sauce and poured it into a pan. He moved easily in the kitchen as he spoke. "My, um…my mom…she used to work at the hospital. It was forever ago. She was in housekeeping. She was a great mom and an awesome worker. She never missed a day, but once when I was young, the babysitter didn't show. She took me to work. I sneaked out of the ER and fell asleep somewhere. You…you found me, and then you covered for her when she could have gotten in trouble for it."

If I hadn't been sitting, I likely would have tumbled over. I didn't show him my shock, though. I didn't want to spook the kid. There was a vague memory of that night in my mind, but it hadn't been something I'd held on to. I'd forgotten it almost as soon as it happened. But Finley hadn't. Had so few people been nice to him in his life? "You remember that?" I tried to soften my tone because I didn't want to embarrass him.

"Yes, but that's not all." He stopped what he was doing and looked me in the eye, fighting to be strong, not wanting to look weak, and I respected the hell out of him for it. "When I was fourteen—it was right after my mom died. I was angry at the world. I tried to steal a candy bar at the grocery store. You were there. You bought it for me…and lunch, and I ran away from you."

My stomach nearly dropped out. *That* I remembered more clearly. I didn't know what it had been about that child that made me do it. It wasn't every day I helped thieves, but something about him had reminded me of myself at his age—alone, angry.

"I remembered the name Dr. Kingsley from your

name tag at the hospital, and you saved my mom that night, so I remembered your face. After the second incident, I looked you up." His cheeks tinged pink.

What were the odds that I would meet this same boy three times? "Did you see me again? Other than at the restaurant the other night? Have you been following me?"

"What? No, oh God. I'm not a *stalker*!"

Maybe I shouldn't have believed him, but I did. "I'm sorry about your mom." The words made my chest tighten, brought back memories I tried to forget. There was nothing like losing a mother. I knew because I had lost my own and she had been my world—she and my little sisters.

"Thank you. She was…she was the best."

I nodded, knowing we both wanted to be off this conversation as quickly as possible. "And Ian? A boyfriend?"

"No!" he rushed out.

"There's nothing wrong with being gay," I told him, figuring he didn't remember our conversation at the bus stop. "I am."

He grinned at my admission. This boy was definitely trouble.

"I'm not uncomfortable with being gay. That's like

one of the only things I'm not screwed up about. I don't give a shit that I like men. You really do too?"

There was hope in his voice that I needed to squash. He was a kid, for God's sake. "That's irrelevant here."

Oh, he didn't like that answer. Finley rolled his eyes, and again, my hand itched, wishing I could spank him.

"Whatever. And no, Ian isn't my boyfriend. We wouldn't be compatible that way, if you know what I mean. We tried when we were younger…but yeah, we're better as friends. Plus, he's kind of seeing someone, this guy at his job. And he's totally not my type. We were in a foster home together. We ran away together, and we've been best friends since. He's my roommate."

"Other family?"

"Grandparents. They didn't want me when my mom died."

I gritted my teeth. What in the hell was wrong with people?

The dryer buzzed, and Finley turned toward it, automatically going over, opening it, and folding the clothes. "Is it okay if I put them in the basket?"

"You don't have to fold my laundry."

"I want to," he replied, again with the red in his cheeks. He was a delight, which I knew wasn't what I was supposed to be thinking.

"Okay." Maybe I should have said no, but I liked seeing him fold my things, and I liked giving him what he needed, and it was obvious he did—need it.

Finley went from the clothes back to the stove to finish cooking. "I figured spaghetti would be easy for you to reheat if you weren't hungry. I made enough that you can have leftovers or…if you like, have a boyfriend or a husband or whatever."

I nodded, not falling into the trap of answering that question.

"Did you lose your job?" I asked, with all the care I could. Finley tensed up…closed his eyes and turned away. It was all the answer I needed.

"I'll find another one."

"I know," I soothed. "There are a lot of restaurants in the city looking for help."

"In case you didn't notice, I'm a shit waiter. I don't know why because I'm decent in the kitchen and I like serving—I mean…" He shook his head. I knew exactly what he meant. One look was all it took to see the submissive in him, and if I hadn't, how he'd done my laundry, dishes, and cooked for me would have told me of his need to serve.

"Do you have anyone…you do that for?" It was a completely selfish question. Not that I planned to do anything about it, and I told myself it was because I wanted to make sure he was okay. There were a lot of assholes in the world who would take advantage of someone like him.

"I…"

"No lying. You can trust me, Finley, and if you don't feel comfortable telling me, say that. Don't lie to me."

He nodded, gave me his back, which wouldn't do if he were mine, and began straining the pasta. "I don't… I've never…but I want to. Do you think that's weird?"

This precious boy would be the ruin of me. I knew it in that moment. I'd made how many absurd decisions where he was concerned? He was so damn innocent, but somehow worldly too. He knew how things worked and followed his instincts instead of running. And he was still alone…and still angry…and in many ways, I was too. Especially the alone part. "No, it's not weird. Maybe some people think it is, and maybe society wants us to believe it is, but it's not. Really, what's more beautiful than what you want? To care and be cared for. To give your service and devotion to someone who deserves it. But they must deserve it."

He paused, and I waited. A moment later, he turned to me. "Is that… Do you…"

"What I do isn't important," I replied, and he

flinched as though I'd hit him. Part of me wanted to take the words back. To go to him and comfort him and give him those things he needed. He was legal, after all. But I knew I wouldn't. I couldn't be who he deserved.

"The food is ready. May I make your plate?" Finley asked, and my body went tight. Those words did things to me they shouldn't—not with him.

"Yes," I answered, even though I should have said no.

He fixed a plate for me and brought it over, but none for himself. "Do you feel like you can eat?" I asked.

"I'm not sure about the sauce."

"Do the pasta with butter and a little bit of salt. We both need ice water. Then join me at the table."

"Yes, Sir," he replied with a smile, and I bit back a groan.

"I'm not your Sir." Another flinch, but it was important he knew that.

Still, Finley did as I said, and a few minutes later we were at the table together, eating. I wasn't hungry but knew it would hurt him if I didn't eat, so I did for him.

"What is it you want, Finley?" I asked him when we were finished.

"Like, in life, or what?" He sounded so damn young.

"Yes," I replied. "Or however you want to answer. If you want it, that's what I mean."

He nodded, took a drink, then said, "This. Like...what we did today? I want that. I don't care about my diploma or college or anything like that. I want this...to like, take care of someone? I watch these videos..."

Porn. Of course it would come back to porn.

"...and I see these relationships where like, one of the guys is the other guy's boy? And he just like, takes care of him. Of his home and you know...whatever his needs are. He fulfills those, and it gives him something too. I would get something out of that, I think. Something I couldn't feel anywhere else. It would make me feel complete, or whatever? I don't know how I know it, but I feel it right here." He touched his chest. "Deep down. It's something I *know*, so don't tell me it's stupid or that I'm too young, because I know what I feel, I know who I am."

It seemed as though now he'd started, he couldn't stop. I waited as Finley continued. "And then I want someone to take care of me too but in different ways. He can hold me and let me kneel at his feet and put his hands in my hair and pet me. When I do the wrong thing, he'll punish me, but I know he'll only do it because it's what's right for me. And maybe sometimes I'll want to hurt, and he'll do that too. I don't know for sure if I want that yet, but if I do, he'll give it to me because I need it. I'll follow his rules because no one has given me those, and I like...need them or whatever. Because I feel that deep inside too. It doesn't matter that I'm only nineteen. I know—" When I hold my hand up, he stops.

Damned if my hand wasn't shaking. I lowered it before he could notice. He would be lovely on his knees. Lovely serving. I'd been with a lot of submissives in my life, too many to count, and I wasn't sure I'd ever seen one as open, as innocent and pure and honest as Finley.

And Christ, a part of me wanted to be what he needed. I'd never had a full-time sub. I'd never had a houseboy or someone who was into domestic servitude. No one took care of my needs at home. When I wanted it, I found someone to dominate and fuck, and then I went home. But when I was with a boy, I was always one hundred percent in charge, and hearing what he wanted pricked at my desires in ways I couldn't explain.

One day, someone would own him the way he needed, and I hoped like hell it was the right person. That he didn't get taken advantage of because that would be so very, very simple to do.

"Did I do something wrong?" Finley asked.

"No, you didn't. You were very honest, which was

what I asked for. That means you were very good, okay?"

His eyes widened, glowed. It was as if I'd given him the answer to all his problems; as if I'd handed him the world. But the world wasn't mine to give him. He was young, and I didn't want anyone full-time. I had too much going on in my own world, and I certainly wasn't going to let this boy have pieces of me I'd never given to anyone else.

"When you're finished, I'll take you home."

His eyes narrowed. He was angry. I could see it. He had a spark to him that interested me. So submissive and so needy to serve, but I knew that he could, and would, be a brat too.

"I'll do the dishes, and I'll be ready." Finley shoved to his feet. I didn't call him on the behavior because he wasn't mine. I also didn't tell him not to clean up because I knew he needed it.

Not long later, my GPS was giving me directions to his apartment. It was…not in the best part of the city. We had been quiet the whole ride, and I knew he was still angry with me. What I didn't understand was why it mattered to me so much.

Because you want to protect him. Because you don't want someone to dim that spark in him. Because you want to be the one to ignite it and watch him grow into who he is supposed to be.

The moment I pulled up to the curb, Finley shoved the door open. He was halfway out when I said, "Stop," and he did. He stopped beautifully, sat back down, and looked at me. "Put your phone number in my cell." I handed it over to him.

His brows pulled together, but he did as told. I sent a text to him so he'd have my number. "Do you have money for the bus?"

Confusion was still etched in the wrinkles of his scrunched forehead. "Yes."

This hadn't been a conscious decision I'd made, but I knew I wouldn't take it back. "Be at my house at nine a.m. on Sunday. We'll discuss your wages and responsibilities then." He opened his mouth but closed it when I held up my hand. "Not now. I need time to think. We'll discuss it on Sunday, but I promise I'll take care of you, okay? You'll work for me." What was I supposed to do? I knew he needed money. That he now had no job. But I was self-aware enough to know I'd also said it for purely selfish reasons. The truth was, the boy fascinated me.

Finley nodded, all doe-eyed and smiling. "I…thank you, Sir…and please…please don't change your mind." He jumped out, slammed the door, and ran away.

What in the hell had I gotten myself into?

CHAPTER FIVE
Finley

I WAS SO jittery, I could hardly contain myself. I felt as if I were going to burst out of my skin, just crack open and spill all the happiness out of me and then be stuck with nothing again. God, I would die, just *die*, if he changed his mind. I didn't know exactly what we would be doing, what Dr. Kingsley even wanted, but whatever it was, I knew I would take it because I trusted him. The only people I trusted since my mom died were Ian and Dr. Kingsley. Maybe it was a mistake. Maybe he would hurt me, but I didn't have it in me not to try.

"Ian!" I called out to my friend as I busted into our apartment. He scrambled up from where he'd been sitting on the futon and rubbed his eyes. He'd worked late last night, and I hadn't even thought of that.

"Holy shit, Fin. Thank God you're home! We talked earlier, but I was still scared I was sitting around while some guy hacked you up."

I fell down onto the bed with him and giggled—fucking *giggled*. "As you can see, I'm very much alive, and…it was him."

"Who?" Ian's brows tugged together. I couldn't remember if I'd ever told Ian about Dr. Kingsley—was that what I was supposed to call him? He hadn't told me. Was he Aidan? When I looked him up, I saw that was his name. Was he *Sir*? It was all such an exciting cyclone in my brain that I buzzed and struggled to calm down.

We lay there together, and I told Ian about the two times in my past when I'd run into Aidan—yes, I was going to call him Aidan for now because it made me feel closer to him. If I was allowed, I would change it to Sir or whatever else he desired.

From there I told Ian about seeing him at the restaurant. Recognizing him. He'd known I felt sick, and I told Ian about what happened and Aidan taking me home. How he'd let me sleep in a warm bed and given me water and medication and how he'd taken care of me. "It was…fuck, it was *amazing*. I've never had someone dote on me that way."

"Wow… That's…wow."

I rolled over and looked at the peeling ceiling. I knew I was smiling like a fool, but I couldn't help it. I didn't want to. "Then this morning I woke up and he wasn't there. I don't know where he was—a home office or something?—but I washed his dishes and his clothes, and I, God, I know it sounds ridiculous and maybe to most people it is, but it felt *good*. Like I was taking care of him and I was needed. It filled this empty place inside me that I've never been able to fill before."

"It doesn't sound ridiculous." Ian reached over and fingered my hair. "We all want different things, and that's never ridiculous. It's just…who we are."

"My best friend is the smartest." I rolled to my side so I faced him. "You haven't heard the best part. He wants me to come back on Sunday. He said he would take care of me, that I would work for him."

"What the fuck!" Ian sat up, and I did the same. We had our legs crossed, facing each other. "What does that mean? Like you're going to be his boy?"

"I don't even know. He said not to ask questions and we'd talk on Sunday." I wasn't sure he was entirely happy about what he'd offered me, but I wasn't going to tell Ian that. Whatever it was Aidan offered, I knew I would take it, but I really hoped he wanted me—all of me.

"Do you think you'll be able to do it? Submit to him?"

There was no doubt in my mind that I could. Aidan

had come into my life at three separate times, and each one, he protected me. I had to believe he would continue to do so. "Yeah. I trust him." Ian nodded, and I added, "But I'm worried I won't be good enough for him. Hell, I've given what? Five sloppy blowjobs in my life, which I'm pretty sure I sucked at, and not in the way you want to suck at blowjobs. I've never been fucked, and I don't really know how to do all the things I want, even though I know I want them. And what if he doesn't even want me that way? I'm getting ahead of myself." Which I had the tendency to do. "He probably just feels sorry for me. It'll likely only be household things he wants from me, anyway." I'd find a way for that to be enough.

"You're gorgeous. I'm sure he wants in your ass." Ian rolled his eyes playfully. "So will you move out? Will he want you to move in with him?"

Shit. I hadn't even thought about that. "I...I don't know. I wouldn't want to leave you."

For the second time, Ian rolled his eyes. "Fin, I'd be fine. I'm a big boy. I can live by myself."

He would be able to do so easier than I would. Money would be an issue, of course, but Ian was more independent than me in other ways. Plus, he had a regular fuck buddy he stayed with sometimes too. "I'll still help you with rent and shit. You know that, right? It could still be our place."

"I'm not your responsibility."

"Ian."

He waved off my concern. "We'll figure it out. We don't even know what he wants yet, but I have to say it—if things don't work out, you know you always have a place with me, right? No matter what."

"Yeah." I smiled at him. "I know."

THE DAYS WENT by at a snail's pace. I seriously wasn't sure they had ever gone by so sluggishly. Finally, it was Saturday night, and I was up most of the night. When I rolled off the futon in the morning and looked in the mirror, I saw the dark circles under my eyes. "Shit." I was going to go over there looking so used up, he wouldn't want me.

I showered and dressed in my best clothes. I couldn't eat anything; my stomach was too nervous. Ian was going to walk me to the bus stop, but the second we got to the busy sidewalk, I saw Aidan's car waiting there. He was leaning against it, his hands in his jeans pockets.

"Umm, he's fucking hot," Ian whispered.

"I know, right?"

Aidan walked over, taking off his sunglasses as he came. When he reached us, he held his hand out for Ian, and I didn't know why, but that made me smile. "I'm Aidan Kingsley. It's nice to meet you."

"Ian, nice to meet you too." But Ian wasn't smiling. I nudged him and heard a soft chuckle from Aidan.

"I'm only making him an offer. If Finley doesn't want to take it, he doesn't have to, but I won't hurt him. You're a good friend to him."

"Sorry. I just worry," Ian replied.

"Jesus, Ian. I know what I'm doing."

Aidan looked at me and cocked a brow in a way that told me he wasn't happy with me. "There's nothing wrong with him worrying. He should. I'm glad he does. It's not a slight against you. It means he cares."

Guilt tumbled around inside me as I shoved my hands into my pockets. "You're right. I'm sorry."

Aidan simply nodded. "I'll have him home before this evening. Finley will text you my phone number from the car," he told Ian.

"Okay…thank you," Ian replied.

We walked to Aidan's BMW together. He opened the door for me, and as simple as that gesture was, it turned my insides to mush. I climbed in and clicked my seat belt into place as he walked around and got in. "You came to get me," I said.

"Obviously."

"Why?"

"Because I wanted to." He pulled onto the street. "Did you eat?"

"No."

"You need to eat. It's important. We'll go home. You can make breakfast, and we'll talk."

Home... Did he mean that because he planned to move me in with him? I trembled with need at the thought, but what I said was, "Does that mean you didn't eat? It's important to eat."

I was sure it was the wrong thing to say, and silently chastised myself, so I was surprised by the sound of laughter coming from Aidan. It pushed through his lips, almost as if he had been shocked about it too. "I knew you would be a brat. Mind your manners, though."

"But isn't that what this is about? You take care of me, and I take care of you too? So if you're reminding me that I need to eat, I should be doing the same for you."

Aidan didn't answer for a moment. I wondered if he was already regretting this, whatever this was. What felt like an eternity later, he finally spoke. "That depends on a few things. First, if we go through with this, and second, the nature of what we do. There are no rules we have to follow; we'll do what's right for us. And I haven't decided what that is yet—or what I want."

I nodded. "Yes, Sir." His hands tightened on the steering wheel, but I wasn't sure if it was because he liked hearing me say that or because he didn't.

We were quiet the rest of the drive to his house. The second we pulled up to it, I was reminded how out of my element I was, that I didn't belong there. It was a beautiful home, this creamish color, with palm trees along with other trees surrounding it.

Aidan killed the engine and got out, and I took a deep breath, forcing my limbs to work, and did the same. *He invited me here. It doesn't matter if I belong or not.*

I followed him to the front doors. They were french, a dark brown with frosted glass in the center so you couldn't see inside. Aidan unlocked the door, then tossed the keys into a bowl on the table in the entryway.

"Should I take off my shoes?" I asked.

"It's fine. Whatever you want."

"Can I take off your shoes?"

His eyes flared with something—desire, I hoped—but he shook his head. "Not now. Let's go have breakfast." He began to walk down the hallway, and I followed as he continued. "There are eggs, ham, peppers, and onions in the fridge. Can you make omelets?"

I rolled my eyes, and he clicked his tongue as if to chastise me. "None of that. Just answer the question."

"Yes, I can make omelets." What did he think I was? I might have been young and uneducated, but I sure as shit knew how to make breakfast.

It took me a moment to realize we had stopped walking. Aidan nodded toward the kitchen and said, "Come."

And I went…eagerly and obediently, silently hoping he would want me to stay.

CHAPTER SIX

Aidan

I STILL WASN'T sure what in the hell I was thinking. I hadn't been sure I would go through with it until I found myself getting into my car and going to get him. Hell, maybe I still hadn't known until he'd come out with his friend and I'd seen the hunger in him...and the relief. Not because I'd picked him up rather than have him take the bus, but because I hadn't changed my mind.

I was being a fool, but I was fairly certain I was going to continue being a fool where Finley was concerned. He'd touched something inside me that ignited my need to protect him.

"Do you have your high school diploma?" I asked as Finley pulled items from the fridge. From where I sat at the table, I saw his body tense up. Not everyone would have noticed, but it was my responsibility to look for signs and read him.

"I don't see why that matters."

"It matters because I want to know. I'll expect you to answer my questions, unless they're a hard limit for you. Is this?" When he didn't immediately reply, I added, "There is no shame to your answer. It's important that I get to know you."

Finley set the food on the counter and looked around for a cutting board, knife, and bowls. I could have told him where they were, but I didn't. He would want to do this on his own, and I intended to let him.

"No," he finally replied. "I don't. And I don't care because how is it going to help me with this? With what I want?"

Rather than setting him straight, I nodded. "And no family?"

"None." Finley washed the peppers and began cutting them.

"And you've never done this? Submitted to a man? Or been a houseboy—if that's what you're looking for?"

"No, but that doesn't mean I don't know I want it. I'll walk out right now if you think that. Like I said before, I *feel* it, deep inside me."

Oh, he had spunk, and I liked that entirely too much. It was refreshing and made me want to smile, but I didn't. "I won't tell you who you are," I replied. I didn't plan to fuck the boy, but still I asked, "What's your sexual experience?"

Finley was cutting as I asked. His hand slipped, and he cursed as the knife tumbled to the floor. Immediately, I shoved to my feet. "Did you cut yourself?"

"No, no. I'm fine. I just…" His cheeks were pink, and it was delicious. I couldn't deny that I wanted him.

"Continue." I sat back down. Finley washed the knife, then did as I said. As he cut, he squared his shoulders and held his head high.

"I've given a few blowjobs. I've never been fucked, if that's what you're asking, but I want it, and I sure as hell know I'll be good at it."

Yes, I was in so much trouble with him. My dick twitched, and that damn smile threatened to curl my lips again. "I don't doubt it."

"Because I know I can and—wait, you don't?"

That was the extent of how far I was willing to go with that at the moment, so I said, "Tell me about Ian."

Finley cooked as he told me about Ian, his job and his fuck buddy and their history together. Ian was a year older than him, and Finley had been seventeen when they'd run away together.

Soon the omelets were done, and Finley plated them for each of us, along with a glass of orange juice. He watched me as I took a bite. I had a feeling he was holding his breath, and I said, "It's delicious. Good job, boy," knowing he needed to hear it. He gave me a thousand-watt smile, and I added, "Eat," and he did.

He didn't ask me questions, which pleased me. We ate, and then he did the dishes before I moved us to the living room. I sat down on the couch and bit back a groan when he knelt on the floor beside me. "I didn't ask you to do that."

"I want to. May I?"

Shit. This was bad. Incredibly fucking bad, but I nodded. He was young, so young, and I feared I was taking advantage of him, but he was so eager, I told myself better me than someone else. I knew I wouldn't hurt him. That I would do what was best for him, even if he didn't always agree with me on what that was.

He was beautiful there, his blond hair like a halo, his blue eyes crisp, open, and needy. I wanted to tell him to unbutton my pants and nurse my cock before fucking between his plump lips. Instead, I said, "If it were up to you, tell me exactly what you would get from me. What you're looking for."

He shrugged as if the answer were so simple. "I want to serve you…in all things. I want to cook for you and clean for you. I want to help you get ready for work in the morning and be here when you get home. Whatever you need, I want to provide it. I want to kneel at your feet, and rest my head on your thigh, and feel...safe, and to please you. Always to please you."

My breath hitched at that.

"Is it wrong? To want that?" he asked, so innocently.

"No. No it's not. Continue."

"I want to know what's expected of me. I want to know that you're there if I need you, and like I said, to feel cherished because you know I cherish you. I want you to push me to my knees if you want my mouth, and to take my ass when you need a hole, and for you to fill me when I need that as well. And I want your control in all aspects of my life. It's all too much for me sometimes."

Blood rushed to my cock, making it ache. *Oh, precious boy. The things I could do to you...*

"You got all this from porn?" I asked, and he snickered.

"Porn...books. I like to read, and just...my instincts. My gut. I want you to own me...to make me feel whole."

"And you don't? Feel whole right now?" I asked, knowing what his answer would be. Still, I needed to hear it.

"No, Sir. I never have."

It was difficult, but I fought to control myself, to keep a clear head. "Have you tried to get this with anyone else?"

"Not really. I've found guys on the internet to hook up with—not the domestic part, but the sex and submission. I can never go through with it."

"What makes you think you can follow through with me?" Maybe this would be it; maybe this would be the thing that made me scratch this foolish idea from my brain.

But then…then he opened his mouth and so sweetly and softly said, "Because I trust you. Because you've never hurt me. You've saved me, and I think that's for a reason. Why else would it be you who's always there? And every time you could walk away, you don't. You're there to give me exactly what I need." He closed his eyes and dropped his head to my thigh. Damned if I didn't tremble, fucking shake as my heart pounded and blood rushed through my ears.

He was going to break me, I thought. He was already hammering away at the walls inside me, this sweet, pure, honest boy who trusted me to take care of him and protect him.

"Please," Finley whispered. "Please don't turn me

away. I need it, and I don't know how to get it without you."

It wasn't a conscious decision, but before I knew it, my fingers were in his hair. I was petting him, comforting him. Nothing he'd said had come as a shock to me. He'd told me most of it before, but somehow it felt different. Maybe it was the naive trust he had in me, or the feeling that I'd done something special when I hadn't.

"You'll move in here, if you'd like. The room you had before will be yours. You'll be paid a fair wage for your work. The house will be your responsibility, maybe a few other things we'll discuss, and you'll take care of some of my personal needs too. I'll discipline you when you need it—spanking, taking away privileges, or whatever I feel is necessary. I'll help lead you in the way you need, guide you and care for you. And you'll also work on getting your high school diploma—"

"Wait. What?" Finley jerked his head up.

"Nonnegotiable if you want to move forward with this. It's up to you. Now, put your head back down. I wasn't done."

Finley nodded. "Yes, Sir." He laid his head on my thigh, and I continued to card my fingers through the soft strands.

"But I won't fuck you. No sex. You'll be my houseboy, domestic servant or however you want to put it, in all other ways, but I won't give you that. If you need it, I'll help you find someone I approve of, someone I can trust. My friend David from the other night, likely. But I have to admit, I'd like you to wait for a while. You have so many things to sort out about yourself."

He was so inexperienced and vulnerable. I didn't want him to feel tied to me, to know that his livelihood was tied to me and then feel obligated to fuck me. My mother had married my father when she was eighteen years old, and he had ruined her, broken her, made her feel like she had nothing without him, and I wouldn't ever do that with anyone.

Plus, there were too many lines we were crossing already; they were already blurred, my rules getting broken. I had no desire to have someone permanently, I never had, and certainly not someone as young as Finley.

"And when I want to fuck, I'll go elsewhere too." It needed to be said. I didn't want him to get the wrong idea. He could be my houseboy. I would be his…Master, for lack of a better term, but there would be no sex.

Finley nodded against my thigh before slowly raising his head to look at me. "You won't change your mind, will you?"

"No, precious boy." And he really was that.

"But I can do this? Kneel for you this way?"

"Yes."

He smiled. "I don't have anything to sort out, and you'll change your mind eventually."

Why did that not surprise me? He was a blend of innocent and worldly, insecure and confident. "No, I won't."

"Okay," he said, but I could tell he didn't believe me. "When do I start?"

I chuckled, fearing he already had me wrapped around his finger. "Today, if you'd like."

"I'd like," he replied, laying his head on me again.

CHAPTER SEVEN

Finley

IT WAS A whirlwind from there. Aidan was going to be paying me more than I'd ever made in my life. I still couldn't believe it. Maybe it wasn't much to some people, but to me, it felt like I'd hit the jackpot. I definitely still planned to help Ian, even though he said he didn't want to accept it.

Aidan drove me back to the apartment and, to my horror, actually came up with me. It was so odd seeing him there. He didn't fit at all, but he didn't seem uncomfortable, and he was friendly again with Ian. He got Ian's number as well and told my friend he could visit me anytime; that if there was anything he could do for Ian, he would.

I wondered if he knew what a caretaker he was. Maybe that was typical of Doms. It made sense, but I had no experience and didn't know what to expect. Even if it was, I still thought Aidan was special. He was a good man who'd helped a boy in need when he didn't have to.

Aidan helped me pack. I didn't have much anyway, and no luggage. He seemed horrified when I threw my clothes into a trash bag, but like, what harm could it cause? It wasn't as if I had fancy things like he did.

Before I knew it, he was driving me back to his home, and I would never tell anyone this, but I felt like a prince who'd been saved and was now being taken to my castle. Princes could be saved too, damn it.

There were things I was obviously upset about—the high school diploma and the no sex, because…why? What good was a stupid piece of paper going to do for me? I wanted to serve the way I would with him, and if I wasn't doing that, I'd work fast food or wait tables like I did before. Not that there was anything wrong with those things. I just knew what I was cut out to do.

And I really didn't understand why he didn't want to fuck me or let me serve him sexually. I would have thought it was personal if I hadn't noticed the shake in his limbs and seen his cock get hard.

Aidan explained his work schedule to me—the set hours he worked but that sometimes he was on call.

We were back at the house now, my bag of clothes over my shoulder. "What kind of doctor are you?"

"A trauma surgeon, and I have routine surgeries I do

as well. It's mostly abdominal stuff. I don't do head or bones."

He said that as if it were nothing. As if he *only* did certain kinds of surgeries, so it wasn't as special. "Holy shit!" I gasped. He was… "You're amazing. You save lives."

His forehead wrinkled. "You knew I was a doctor."

"Yeah, but…I guess I didn't let myself think about it much." He'd spent how much time in school, and he worked long, crazy hours sometimes without sleep in between. He operated on people, sometimes in emergency situations. I both wondered what he was doing with me there, was so incredibly thankful, and…I felt a sense of pride because I would get to serve him. Because I would care for a man who saved the lives of others, even if I did that in the most simple of ways.

"You're a hero."

He waved me off as I knew he would. "Do I also wear a cape and have a lair?"

"No, but you *save lives*. Do you not think firemen or police officers are heroes? I thought surgeons were supposed to be conceited assholes." I rolled my eyes and went to take a step. One *tsk* from him, and I stopped where I stood.

"You're being disrespectful. Am I going to have to

punish you already?"

Yes, oh yes, please do! What came out of my mouth, though, was, "But how will you spank me? I mean, if there's no sex, will you still spank me with my pants down?"

He stepped closer to me, tall and imposing, making my pulse race. I wanted him to devour me, to punish me, to possess me in every way, but he was intimidating too.

"Precious boy, you're in for a world of surprise if you think the only way I have to punish you is to spank you. And you're also in for a surprise if you think you can manipulate me. Unless that's a limit for you, if I want to spank your bare ass, I will. I can do that without fucking it…and if I don't want to, I won't. Now go to your room, nose in the corner for ten minutes—there's a timer on the dresser—and then put your clothes away."

I gulped, something heavy and round in my throat, refusing to be swallowed down. Aidan cocked a confident brow, and I longed to drop to my knees for him right then and there, beg him to take possession of my body and soul.

Then it hit me what he said. "Nose in the corner?"

"Yes. They don't do that often in porn, do they? There are many ways to punish. Do you plan to argue with me already?"

No…no I didn't, but standing in the corner wasn't the hot sort of thing I was expecting. "No, Sir. I won't argue."

I kept myself calm as I walked upstairs to the room I'd stayed in before. I dropped the bag, set the timer, then went…went to one of the corners of the room and pressed my nose to it. I had no idea if he would check on me or not, and I felt absolutely ridiculous doing this. I was nineteen years old and I was standing in the corner, but then…then I remembered Aidan had wished it, and he was correcting me, and that helped.

When there was a *ding* from the dresser, I ran to the bed, threw myself down on it…and laughed. My cheeks hurt, I smiled so widely, looking up at the craftsmanship on the bed, and the ceiling that didn't peel, in a home where a beautiful man was going to be my… I didn't know exactly what. But again, I felt like the girl with the red hair in the hooker movie or a servant who became a prince.

Once I had it all out of my system, I stood up, went to the trash bag, and began to fold my clothes.

I'd be wise to take this seriously so I didn't lose it.

After arranging my clothes in the drawers and my toiletries in my *own fucking bathroom*, I went into the hall to find Aidan. "Hello?" I called out.

"Down here," he replied. Damn it. I'd hoped he was in his bedroom because I really wanted to see it.

I went downstairs, and he met me there. "Let me show you around."

"Yes, Sir!" I replied, giddy that I was there and got to call him that. He smiled, and already I liked Aidan's smile. I wanted to make him do it all the time.

"You know the living room, kitchen, and laundry room." He led me down the hall behind the stairs. "My office." He pointed to a room on the left. It had french doors too, in dark wood. There was a desk and chair, with two other chairs across from it and a leather couch against the wall…and bookshelves. Jesus, there were a lot of bookshelves, and they were all filled.

"Do you like to read?" I asked him.

"Some, yes. I'm a fan of mysteries, but I have a lot of medical books too."

He was smart, so damn smart, and suddenly I felt very much as if I didn't belong there with him.

"Hey, look at me," Aidan said. I hadn't needed to tell him how I felt; he just knew, and that did twisty things to my insides—good kinds of things. "There's no shame here, not for any reason, okay?"

"Yes, Sir." But I wasn't sure I believed him. If that were true, why was it so important I went back and got my diploma?

We continued down the hallway, and he led me to a small home gym next. "I'd like you to exercise five days a week."

"Do you think I'm fat?" I said sarcastically. I knew I wasn't. I was too bony in some ways and slight in my stature.

"No, but there are a lot of reasons to work out. It's healthy. It's good for the mind. Who knows, you might end up enjoying it."

I highly doubted that. We went around and then through the dining room and to the kitchen again, before heading into his backyard. "Holy fuck." My eyes scanned the area—foliage and palm trees; a pool, hot tub, large built-in grill, patio cover, and lots of chairs and tables; rock work along the ground, and a small wall with large rocks and a waterfall that went into the pool.

"Do you know how to swim?"

"Yes." I walked over, bent, and stuck my hand in the water. "I can use it?"

"Of course. This is your home."

Did he know what he was giving me? That I felt as if I was living in a fairy tale? I'd never seen anything like his home, and now I would be working out in it and could relax by the pool...

I didn't know what came over me, but I turned…and then crawled over to him. It was likely weird, but it was what I felt I should do, what I wanted to do, what I hoped pleased him.

Aidan sucked in a sharp breath, and I knelt at his feet, knowing I would do it even if there wasn't a privacy fence around us so no one could see. "Thank you," I whispered with my head bowed.

For a moment I thought he would tell me to stand, or say I didn't have anything to thank him for, and somehow, that would have hurt. But then I felt his hand in my hair, Aidan's strong yet gentle fingers caressing me. "You're very welcome, precious boy."

It was exactly what I needed to hear.

"Now, stand up, please, and not because you don't look beautiful down there, but because the ground isn't good for your knees."

"Yes, Sir," I replied, even though I didn't want to stand.

We went back inside, and Aidan told me there were more bedrooms upstairs, but his was the last one at the end of the hallway. He said he had some work to do, but I was free to do what I wanted until dinner. On his days off, dinner was to be done at seven, and on days he worked but would be home, at eight. "When you start your classes, that can be rearranged if need be."

Ugh. That again. I rolled my eyes.

"No kneeling for me tonight," he said firmly.

"Wait. What?"

"You rolled your eyes, and that's your punishment."

"Oh my God! I didn't know. That's not fair!"

"Maybe you'll think about that before you disrespect me next time. Now go. I have work to do."

It was on the tip of my tongue to argue with him. Everything inside me was screaming for me to do so, but the smug expression on his gorgeous face held me back. He knew I wanted to…and maybe he wanted me to so he could punish me again. If it wasn't a spanking, I wasn't digging this whole discipline thing. "Yes, Sir," I replied tersely and went upstairs to my room.

My old laptop sat on my bed, and I thought about watching porn, but I didn't. Instead I found myself in the bathroom, looking at the huge tub with bottles of soaps and bubble bath around it.

It was the middle of the day, but I didn't care. I hadn't taken a bubble bath since I was a child, and I'd loved them then. They had made me feel cozy and warm.

So I started one and stripped out of my clothes. Fucking Aidan. I couldn't believe he wouldn't let me kneel for him just because I'd rolled my eyes at him.

I lounged in the bath for over an hour before getting out, getting dressed, and cleaning up after myself. Plopping on the bed again, I opened my laptop but realized I didn't know the Wi-Fi info and closed it. So I called Ian and complained about my punishments, then told him about the pool. "Maybe you can come and swim one day."

"I can't believe you're living in a mansion."

"It's not a mansion." But it was a beautiful home.

I kept myself busy until it was time to start dinner. I rummaged around and decided on fried chicken, mashed potatoes, and zucchini.

Aidan joined me about fifteen minutes before it was done.

"It smells good." He looked at the stove. "I'll definitely need to up my workouts."

"I won't cook like this all the time." I didn't tell him it was my mom's favorite and that she taught me how to make the best gravy.

I loved that he sat at the table and allowed me to serve him. I made his plate first, and knew I always would, because I wanted to take care of him.

"Do you want wine?" he asked, and I frowned.

"I've never had it, and I heard it's gross."

"I forget how young you are."

I could already read him, and I could tell he was uncomfortable with that fact. What mattered was that I was legal and knew what I wanted, so I didn't understand his hesitation. I almost rolled my eyes but held off because I sure as shit didn't want to be unable to kneel for him the next day as well.

He poured himself wine, and I got water before I sat at the table. Aidan went over some more of my responsibilities: laundry, washing bed linens twice a week, cleaning bathrooms, making the beds, sweeping, mopping, vacuuming, dishes, and meals. All standard stuff.

"I'll add you to my car insurance," he said, and my fork clattered to my plate.

"I don't have a car."

"I guess it's a good thing I do. Two as a matter of fact. You can use the BMW."

"Are you out of your mind?" jumped out of my mouth, and by the tic in his jaw, I could tell he wasn't happy. "I'm sorry...I didn't mean that, but I can't drive your car."

"How do you plan to do the shopping and run errands?"

"Um...I don't know...a car service or something?"

He rolled his eyes, and I wondered why it was okay

for him and not me but didn't ask.

"That's ridiculous. You'll drive the car."

"I don't want to drive the car, but I want to do your shopping."

"You're not taking a car service."

"What if I wreck?"

"Hence the reason you'll be on the insurance." He said it like it was the simplest thing, but to me, it wasn't.

"That car is worth more than I could ever pay for." Worth more than me.

Aidan sighed, and I could tell he was getting frustrated with me. "You won't have to pay for it. You'll be on the insurance. That's what insurance is for. This is what I want, Finley. You'll be responsible for shopping and dry cleaning or whatever else I need. You must be able to drive." He paused, looked at me, and added, "It's just a car. There's no reason you can't drive it. I saw your license when I brought you home the first time. Do you not like to drive?"

"I can do it. I haven't done it a lot, but Ian used to have a car before it broke, and he taught me to drive it. I used that to get my license."

"It's settled, then. I trust you, and if something happens, all that will matter is that you're okay."

My cheeks flushed, my whole damn body, maybe. I

felt warm all over and gooey inside and…cared for. I felt deliciously protected and important. "Yes…yes, Sir. And thank you."

"You're welcome." He took a bite, chewed and swallowed. "You're a good cook. The gravy is wonderful."

I smiled. Mom had been a good cook. She'd wanted to be a chef and had taught me so much. I loved cooking because of her. "Thank you," I replied again. Then, because the mood needed to be lightened and because I really hoped he said yes, I added, "Should I do my chores naked every day?"

He chuckled, and I felt accomplished that I was able to make him do that. I had a feeling he didn't do it often. "No, boy, you shouldn't."

"French maid uniform, then?" I waggled my brows.

"That won't be necessary."

"Who cares about necessary? It will be fun!"

I got another laugh. "You're going to be a handful."

I was, but I knew that Aidan was up for the challenge.

CHAPTER EIGHT
Aidan

IT HAD BEEN a week since Finley had moved in, and we were beginning to fall into our routine. He did everything that was expected of him, and he did it with pleasure like I'd never seen, not for activities like cleaning the house and cooking meals.

I'd had many playmates over the years, more scenes than I could count, but I'd never had something like this—someone who fulfilled all my needs that weren't sexual; someone who lived in my home, and folded my clothes, and loved nothing more than sitting at my feet with his head on my thigh.

And I found that having him there helped me too. When I'd had a busy day at work, eating the meal he prepared and having him kneel for me helped me come down as well.

He was a spitfire. Beautifully obedient but also a brat, making me laugh and smile more than I likely had any business doing.

Tonight was the first time I would be seeing David since I'd taken Finley in. I'd told Finley I wouldn't be home for dinner, and he'd frowned as if he hadn't expected it, but hadn't questioned me.

I wasn't in the mood to go out, so I was at David's in Santa Monica. We ordered Chinese and were sitting by his pool, eating and drinking wine.

"So, what's new with you?" he asked.

"Remember the boy from the restaurant? Finley?" He nodded, and I continued. "Well, he lives with me now, and I have my very own houseboy."

David's eyes widened. "Excuse me, can you repeat that?"

"You heard me." I'd known he would react that way, and I understood why he did. This was very out of the ordinary for me, but I knew I had to tell him. It was a bit like ripping a Band-Aid off, and now it was done.

"But you've never lived with anyone before."

"I'm aware."

"And you've never had someone permanent for anything."

"I'm aware of that too."

"And you've never wanted it."

"Will you stop stating the obvious? These are things

we both know," I snapped. I knew I was one of only a handful of people who could speak to David that way.

"I'm sorry, I'm just...wow. I can't believe you're fucking that kid."

I bristled uncomfortably. "First, he's not a kid. He's nineteen. And second, I'm not fucking him."

David frowned. "Wait. Now I'm really confused."

I sighed, knowing I had to get this over with. I understood David's confusion, and honestly, it felt good to talk to someone about this. "He lost his job. He doesn't have much money. He's young...so very young, and innocent, and beautifully submissive. He wants to serve. In fact, that's all he wants. He wants to be a houseboy, and he wants a Dominant to take care of him. He needs me...and he trusts me, no matter how foolish his reasons for doing so. I couldn't walk away, and I didn't want him to turn to someone who would hurt him to get his needs met. There was nothing I could do."

David huffed. "There's always a choice. You took that boy because you wanted to. You can lie to yourself and maybe to him about it, but not to me. If you didn't want to take care of him, you wouldn't be. But why not fuck him? As you said, he's legal, and it sounds like you want him."

This part was harder to explain, especially as I'd

never spoken to David about my childhood. I sipped my wine and thought for a moment. "The lines are too blurred. He works for me. I pay him. I don't pay for sex, and he… The way he looks at me…" It was as if he worshipped me, which was exactly how he was supposed to look at me, but to fuck him too? It would be too much. "He needs to be able to explore. I don't want him to feel tied to me, like I'm his only option." My mother had felt that way. My father had swooped in and been everything to her, made her think he was something he wasn't, and she had been young and innocent and he had taken advantage of that. "I told him if he needs to submit sexually, I would speak to you."

"Yeah…yeah, of course. I'd love to play with him, but I still don't understand why you won't do it."

I shrugged. "You don't have to."

David sat back in his chair. "I feel like I stepped into an alternate universe. I can't believe you have a nineteen-year-old, live-in submissive."

Him and me both. "I underestimated what it would be like—living with someone, being responsible for someone that way." It wasn't that I disliked it. I quite enjoyed it. But I was used to having my space, and I already found myself wondering how everything I did affected Finley.

"You'll be great, as you are at everything. And actually, even though it's not something I ever thought you would do, it fits you, caring for someone at that level."

I wasn't sure about that, so I took a bite of my fried rice and didn't reply.

I stayed at David's for a few hours, then made my way home. The porch light was on, and the door opened before I reached it. "I made a cake!" Finley said and smiled, but it didn't reach his eyes. He was hiding something, that much was clear.

"What kind?"

He took my keys and put them in the bowl, then reached for my suit jacket. "Let me get this." I allowed him to remove it from my shoulders. "Your shoes?"

"They're fine," I replied, and he winced. "The cake."

"Oh, it's chocolate. I love chocolate. I hope you do too."

"My favorite." And it really was.

"I'll get you a piece."

I nodded and went with him to the kitchen. Finley cut me a piece of cake, and I sat at the table to eat it. He surprised me by kneeling by the chair. He'd done it in the living room but never at the table. *Oh, precious boy.* He'd missed me. I was both honored and worried about that. "Are your knees okay on this floor?"

"Yes, Sir."

"We'll get a pillow for the room," I said, then ate while he sat there. "How was your day?"

"Good. I got all my chores done, obviously, but I was bored this evening."

He should have looked into the credits he needed for his diploma, but I didn't say anything. Not yet. "You should have had Ian over."

"I wasn't sure I could."

"I told you he can come anytime. This is your home too, Finley."

He nodded, and I finished my cake. "It was delicious," I told him as he took my plate to the sink and washed it. He had his back to me, and I waited, knowing there was something on his mind.

"Did you... Did you go...you know...do your thing?"

Ah, so that was what this was about. "What thing is that?"

"Sex, of course." He turned around. "What do you do? I know you're a Dominant, but do you go have scenes with people? What kinds of things do you do with them?"

I sighed, standing and walking over to him. Finley looked up at me, needy and hurt. I hated the hurt. I was supposed to protect him, not hurt him, unless it was in a scene and something he wanted. "I wasn't with a boy tonight. I was with my friend David. But if I had been, that would be okay, remember? Those are the rules we agreed on."

"The rules you made."

"Yes, but you agreed to them. I'm supposed to make the rules, yes? And I'm supposed to do what I feel is best for you, which I am."

He crossed his arms, obviously unhappy, but he still said, "Yes, Sir."

Finley turned to walk away, but I reached out and held his wrist. "You don't want to be alone." I knew he didn't. He was feeling needy, lonely, and it was my job to make him feel protected.

"No."

"Go change into something more comfortable. We'll watch that show—whatever it is you're always watching." I hated television, but that wasn't what mattered then. What mattered was being what he needed as best as I could.

"Really?" Finley asked, almost giddy.

"Yes. Go."

He turned and ran upstairs. I went to the entryway and removed my shoes before going to the couch. He was downstairs a few minutes later, in sweats and a T-shirt. He knelt on the floor and put his head on my knee, my fingers automatically going to his hair.

After plucking the remote from the table, I went to Netflix. "Now tell me what this is about."

I couldn't see his face, but I heard the smile in his voice as he told me. I fingered his hair, comforting him as we sat there and watched.

CHAPTER NINE

Finley

"I FEEL LIKE we're on one of those TV shows…rich housewives or something like that," Ian teased as we sunbathed by the pool. He held up his glass of pink lemonade, which we'd put those little umbrellas in, and we clanked them together.

"Right? I think that shit all the time. It's like a dream. I mean, I know I don't belong here, and eventually I'll turn back into a pumpkin, but the past three months have been…" I didn't even have the words for what they had been. I was happy, and being happy made me realize that I truly hadn't been before. Logically, I had to have known that, of course, but I didn't realize how bad it was. But even beyond happiness… "Fulfilling." I felt fulfilled in too many ways to count. Like this rightness had settled into my bones, and I finally fit into my skin the right way, my thoughts soothed and steady.

I was me. The real me. The one who had always lived inside me but had no idea how to break free. Every day I woke up and knew what was expected of me. I made coffee and breakfast. I ate and cleaned and worked out. On certain days I grocery shopped, on others I washed linens, and others I ran errands. My life fit exactly into the schedule Aidan created for me, and that made me feel important.

"But still no sex?" Ian asked.

Okay, so I was happy and fulfilled and all that other stuff minus that one part of it. That was still missing, and the ache was a constant in my bones…in my soul. "No. I haven't tried to hint or anything. I've wanted to. I just hoped it would progress naturally, but it hasn't. I want to respect him, and I'm scared of pushing him away, but he's…" God, Aidan was everything. Gorgeous and kind, protective and dominant, and he made me feel as if I really was the precious boy he called me.

I wanted him. I wanted him so badly, sometimes it felt like it would kill me.

"Tell me again why he doesn't want to fuck you?" Ian asked. He lifted the edge of his Speedo to check his tan line.

"I don't know. Something about my age and feeling indebted to him and blah, blah, blah. It's annoying as shit."

"That's kind of...sweet."

"No, it's not. It's stupid, and I'm horny, and I so want Aidan to be my first."

"Sweet virgin Fin."

I rolled my eyes.

"Try seducing him. You can even do little things like...*Oops, did I leave my dildo out where you could find it? Maybe you should use it on me.*" A dildo was something I'd purchased about six weeks before. I was horny, damn it.

We both laughed, and it struck me for the millionth time how lucky I was to have him. I was lucky to have both Ian and Aidan. They were the only two people I would ever trust.

Ian set his glass down. "Come on. Let's swim." He jumped up, ran to the pool, and leaped in. I was right behind him, and we swam for I didn't know how long. There was a freedom to living with Aidan and being his boy. I had a job, responsibility, a purpose, but I also had protection and care and what felt like love even though I knew it wasn't that.

Eventually we got out of the pool and went back to our chairs. I glanced at my phone and saw that Aidan would be home soon. I mentally ran over my checklist, making sure I had all my responsibilities done for the day. It was linen-washing day, and I'd grocery shopped and put together a casserole I only needed to put in the oven.

"I'll be right back. I need to get dinner on."

Ian nodded, rolling over to lie on his stomach. I dried off as best as I could, warmed the oven, and put the food in before joining him again. I closed the screen but left the sliding glass door open to get a bit of fresh air and so I could hear the oven timer.

We lay there enjoying the kiss of the warm sun on our skin, and for the first time in my life, things felt almost perfect.

A few minutes later Ian asked, "What about the school thing? Is he still making you get your diploma?"

"Ugh." I groaned. Besides the no-sex, that was the worst part—the thought of figuring out how many credits I needed to make up and registering to do it, along with actually going to class for what felt like absolutely no reason. "He's mentioned it a couple of times over the past few months. I know he wants it, but I'm trying to hold off as long as I can. I'm hoping eventually he lets it go. It's really fucking stupid. Why do I have to get my diploma if I don't want to?" What if I couldn't do it?

"So you're basically disobeying him?"

I shrugged. "I guess, but like I said, I think it's dumb, so if I don't have to, I'm not going to do it."

The sound of the screen door opening made me scramble to sit up. Aidan was there, in jeans and a short-sleeved button-up shirt, his arms crossed and disappointment in his eyes. One look was all it took for me to know he'd heard me and that he was *not* happy with me.

"Ian...I think it's time for you to go home. I'll order a ride for you." Aidan's voice was calm, steady as ever. He didn't look at me, but I silently begged him to. God, I didn't want to anger him. Not really. More than that, I didn't want to let him down, but I had. I'd disobeyed him and let him down.

Without a word, he turned and walked into the house.

"Oh shit. I think he heard us," Ian said.

"You think?" I snapped. Suddenly, I wanted to cry. Wanted to crawl to him and kneel for him and beg him to forgive me, not to be mad at me. "Come on, let's go."

Aidan was in the kitchen when we got there. He had a glass of ice water in his hand that I wished I'd gotten for him.

"Your ride will be here in five minutes," Aidan told Ian.

"Okay…thank you. I'll get dressed and see myself out."

The moment Ian was gone, I walked toward him. "Aidan, I—" He held up his hand, and I immediately stopped speaking.

"Get changed. Finish dinner. I'll be in my office. Let me know when it's done."

"Yes, Sir," I replied with a nod, missing him the moment he walked away.

I ran upstairs to get dressed, needing to do as told. Afterward, I was back downstairs, finishing dinner and drying any water off the floor from Ian and me. I threw the towels into the washing machine and paced the room, wanting Aidan, needing to serve him, scared he would toss me away.

When dinner was done, I plated our food and set it on the table. I opened one of his favorite bottles of wine and poured him a glass, then got water for myself.

My heart thudded as I knocked on his office door. "Dinner's ready."

"I'll be out in a moment."

I wanted to wait for him but didn't think I should, so I went to the table and sat in my chair, the one I always sat in. We had our own spots, and I loved that, knowing there were things in Aidan's home that were mine.

As soon as he joined me, I said, "Aidan, I—"

"Eat. We'll discuss it after dinner."

"Yes, Sir," I replied, but I didn't like it at all.

We ate in silence, and when we were finished, he said, "Wash the dishes, please, then go to your room. I'll be there in a few minutes."

My room? Aidan never joined me in my room. "Yes, Aidan."

I was quick to do as he said, and then I was there, waiting, standing in the middle of my bedroom, and felt…wrong. This wasn't where I wanted to be, so I knelt down, let my knees kiss the carpet, and the simple action soothed some of what ailed me.

It felt like an eternity before Aidan entered the room, but I knew it had only been a couple of minutes. He walked over and sat in a chair that wasn't usually there; I hadn't noticed it when I'd first come in. It was a comfortable chair, upholstered in soft, gray fabric, but without armrests. It was usually in Aidan's room.

"I've been patient with you on the school issue. I wanted you to get adjusted, to fall into your routine. I thought a little time would be beneficial and that eventually you would do as you promised, if not because you wanted to, then because I said it. What I didn't expect was to come home and hear you've been disobeying me on purpose, laughing while saying you would go back on your word and that you were trying to put me off."

My head spun, and tears already pooled in my eyes as fear clung to me. Not of Aidan. I would never be afraid of him, but of losing this, losing myself, because serving made me feel complete and…and because I'd failed him. That was the last thing I wanted. "Aidan, I didn't…" But what could I say? I had done exactly what he'd said I'd done, and I'd planned to keep doing it. "I'm sorry."

He nodded. "I know you are, but that doesn't change the fact that you did it. Unless this is a hard limit for you, stand up, please, take off your clothes, and lie over my lap. Say *red* if you want me to stop, or *yellow* and I'll ease up. You'll take your punishment, and then we'll discuss where things go from here."

My heart dropped to my feet, a heavy weight making it difficult to move. Where we went from there? Did he mean he was sending me away?

"Yes…yes, Sir." I couldn't even be excited about being naked around him, something I'd wanted so badly, because I hated upsetting him. Hell, I loved the idea of being spanked, and I'd wanted it for…forever, but my dick hung soft because this wasn't for fun; this was because I'd done wrong. I'd let him down, and that hurt me soul-deep.

I took off my clothes, walked to him on shaky legs, and lay over his lap. I took in Aidan's scent—the light hint of sweat on his skin, twined with the subtle musk of his cologne, the ocean, and what I thought safety probably smelled like. I took comfort in that, inhaling it, then letting it out.

"I'm going to start slowly." He rubbed his hand over my bare ass, and I hated that I couldn't enjoy this, that it couldn't be a moment of desire between us instead of a reminder that I'd disobeyed him.

"Yes, Sir."

"You're not allowed to come. If you do, you'll dislike your punishment. Count them for me," he said, and then his hand slapped down on my right cheek.

"One."

Left cheek.

"Two."

Lower on my right cheek.

"Three."

He kept going, and I kept counting, each sharp sting of his palm part of an intricate pattern that I knew deep inside was to protect me. He spanked and I counted, at some point slipping into this foggy place in my mind that I'd always known was there but had never lived in. I cried out, tears coming harder and harder, and somehow I knew they were less because it hurt and more because I'd let him down. I counted without true knowledge I was doing so, following instinct into this place Aidan was leading me as he punished me the way I needed, showing me in the simple act how much he cared for me.

The sting went deeper, spread out, and I felt it from my ass all through my body.

Then suddenly I was in his arms. He was holding me, and I was straddling him, my face buried in his neck, salty tears on my lips and tongue and Aidan as I clung to him with everything I had inside me. "I'm sorry. I'm so sorry. I'm sorry…I'm sorry…I'm sorry."

"Shh. It's okay, precious boy. I have you. I'm not going to let you go. You took your punishment so well. I'm so very proud of you."

Aidan stroked my back, my ass, my nape, and petted my hair the way I loved so much. His hold on me didn't loosen as I cried into his skin and allowed myself to be lulled by his soothing words.

Finally, when I came down and my vision began to clear, he stood with me, my legs around his waist and my arms around his shoulders. Aidan set me on the bed, and I clutched him, needing him close, needing his presence to ground me. Wanting to make up for what I'd done. "Don't go. Please don't go. I'm so sorry for what I did."

"Shh. I'm not going anywhere, okay? Roll to your stomach and let me see your ass."

Oh, how I'd longed to hear those words from him so many times, but not under these circumstances. I wanted it to be out of pleasure and need. I did as he said and shuddered when his warm fingers danced over my tender skin.

"It's not bad. Will definitely be sore, but that's it."

"Okay," I replied softly, moving to wipe my tears. Aidan's hand was there first, and he did it for me, drying my face and making me feel so very treasured.

"I'm sorry," I said again.

"Shh. It's over with. You took your punishment, and the slate is clean."

I cuddled into the pillow and closed my eyes as Aidan took care of me.

CHAPTER TEN

Aidan

FINLEY RELAXED AS I danced my fingers over his pinkened ass. I didn't allow myself to focus on how pretty the shade was along his pale skin. All I saw in it was that I'd failed him somehow in not nipping this in the bud earlier.

Pulling away, I sat on the bed, with my legs out in front of me and my back against the headboard, knowing he still needed me close, that he was still in that delicate place where he needed my care.

"You can put your head on my lap," I told him, and he did, wrapping an arm over me as he rested there. Because I knew he liked it, knew it soothed him, I carded my fingers through the blond strands of his hair. "Do you understand why you were punished?"

"Yes, Sir," he whispered.

"Before we go on, I want you to know I'm very proud of you. Of how you've taken care of my home and me. I'm not proud of your actions today, but I'm pleased with how you accepted your discipline."

"Thank you."

"Let me explain something to you. Maybe this is my fault. Maybe I should have done it before, but we'll remedy it now. We are a team, you and I; we have to work together. That doesn't mean everything will always go smoothly. It doesn't mean I won't ever make mistakes or that you won't ever give me reason to tan that pretty ass of yours, but we have to work in a rhythm together. In many ways, you lead the way, even though it doesn't seem like it. It starts with your limits and what's best for you. I guide you based on that, and then it's your job to follow me."

He nodded, and I continued caressing him. I thought maybe I needed it as well.

"Now, let me explain why I think it's important for you to get your diploma, even if technically that isn't something that should be up to me—though you'll remember I said it was nonnegotiable before we even began this. I likely should have done this from the start, and that's my mistake.

"I know we aren't in a sexual relationship and your primary concern is our home—as a houseboy of sorts, but I think we both know that the lines have been blurred from the start—and that's something we have both agreed upon, something we both needed."

"Yes," he replied softly. "I want you to make most decisions for me."

"Which brings us back to here. My role in this, maybe my most important one, is to guide you to reach your full potential. It's to do what's best for you, even if you don't see it or believe it. It's to help you be the best you can be in all areas of your life. That doesn't mean a diploma shows your worth, precious boy, but it's a tool I'm helping you arm yourself with. It will help you take care of yourself when I'm not there."

"But—"

"Shh. Don't interrupt." I twisted his hair gently around my finger, then brushed the back of my hand against his cheek. Finley smiled and nuzzled closer to me, and it felt so very good. "I think you need to see that you can do it. I know you can."

Finley gasped, his hold on me tightening. "But what if I can't?" he asked, and my heart broke for him.

"Oh, sweet boy. You can. I know you can."

"School was hard for me, and I'm not...not as smart as everyone else. What if I'm too stupid? What if I fail?"

"You're not too stupid, and if you fail, you try again." Because, whether he saw it or not, Finley needed this. He needed to see he could accomplish it.

"I'm scared. And when I start to think about it, about everything I have to do, my thoughts go too fast and…what if I can't do it? What if I let you down?"

"Hey. Sit up and look at me."

Finley did as told, and I pulled him over so he was on my lap, straddling me, his eyes on mine. I didn't allow myself to think about the fact that he was naked…and that even though I told myself I didn't, I'd spent three months wanting him.

"It's okay to be scared. Do you think I've never been scared?" Maybe I was scared too often, but now wasn't the time to think about that.

"I don't know," he replied simply.

"Well, I do get frightened. Everyone does. What matters is how you react in the face of fear, and I can promise you, trying will never mean you let me down. Giving up? Yes. Trying? No." He nodded, and I continued. "How about this: on my next day off, I'll get some information from you, and we'll look into getting your old school records together. We can figure out how many credits you're short and what they are. Then we'll figure out the next steps we have to take. It might even be something you can do online. Does that help?"

Finley cocked his head slightly and looked at me. He

blinked a tear from his eye, and it slowly trickled down his face. I reached over, wiped it, and sucked my finger into my mouth. He gasped…then smiled, falling against me and burying his face in my neck again.

"Thank you! God, thank you so much!" He sighed, relaxing against me. His cock had hardened and was pressing into my stomach. "So…do we get to make adjustments for sex?"

I chuckled and felt him tremble, my joy radiating from my chest and vibrating through him. "Be good."

"Ugh…fine." He nuzzled in deeper and inhaled. "I like the way you smell. It relaxes me. Makes me feel safe and at home."

Damned if my pulse didn't beat wildly against my skin, my body feeling a little too sensitive. "Stay as long as you need to."

So he did. We sat there for who knew how long, Finley giving me his weight and me carrying it. And in the bearing of his, some of mine was carried by him too.

Eventually, he said, "I'd like to take a warm bath."

"I'll start it."

"But aren't I supposed to do those things for you? If I'm your houseboy? You shouldn't serve me."

"I should care for you, no? This is just another way for me to do so." It was a reminder of how young he was, how inexperienced.

Finley climbed off me, and I didn't allow myself to look at him as I rose, went to the bathroom, and drew his bath. A moment later he walked in, and it was impossible not to see his dick was hard and his balls tight. His ass was deliciously pink, and he had light hair on his legs but none on his chest or belly.

He smiled when he saw me looking, and I shook my head. Naughty, naughty boy.

I stayed with him as he bathed, then helped him dry off afterward. It was early, but I could tell his body was exhausted from the long day and all the emotions.

"You need your sleep. Put some sweats on and go to bed."

Finley didn't argue. He dressed, climbed in, and I brushed the back of my hand against his smooth cheek again. "Good night, precious boy."

"I wish you could stay with me."

"Good night," I repeated, then turned off the light and slipped out.

Alone in my office, hours later, I realized I still felt him, that he was beneath my skin already, and I wasn't sure what to do about it.

CHAPTER ELEVEN

Finley

It was Aidan's day off, and I wanted to do something special for him. It was clear the day would be spent doing the school stuff, which I couldn't say I was excited about. I still didn't think it mattered, in the grand scheme of things, if I had a high school diploma or not, but I did feel better about it after what happened the other night.

It had been… *God*, I trembled at just the thought. It had been so many things I wanted and needed and didn't fully realize I wanted and needed until then.

The way he had punished me hurt, obviously, and I could have done without it, but the fact that he did it pleased me, because it was a way for Aidan to take care of me and do what was best for me, and that made my heart swell and my thoughts calm down. There was also a part of me that liked the pain and was curious about it, but I wanted to explore it in the context of pleasure, not punishment.

I had set my alarm clock for earlier than usual so I could set about my day. I made my bed before going downstairs to the laundry room. The basket had laundry in it, which Aidan had thrown down the laundry chute. Until I moved in with him, I didn't even know people still had those nowadays. It was a little funny. Aidan came off as such an old soul in some ways.

Once his laundry was in, I started coffee and breakfast, a foreign sort of pride swelling within me at the fact that I was serving him in these ways. Logically, I knew most people wouldn't understand that. Maybe it was a little weird to desire these things and feel complete because of them, but I did, and I hadn't felt fulfilled in my whole life before Aidan, so I didn't care what anyone else thought.

I made a veggie omelet for him, with a blueberry bagel. Once it was done, I plated the food and put it on a tray along with orange juice and his coffee exactly how he liked it—milk and two sugars—and then prayed like hell I didn't carry a breakfast tray as terribly as when I'd been a waiter because it would be just my luck to drop it and ruin the morning.

The tray didn't tumble from my hands, and I didn't spill anything before setting it on the floor in front of

Aidan's bedroom door. I'd never been in his room with him. We didn't cuddle on his bed the way he often let me do with him on the couch, and an excited sort of vibration ran the length of my body. Of course, it would suck if he sent me out, but I hoped he didn't, hoped he saw this for what it was.

Once I had the door open, I picked up the tray again and walked inside. He lay on his side, surrounded by the thick and fluffy white bedding, stubble along his jaw that I wanted to feel scrape against my skin, especially my ass, which was still deliciously tender. I willed my cock not to get hard.

His dark-brown eyes fluttered open, making me wonder if he'd already been partially awake. "Surprise. I made you breakfast in bed! I hope you don't mind."

He gave me a small smile that didn't reach his eyes, but I didn't think he was disappointed in any way.

"Thank you," Aidan replied, sitting up.

I set the tray on the bed, my eyes darting between Aidan and the food, wanting to watch him and take pleasure in him enjoying the meal I cooked for him.

"Did you eat already?" he asked.

"No, I didn't make anything for myself. I can eat some cereal later. I wanted to do something special for you." Because I was there with him and he had punished me and then held me before making me understand why he did the things he did. For wanting the best for me when no one had in so very long.

"Sit down." He nodded toward the bed, and I did so. "Give me just a moment." Aidan stood, wearing a pair of tight, black boxer trunks that hugged his ass deliciously and showed me his very large bulge. God, I wanted it. Wanted to kneel for him and inhale the scent between his legs, suck him off and choke on his cock before nursing it while he played with my hair…

He walked to the bathroom, and I watched him go. Aidan pushed the door partway closed; not all the way, but enough so I couldn't see him, and I heard him as he began to take a piss. I wanted in there with him while he did that too. I yearned to hold his cock for him while he went, which again, maybe that was weird, but I didn't care.

The toilet flushed, and then the faucet ran, I assumed to wash his hands. A moment later he was sitting on the bed, leaning against the headboard with his tray on his lap. Aidan cut the bagel in half, then did the same with the omelet. "Eat." He handed me half of the bagel while he used the fork to begin eating half of the omelet.

I took a bite but wished he would feed me from his hand. I wanted that right then, to be fed by him. I would feed him as well. Was that something a houseboy was supposed to do? But then I remembered what Aidan had said, about doing what worked for us and that the rest of it didn't matter.

"Did you sleep well?" he asked.

"I did. How was work yesterday?"

Aidan shrugged. He didn't like to talk about what he did. Sometimes I thought maybe it made him sad.

"Everyone lived, which is what matters."

We sat there, eating together, talking about nothing in particular, but it felt like one of the most important conversations of my life. When I finished the bagel and he the omelet, we switched, and he went for the carbs while I used his fork to eat the eggs.

I loved being in Aidan's space like this, just talking to him and eating with him as if this had been our life for a hundred years. He laughed when I told him a story about Ian, and I was reminded how much I loved the sound, the way it settled inside me like a hug from within.

He shared his orange juice with me too, and when we finished eating, he said, "Thank you, boy. That was very good."

I felt my skin glow and my smile get too bright. "You're very welcome, Sir."

He chuckled. "You are so eager to please and a bit of a slut for praise. It's utterly adorable." Aidan brushed the back of his hand against my cheek. I was beginning to notice it was his thing, and I liked it very, very much. "Go downstairs and take care of your morning responsibilities, please. I'll be down soon."

"Yes, Sir."

I was giddy as I took the tray back downstairs, put his laundry in the dryer, washed the dishes, cleaned the counters, swept and mopped the kitchen. Aidan came down not long after in shorts and a T-shirt. "Have you done your workout yet?"

"No, Aidan."

"Get changed. We'll do it together."

"Oh my God, really?" I still wasn't fond of exercising, but I liked the idea of doing it with Aidan. I wanted to do anything and everything with Aidan, and I would if he'd let me.

"Of course, silly boy. You say that as if I never spend time with you."

"No, I just want to spend all the time with you, and if you're forcing me to like, be healthy and sweat, then at least I should have a nice view when I do so." I waggled my eyebrows at him, which earned me another Aidan snicker.

"There's a gorgeous view out the window, you know."

"Yes, but it's not you…all glistening and sweaty and muscular." Now if he would just let me lick him up afterward, it would be perfect. "But I'll go get dressed before you change your mind!"

"That's what I thought!" he called after me as I jogged away. Playful Aidan was the best.

I used the elliptical while Aidan ran on the treadmill. From there we lifted weights and he spotted me, cheering me on with things like, "One more. You can do it, Finley," which made me all melty inside.

Afterward, Aidan got on his laptop as I cleaned bathrooms.

That done, I went back into the kitchen, where he'd been in the meantime. Aidan stood and stretched, saying, "Shower and dress, then meet me in my office."

"Yes, Sir." Which meant school stuff was next, and the thought made my stomach tumble in a *fuck this* sort of way. Still, I obeyed him because I trusted him, and Aidan said this was for the best.

When I got to his office, he had pulled up another chair next to his at the desk. My grades had been shitty when I was in school, and I hated that he would likely see them. "No shame, remember?" Aidan said as I sat beside him.

"Are you a mind reader?"

"I wouldn't be very good at this if I didn't learn to read you. That doesn't mean you don't have to communicate, because you do. I'm not perfect, but I do my best."

"I know."

It took a few hours to get the information we needed. I had to give Aidan school names and my personal information as he requested transcripts. He researched local programs for getting your diploma. They had programs at community colleges, and some high schools also did continuing adult education.

Aidan made phone calls, and then we left for appointments, and before I knew it, I was going to be taking summer courses to get my high school diploma.

"Are you hungry?" Aidan asked.

"Starving."

I was quiet after that, and I figured he noticed, but I was trying to sort through the day, the future, and deciding how I felt about it all. What Aidan had done for me was…unexplainable. No one had ever gone through the trouble for me the way Aidan had, no one had ever made me feel loved the way Aidan did, even though I knew he didn't love me. He was my Dominant, my Sir, my employer, my…friend, in many ways. The man who watched TV shows with me when I knew it wasn't his favorite thing; the guy who let me rest my head in his lap and stroked my hair. But knew I didn't love him either. It was surprising how he could be my world while I wasn't in love with him, but I also knew I could be. Very, very easily, I *could* be, because he was kind, made me feel secure, and was funny when he wanted to be. Was the fact that I *could* love him why he didn't want to fuck me? Or was it something more?

Aidan took me to a burger place for a late lunch/early dinner. It was the first time we'd gone out for a meal together, and I felt proud that people would see me with him.

When we got back home, I lost myself in cleaning things that didn't truly need to be cleaned, because it centered me and cleared my head.

At about eight o'clock, Aidan found me and said, "Meet me in the living room. We'll find a new show to watch together."

It was things like this—Aidan telling me to choose a show because he knew I enjoyed it—that made me see how much more there really was to Aidan.

He allowed me to kneel for him as we watched the first episode of *Spartacus*. "The special effects are badass,"

I said, and he chuckled, his hand finding its way to my hair, petting me.

We ended up watching two episodes before Aidan turned off the television. My instincts took over as the day washed through my mind and heart, making me lean into him, push my nose farther between his legs as I inhaled. "Please...please, Aidan."

I wanted to serve him. I wanted to thank him because this day had been...the best day of my life, and I realized as I sat there on my knees that I truly did want what he'd said. I wanted my diploma, even if I never used it, even if it didn't get me anything. A part of me wanted to know I could do it, and another part wanted it because Aidan desired it. "Please," I begged again as my nose rubbed over his full balls and thick erection. Pride rushed through me that I'd gotten him hard, that he wanted me, and I kept breathing him in and trying to push in as close as possible. *God*, I loved the way he smelled, masculine and dominant, heady.

He inhaled a deep breath. His hand tightened in my hair. *Yes, yes, yes!* He was going to give me this. He was going to allow me to serve him this way. "Please, let me thank you for today."

It was as if I'd thrown cold water on him. I felt the change in Aidan's body as he stiffened, then gently eased my head back. "No. Go upstairs for the night, please. I'll take care of turning off the lights and locking up."

"Aidan… I…"

"I said no. If you don't obey, you'll get punished, and I promise you, you won't like it."

I stood, crossed my arms, almost told him I hated him, but instead said, "Yes, Sir," and walked away.

CHAPTER TWELVE

Aidan

I WAS SPENDING more time than I should thinking about Finley. Not that I shouldn't have him on my mind, because he was my responsibility. He was under my care, which meant I should consider him in all things. But there were other thoughts coming more and more frequently, especially in the weeks since he'd knelt for me, inhaled my scent, and begged to let him serve me. I'd been right there, ready to throw my rules out the window, until he'd whispered the words that had doused the flames of my lust—*"Please, let me thank you for today."*

Did I know the boy wanted me? Or wanted someone? Yes, I did, but I also refused to let him become to me what my mother had been to my father. To take someone young, who had nothing, and to make him feel trapped, to make him feel as if he owed me, until he had little choice but to stay with me. I wanted to care for

Finley, yes, but I also wanted him to have options. I wanted him to always know he had a choice in being mine or not.

My mother hadn't felt she had that choice. My father had been ruthless in beating her down until she felt she was nothing without him. And no matter what ugliness he showed her, she had never shown it to us. She had loved us, my sisters and me, until the three of them died because of my carelessness.

I shook my head, unwilling to let my thoughts go there. I had a job to do, and I damn sure planned to do it. If I couldn't save them, I needed to save others.

The next few days went by without any major incident. Finley was doing well with school and keeping up with his chores around the house. He did well when given a routine and responsibilities, desiring so very much to do a good job for me. It was one of the most stunning things I had ever seen—his need to please and his passionate submission.

But my desire to dominate someone sexually was plaguing me more and more each day. The months Finley had been in my home were the longest I'd gone without playing with someone in a long time. I was on edge, the tension inside me coiling tighter, sharper, as I denied myself something I very much needed. Something I'd told myself I would continue to do, even with Finley as my houseboy, because our relationship wasn't going to be about sex.

After work, I met David. "You okay?" he asked.

"Fine, I just…"

"You're still not fucking that kid, are you?"

I groaned. "Because wording it like that is going to make me want to. Christ, David."

"You already want to." He shrugged. "You should do it since it's what you both want."

"It's not always just about what I want. Maybe you live that way, but I don't."

David flinched, and I felt a familiar stab of guilt. "I'm sorry. I'm being an asshole."

"No, you?" he teased.

I chuckled but didn't truly feel it.

I wanted to get laid. I wanted to fuck. To demand. To dominate. To lead someone into that exquisite space where they lost themselves to my control.

When my meal with David was finished, I sat in my car and sent a text to Finley.

I won't be home until late tonight. Continue with your normal responsibilities, but I would also like the equipment and mirrors in the gym cleaned and the fridge cleaned out.

I knew he would wonder where I was and would

need something extra to take his mind off things. His response came almost immediately.

Sir?

Do as you're told, Finley.

There was a pause before his reply. **Yes, Sir.**

I made a phone call after that, to a boy I'd played with before. I asked him if he was busy that night and if he wanted to meet me. He invited me over, and I knew he had a closetful of toys we could play with. "Clean yourself out for me. Unlock the door and be naked and kneeling for me when I arrive."

"Yes, Sir," he replied, and hearing the words from Les made my insides twist. It was uncomfortable hearing it from anyone other than Finley, as I hadn't in so long.

Les was exactly where I told him to be when I arrived at his apartment. Once I had the door closed and locked, I looked at him, at his dark, curly hair and perfect posture. There was no reason I shouldn't do this. No reason I shouldn't want it. "Open my pants and get me hard," I ordered, and Les crawled over to me and did just that.

THE HOUSE WAS quiet when I arrived. It wasn't the first

time that had happened, obviously. There were times I worked late or was on call, so Finley wasn't there to greet me as he would already be asleep, but this was...different.

My night with Les had gone as it should. I was good to him and read him and gave him what he needed. In turn, a part of me found what I sought in the dance of dominance and submission, but I wasn't sated, and there was a heaviness in my chest, one that was even more potent than what I had felt before.

I locked up and went through the house, which was spotless as Finley was so good at keeping it. I took my shoes off and put them away before plucking a bottle of water from the fridge.

I paused when I got to Finley's bedroom door. The lights were off as they should be, because it was long past the time I gave him for going to bed. The door wasn't closed tightly, though; it was opened just a crack, and I found myself slipping inside, going to his bedside, and looking down at him.

He had the blinds open, the moon shining in the room. He lay on his side, curled in a ball, and he was...incredible, as I'd always known he was. His skin looked soft, unblemished and smooth, and his face almost boyish, but with strong, defined cheekbones. And that halo of blond hair…which he so very much loved for me to pet. It was something I loved too.

There was a bottle of lube and a dildo on his nightstand, and I wanted to wake him, wanted to tell him I owned him and his orgasms were mine. That he was not to come unless I said he could. But I hadn't allowed myself that kind of control over him, had I?

So instead, I turned to leave. I made it two steps before there was a soft, "Aidan?"

I paused, took a deep breath, then turned to him. "Someone is being very naughty right now. You're not supposed to be awake."

"I'm sorry. I tried to follow the rules, but I couldn't sleep. Are you angry with me?"

A long sigh escaped my lips. I set the water on his nightstand and ran my fingers through his hair. "No, precious boy. I'm not mad at you." If I wasn't mistaken, I was angry with myself. Tonight had felt…wrong.

"Will you lie with me?" It wasn't something we had done in bed, except the one time I'd spanked him, but I found myself nodding regardless.

Finley scooted over and lifted the blanket. I climbed in beside him and lay on my back.

"Will you hold me, Sir? Please?" Without me having told him, there wasn't a doubt in my mind that Finley knew where I had been tonight, that I had been with someone. The wrongness of it settled in my chest. It wasn't supposed to feel this way. These were the terms we had agreed upon, but the night was like a heavy weight around my shoulders.

"I will," I told him, opening my arms for him. He was still on his side and tossed a leg over me, rested his head in the crook of my arm, and buried his face inside my armpit.

We lay there for one moment after another. His cock was hard against my hip, and mine throbbed behind the fly of my jeans. Finley nuzzled in deeper, breathing me in. He took comfort in my scent, which made the Dominant in me roar…want to claim.

And then…then he quietly began to cry, and everything inside me raged against this kind of tears. I was supposed to care for him, protect him, not hurt him, not in this way.

I shushed him and kissed the top of his head, squeezed him tighter against me. "It's okay. I'm here," I said softly.

"I'm sorry. I know it's not cheating because we're not in a relationship, and it's something you told me you would do from the start, but…"

"You have nothing to be sorry for. I do. I should

have known it would hurt you. That wasn't my intent, but intent doesn't matter. I failed you tonight, and it's me who's sorry, okay?"

"I—"

"Shh. Your Sir is speaking," I chided. "Nothing else is changing between us, but this, what I did tonight, I won't do that again, okay?" It went against my better judgment, but I also couldn't hurt him this way. And I hadn't been fully in the scene with Les either, which wasn't fair to him. I'd known from the start it felt wrong for me.

"Yes, Sir. But what if you need—"

"I'll worry about myself. You just be a good boy and keep doing as you're told." But it was a good question. There was no end in sight to what we were doing, and I couldn't be celibate forever.

"Yes, Sir," Finley replied, burrowing himself into me farther. "I love the way you smell. It makes me feel safe. I know I said that before, but yeah, just wanted you to know."

"While you're mine, I'll always protect you." I hadn't done that tonight, and I wouldn't allow myself to do it again.

"I know. Will you stay with me tonight?"

"Yes," I replied simply, petting his head until he fell asleep…and maybe long afterward.

CHAPTER THIRTEEN

Finley

TIME PASSED BY in this sort of whirlwind. I was happier than I'd ever been, more fulfilled than I'd ever been, even though there was more I wanted too. Sometimes I felt greedy for not being completely satisfied. Aidan took such good care of me. He was different with me than others—somehow I knew that. Even small things were changing, little things like sitting around the table and playing cards or board games. We'd begun spending time like that together, and honestly, I couldn't imagine seeing Aidan do those things with others.

He told me daily that I served him well, which was the best kind of compliment. I took my position as his houseboy, his submissive—without any sexual play, of course—very seriously. I loved that Aidan and I were making our relationship fit our needs, even though I was still hoping I got some of those other needs fulfilled soon.

It was the first week of December, and I'd noticed some of the other neighbors begin decorating for the holiday. Mom had tried to make our apartment as festive as possible growing up, and I'd loved it. I missed that.

I couldn't imagine seeing Aidan's home decorated. It would feel like a winter wonderland.

I'd just finished my cleaning for the day. Aidan was home, sitting at the kitchen table with his laptop. I walked over and sat in one of the chairs beside him, not sure exactly what I planned to accomplish.

His eyes darted to me a few times, then back to his computer before he asked, "What is it? Something's wrong?"

"Nothing's wrong. I was just wondering…do you ever like, decorate for the holiday or anything?"

"Christmas?" he asked, his expression pinched.

"No, Easter. Of course Christmas." He cocked a brow at me, and I said quickly, "Sorry, Sir."

"I don't have a tree or anything."

"Aidan! Oh my God. I can't believe you don't have a tree!" I exclaimed. I swear, was he the Grinch or what?

"What did I ever need one for? I live alone."

That made me feel…heavy. "Just because you live alone doesn't mean you can't have a Christmas tree. Can we get one? I can buy it myself. We can get a huge one. You have so much space!" I was feeling slightly giddy at the thought now. I wanted this, so badly, but I could tell by the expression on his face that he didn't get it. I fluttered my lashes at him playfully. "Please!"

He snickered, but as he did so, he shook his head, then closed his laptop. "Go get dressed, then."

I shoved to my feet and flung my arms around him. I didn't think Aidan realized how sweet he was, how caring.

"Dress warm!" he called as I went for the stairs. That surprised me, but I did as he said.

A little while later, we were in his car. "Where are we going?"

"Big Bear. I thought… My mom used to enjoy cutting a fresh tree. I thought we could do that."

A million questions swam around in my head. I wanted to know about Aidan's family, but I could sense it was a sore spot for him, and the last thing I wanted to do when he was being so nice was hurt him.

And *God*, was he the best. He never had a tree, but obviously he had fond memories of them, and now that we were doing it, Aidan went there with all his heart.

"I've never cut a fresh tree before."

He glanced my way. "Then I'm glad we're doing it."

"There isn't snow on the pass or anything?"

Aidan shook his head. "No, it's colder, but they haven't gotten any snow yet. You can turn music on if you like, whatever you enjoy."

"I'd rather talk if that's okay with you." It was nice just getting to talk to him.

"It is."

"What kind of music do you like?" I asked, out of curiosity.

"Hmm… I don't know. I'm not much of a music person. I like some older jazz and blues." He was quiet for a moment, then asked, "You?" as if nervous about being interested in me.

"Oh, anything I guess. Mostly pop."

"Why am I not surprised about that," he teased.

"Hey! Popular music is good!"

"If you say so."

"I do, thank you very much."

"Um-hm. Whatever you say."

"I can't believe you're insulting my musical choices," I joked, and we went back and forth like that for a while, then chatted about random things like books we read, or funny things Ian and I had done, and how there had never been anything Aidan had wanted to do other than be a doctor. He'd been a bit more subdued when we'd spoken about that, so I knew there was a story behind it.

I noticed him looking at me every now and again, especially in quiet moments, and it was *killing* me not to know what he was thinking. But he was enjoying himself, and I was too, just having this simple moment of getting to know each other.

"Maybe next year we can decorate the whole house. The outside and everything," I said without thinking. As soon as the words left my mouth, I scrambled a bit. "I mean…if I'm still living with you, obviously. I know that's a long time."

"We'll see what happens," Aidan replied, but I had a feeling he was just placating me, that he didn't think I would be there with him. "Here we are," he added a moment later as he pulled up next to a cabin with tons of cars parked out front. Behind it was a large Christmas tree farm full of families and couples, all picking out their perfect tree.

This overwhelming happiness took me over, and I was so glad to be sharing this moment with him—with the bighearted man who was changing my world in more ways than he would ever know.

"Come," Aidan said, getting out of the car.

I followed along behind him as we went into the cabin and found out what we had to do. Aidan signed some forms and got a saw, and we made our way out back.

"What's your favorite holiday?" I asked as we browsed the trees.

"Hmm..." He tapped his temple playfully, as if thinking. I was pretty sure he was covering for something, maybe for mentioning his mom? "Christmas, I guess. It's not something I've thought about much."

"Oh my God, Aidan. You totally should. And Christmas is second to my birthday, which is on Christmas Eve."

"I know," he replied with a grin.

My pulse sped up a bit. "Wait. You remembered? Like, is it something you've thought about?"

Aidan chuckled. "Relax, boy. There's no hidden story there."

Crossing my arms, I pouted playfully.

"Which tree do you want?" he asked a moment later.

"I don't know. Which one do you like?"

"You choose," he replied, and I felt a bit light-headed as another rush of happiness swam through me.

Aidan didn't rush me. It took me over thirty minutes to find the perfect tree, and he waited patiently as we browsed and chatted. When I saw the perfect one—probably eight feet tall and incredibly full and wide—I stopped. "This one. It's perfect!"

"Looks like a good choice to me. Let's do this."

We took turns with the saw, cutting down our tree. Aidan wouldn't let me pay, and a little while later, with the tree strapped to the top of the car, we were driving home and chatting about all sorts of random things.

This felt…different from any time Aidan and I had spent together, and I wanted nothing more than to live in moments like this with him for as long as I could.

CHAPTER FOURTEEN
Aidan

I WAS ABSOLUTELY ridiculous. I felt a bit silly, but that didn't stop me from researching light companies to have someone come to decorate the outside of the house while Finley was out.

I'd enjoyed our spontaneous trip to Big Bear more than I liked to admit. We had to shop for decorations afterward, and he'd loved it. It felt good to see him smile and know I was the one making it happen. He hadn't had enough happiness in his life, and while I couldn't give him everything he wanted, I took delight in giving him what I could.

And I knew he wanted the outside of the house decorated. I knew it would please him.

This was all…not what it was supposed to be. I didn't mean my promise not to be with anyone else or picking out trees and holiday ornaments together, but the fact that I liked spending time with him more than I thought I would. Having Finley around had become more than just a routine. We'd slipped into this sort of life together. That was something else I hadn't expected, and again, I didn't know what to do with it.

Once I made the phone call and was able to get someone out quickly to take care of decorating the house, I went to work.

Absurdly, I continued to check my phone when I knew Finley would be home. The lights wouldn't be on, so maybe he hadn't noticed? But he paid attention well to detail, and I knew that wasn't the case. He would have seen them, so I was surprised he hadn't called or texted. What I didn't want to acknowledge was that it disappointed me he hadn't.

Forcing those thoughts from my mind—they had no business being there anyway—I finished up at work and headed home.

When I pulled up to the house, it was after dark. The Christmas lights were glowing…and were a bit obnoxious, if you asked me. It was…a lot. But the second I got out of the car, the door to the house opened and Finley came running out.

He jumped at me before I had a chance to do or think much of anything. "It's perfect, Sir! I…I can't believe you did this for me. Thank you!"

"It's not a problem." I patted his back awkwardly before letting him go. "Why wouldn't I do this for you?" Forget that it wasn't the kind of thing I did. I knew that wasn't what he meant.

"I just know it had to be expensive…and you don't care about it. I'm not sure I'm worth that kind of—"

"Stop," I cut him off. "I'm going to make you say nice things about yourself every time you say something negative if you don't stop." Cupping his cheek, I angled his face toward me. "You're worth Christmas lights. You're worth more than that. Don't feel differently, and don't let anyone ever treat you differently either."

Which included me…and whoever he was with after me. The thought made my insides feel hollowed out.

"Okay," he replied. "I…I love it. And I made double-chocolate-chip cookies, your favorite, to celebrate."

He grinned, and then I did, something I was noticing I did entirely too much around him. "I'm glad you like it, boy."

We stood there and looked at them for a moment, and…I wasn't sure they were as bad as I'd originally thought. When we went inside, I thought maybe I actually liked them.

CHAPTER FIFTEEN
Finley

IT WAS MY birthday. My mom always said I was the best Christmas gift she'd ever received, which I never understood. She'd been sixteen, and having me had gotten her kicked out of her parents' home. There was also the fact that I'd been born a month early and had almost died, but she said that since I hadn't, that just went to show how special I was.

It had been months since the one and only time Aidan had shared my bed. That night…it almost wrecked me. I hated how weak I was, how needy, as I'd cried and imagined Aidan with someone else, wishing he'd wanted to use me instead. I would do anything to be used by him, to be possessed and fucked and shown all those sexual activities I'd only seen in porn and longed to know firsthand.

But he hadn't come to me. He'd gone to someone else, and then I'd cried and forced him into bed with me, when it obviously wasn't where he'd wanted to be. And then he'd sworn to me he wouldn't do it again, and a stronger boy wouldn't have needed that. Aidan was a Dominant and deserved to be served by whomever he wanted, but I'd clung to that promise, knowing that in the months that passed, Aidan hadn't gone back on his word to me.

"It feels weird, not cooking for you," I told Aidan as I went downstairs that evening. He hadn't allowed me to do any of my chores either.

"It's your birthday. It's my job to take care of you, yes? I want to give you this. We didn't celebrate when you got your diploma. I'm not going to allow your birthday to go unnoticed."

I was such a fucking slut for him. I couldn't hold back the grin that split my face. "Thank you, Sir. You make me feel…" Loved. He made me feel loved. "Cared for."

"You are, and you deserve it." Aidan reached over and threaded his fingers through my hair. Closing my eyes, I savored his touch, while also wondering what it would feel like if he pulled. He'd tightened his grip on my hair before but never tugged it, never let me feel the sting deep in my scalp.

"Thank you."

The doorbell rang, and my eyes jerked open in excitement. "You may answer it," Aidan told me.

"Thank you!" I replied before running for the door.

Ian was there, like I knew he would be, with a package in his hand. "Happy birthday and merry Christmas," my best and only friend in the world said. He stepped inside, and we hugged.

"Hi, Aidan," Ian said when we pulled apart. "Thank you for letting me come over today."

"It's Finley's special day. He deserves to be celebrated."

Oh, I nearly melted right there in the entryway. I loved when he said things like that.

"As do I, and I don't remember you ever having a dinner party for me," another voice said. A tall man stepped up and smiled at Aidan. It was his friend David, with whom he'd been having dinner the night Aidan had taken me home with him. The two of them met up often, but I'd never seen him other than that night. I knew he was coming tonight, and I thought maybe that was because Aidan knew I had no one except Ian and wanted me to feel more like it was a real party.

"Who are you, again?" Aidan asked, and David laughed.

"I used to be your friend, but I don't think I want

that title anymore." They grinned, and I felt honored to be in this moment. I never saw Aidan with anyone other than me or Ian, outside of deliverymen or someone at a restaurant or gas station or whatever. "Are you going to officially introduce me to your boy or what?"

David came inside, and I closed the door behind him.

"David, you remember Finley, and this is his friend Ian. Boys, this is David," Aidan said.

"Hi. It's great to meet you," I replied.

"Happy birthday," David answered, surprising me by giving me a hug.

He and Ian said hello next.

"Well, aren't you pretty?" David said to him, winking. Ian and his boyfriend had broken up a while ago, but Ian wasn't in this lifestyle. I looked up at Aidan, unsure what to do, and he nodded as if telling me he would take care of it.

"I have some good whiskey in my office," Aidan told David.

"Then what are we doing out here?" David replied, and the two of them disappeared down the hallway.

"Sorry about that," I told Ian, but he only shrugged it off, moving farther into the house.

"Holy shit. The Christmas tree is huge." He walked

over to where it stood in front of a window.

"Right? Aidan didn't have one. I can't believe that. I asked him if we could get one, and we went to Big Bear and cut it down ourselves. He had to buy all the decorations and everything. I think it's the best tree in the world." Especially because he did it for me.

"You're so spoiled." Ian playfully rolled his eyes.

I was. There was no denying it, so I didn't try. There were so many things Aidan did for me that I knew were for me and me alone—the tree, this party, the shows we watched together. It was hard, having to remind myself that he didn't do them because he loved me, but because I was his boy. I felt extremely loved, though.

Ian and I played some games on the new system Aidan had purchased, something else that was for me. I felt guilty sometimes, because he gave me so much, but still I wanted more. I wanted to share his bed and serve him sexually. I'd begun doing what Ian had said, leaving my dildo out more often, and even masturbating when he was home and could hear me, but nothing had changed.

"Has he still not fucked you?" Ian asked as if he could read my mind.

I glanced over my shoulder to make sure Aidan or David weren't there. I learned my lesson on that.

Lowering my voice, I whispered, "No, and it's killing me." With another peek behind me, I added, "I'm thinking about asking him if he can control my orgasms…even without fucking me. Maybe that will turn him on and make him want me."

"You are so weird," Ian said, but I knew it wasn't said to put me down. He just didn't understand. "I can't imagine wanting someone to control when I blow my load."

I shrugged. "You're not me."

A moment later Aidan and David returned. I set the controller on the coffee table and asked, "Is there anything I can get for you?"

Aidan cocked a brow.

"Sorry, Sir! I forget. It's so weird, not serving you."

"Bad weird?" he asked, and I knew it was because he wanted to make sure he was doing right by me, that I felt like this day was a treat and not a punishment.

"No. It's…nice. Because you wish it and you want to take care of me."

"Oh, Aidan. He's delightful," David said, and I blushed.

"Yes," Aidan replied. "He is." He smiled at me, and I went to him, asking permission with my eyes. Aidan nodded, and I rubbed my cheek against his chest. It was something he had allowed me to do after the night he slept in my bed.

"Thank you, Sir."

"You're welcome, boy. Are you hungry?"

"Yes."

Aidan ordered food from my favorite Chinese restaurant. The four of us sat in the living room and chatted until it arrived. David was much more talkative than Aidan, and he kept the conversation going with Ian and me.

I felt Aidan's stare on me, on us, but he didn't look upset. I wasn't sure if that was a good thing or a bad one. Part of me wanted him to be jealous as I had been the night he fucked someone.

The food came, and we ate at the larger table in the dining room. Aidan laughed quite a bit, which was lovely. His laugh was one of my favorite sounds in the world.

When dinner was done, he wouldn't allow me to clean up. From there we went to the living room and watched an older *Terminator* movie, because they were my favorite and that's what I'd told Aidan I wanted to do.

"Kitchen," he said simply when the movie was over, and I pushed to my feet. We were all standing by the kitchen island when Aidan went to the garage. He came in a moment later with a cake. It must have been in the second fridge out there. "Chocolate cake and icing with strawberry filling, right?"

I'd told him that months ago, that I loved strawberries with chocolate. The reason escaped me, but all I could focus on was the fact that he'd remembered. Aidan had remembered something so small, and then he'd made sure to give it to me for my birthday. "Yes, it's my favorite. Thank you."

"There's nothing to thank me for."

The three of them sang me "Happy Birthday," and then I blew out the twenty candles on the cake. We ate it along with strawberry ice cream.

Ian gave me my gift. It was a new video game. David gave me a gift card so I could buy whatever I wanted. Aidan's box was a long rectangle, perfectly wrapped. Had he wrapped it himself? It was a silly thing to think.

My fingers shook and my heart thudded as I opened it. "A laptop? It's too much."

"It's what I wanted to give you," he replied, and I knew he did it because I wouldn't argue with that. I wanted whatever Aidan desired.

I slid from the chair and to the floor. Part of me felt stupid, doing this in front of Ian and David, but the other didn't care. I worshipped Aidan and didn't care who knew. I crawled to him and knelt at his feet. His eyes flared with dominance when I looked up at him. "Thank you, Sir. You take such good care of me. I've never…" Never had this. Never been spoiled this way. My mom had loved me so much, but she hadn't had the means Aidan did. Not that I didn't appreciate what she gave me. I would give up everything for her to be there with me, to look at me and hug me and laugh with me the way she had always done.

But this, the way Aidan cared for me, it was so foreign to me outside of him, and it was the very best thing that had ever happened to me.

"I know," he said, understanding what I couldn't put words to. "You're a very good boy. You serve me well, and you deserve this."

"Thank you." I nodded, unsure if I believed him.

When I looked up, Ian's eyes were on me with an interest I'd never seen in him before.

"You may stand," Aidan said.

"Yes, Sir."

We visited for a little while before David said, "I should head out. Thanks for having me."

"Thank you for coming," I told him, and I meant it. He might have only come because he was Aidan's friend, but I appreciated it.

"Anytime," David replied. "Do you need a ride home?" he asked Ian.

"Sure, if you don't mind."

We walked them to the door and said our goodbyes. Ian and I hugged, and then the two of them slipped out the door. The second Aidan had closed and locked it, I looked at him and burst into tears.

CHAPTER SIXTEEN
Aidan

THE MOMENT FINLEY began to cry, I went to him, wrapped my arms around him, and kissed the top of his head, trying to figure out what happened, where I went wrong. "Shh. It's okay. I'm here. I have you."

My words only made him cry harder, so I lifted him, and Finley went easily. He wrapped his arms around my neck, his legs over one arm and his back against the other. If I could, I would carry him upstairs like this, but I knew it wasn't possible, so I went to the couch and sat down.

"I have you. I'm not going anywhere," I told him again, playing with his hair because I knew how much my boy loved it. Finley nuzzled into my neck and breathed me in, his body beginning to relax against me. "Communication, remember? If something's wrong, you need to tell me. I'm just a man. I can't always figure it out on my own."

Finley gasped. "What? No. Nothing's wrong. I'm so sorry. I'm just…" He lowered his voice. "I don't know why I'm crying. It's ridiculous, really. I'm just so happy. This is the best birthday I've had since my mom died."

Oh, this sweet, precious boy. The things he did to me. My body was sensitive, this sort of softening of walls inside me. I should have thought of that, what this meant to him after losing her. "Tell me about your mother," I commanded.

"Really?" His eyes were bright, eager, as if my demand had surprised him.

"Yes, of course."

"I… Okay. Her name was Amanda. I never met her parents, but I know they were wealthy—they came from money—and very religious. Her dad was a minister."

I listened, petting his hair as he spoke.

"She got pregnant with me when she was sixteen. She kept it from her parents for as long as she could. When they found out, they were incredibly angry with her, but at that point there wasn't much they could do. They're from Texas, and I think her mother brought her here so that no one back home would know. When I was born, it was me or them, and she chose me."

Wow. That was a lot to put on his shoulders. "Tell me you know that's not your fault," I urged him.

"Because it isn't."

"Part of me knows that. I didn't ask to be born, but her life would have been much better without me."

I didn't think anything would be better without him. "You were worth it to her. She loved you, correct?"

"Yes, she was the best."

"Exactly. Now continue, please."

"I was born a month early. They didn't think I would make it. I was very sick, and we were in the hospital for quite a while. It's why she named me Finley. It means fair-haired warrior. Even though I was early, I was born with a headful of blond hair. She told me the story often, how I was her little warrior because I survived."

I smiled, kissed his temple. "I like that. It fits. You are a warrior."

"Thank you. Anyway, her mom had arranged an adoption and tried to take me away when I was born, but she said she changed her mind as soon as she had me. Her mom kept trying to get her to give me up, but she wouldn't. She spent the whole time we were in the hospital telling me I would be better off somewhere else. In the meantime, she had met a woman—a nurse in the OBGYN center. She and her husband couldn't have kids. They helped her, gave her a place to stay, and had appointments with CPS and all that. The problem was, eventually she realized they helped her because they wanted me…wanted a child. They basically tried to be my parents. She was young, and they took advantage of that. I was two by the time she ran from them, but at least by then she was eighteen. She bounced around from place to place, doing her best to make ends meet."

What a tragic beginning for such a sweet boy. It made me want to protect him even more, to take care of him so he never had to worry or struggle.

"Were you born in the hospital where I work?"

He shook his head.

"And when she passed away?"

"They found her parents. I guess they didn't want me."

I found myself kissing him again, trying to soothe him. How could anyone not want their family?

"She was the best mom. We never had much, but I always knew she loved me. She liked to sing to me and always laughed. She worked so hard to be able to take care of us, and I remember knowing that what she did, how she took care of me and protected me, was what love meant. Not a day went by that she didn't tell me she loved me, her little warrior. And I'll never forget you saved her once."

"I didn't save her, precious boy. I may have helped her, but your mother, she saved herself and her son over and over during her life."

He snuggled closer, his hand tight on my arm as if he was afraid I would walk away.

"Tell me more," I commanded, and he did. From her favorite song to her favorite movie to her favorite color. I let him talk until there was no talk left in him, and then I held him as he cried. It was clear how much he needed it—to share her and grieve for her. I was angry with myself for not having asked about her earlier.

When he finally stopped crying, he whispered, "I'm sorry. I got your shirt all wet with my tears and snot."

"There's nothing to be sorry for." I adjusted my position, and he gripped me again, making it obvious he still needed me, needed to be cared for. "Come, let's get you in the bath." He took them often, and I knew he enjoyed them.

"I don't want to be away from you."

"Then I guess you better go with me to your bathroom because that's where I'm going to be."

He looked up at me and grinned, and a feeling of calmness filled me. Being what he needed was *everything*.

Finley stood, and I held his hand as we went upstairs. I drew him a bath, added bubbles, and undressed him. I feared he would ask me to get in with him, but he didn't. I sat on the toilet lid while he relaxed in the water, his eyes and face red from crying.

He stayed inside until his body was pruned. "Can I get out now, Sir?"

"You may. Let the water out, and I'll dry you."

Finley, my fair-haired warrior, nodded and did as told. I held a towel out, and he stepped inside it as I wrapped it around him and began to dry him. His cock lengthened in front of me, filled with blood, and he gasped when I ran the towel over his balls and between his legs to dry him. When I slipped my fingers between his ass cheeks, drying him there too, his knees gave out, and I had to hold him so he didn't fall. "Please…" he said breathlessly. "Please, Sir. I need it. I need *something*."

I rubbed the towel over his hole again, and his nails dug into my back as he melted against me once more.

"Just this once…please. I need to come, and I want my orgasms to be yours too. Everything of mine is yours."

My jaw tightened. My dick ached. My body screamed at me to take him, own him. It took everything inside me not to throw him over the bathroom counter and fuck him raw and hard right then and there.

I wasn't going to do that, of course, but I knew I

couldn't deny him. "Go lie on your bed. Get your lube and dildo. I'll be right there."

His mouth dropped open in surprise. It was so adorable, I found myself chuckling as I hooked my finger beneath his chin and closed it. "Go before I change my mind."

"Yes, Sir!"

I watched his cute little ass retreat while I took deep, steadying breaths to control myself. A moment later I went to the bedroom and sat on the bed. He was beautiful, laid out for me, all pale, unblemished skin and eagerness to obey.

"We're going to do this my way, but if we do it, all your orgasms are mine from now on. You can't come unless I say you can. If I'm not home, you call and ask me, and if I say no, you don't."

"Oh God." His head dropped back, and his eyes rolled as if I were already touching him. "Yes, please, Sir. That's what I want. What I need."

"Then it's time I give it to you. Open your legs so I can see you." He obediently did so, holding his legs back so I could see his small, pink hole tucked between his firm cheeks. His balls were tight, with a light dusting of hair there and short, blond curls around his cock.

He writhed on the bed before wrapping a hand

around his cock.

"Stop!"

Finley's eyes went wide.

"Did I say you could touch yourself?"

"I… No. I'm sorry, Sir."

"Don't do it again or you won't come at all." A sort of rightness settled in my bones, my head clear as I took control of him. It felt as it was supposed to and not the way it had with Les. "Do you like your nipples played with?"

"I don't know."

Oh, how innocent he was. "Tell me everything you've done."

"To other people? I've given a few blowjobs. With myself I've just jacked off, fingered myself, and used my dildo." His cheeks turned a delicious shade of pink.

"There's nothing to be embarrassed about. You can put your legs down, and I want you to play with your nipples."

Finley kept his knees bent but pressed the soles of his feet to the bed. He began fingering the small, swollen buds, pinching and rolling them.

"That's good. You're so very good at this," I praised him, and he bucked his hips off the bed, seeking friction that wasn't there, as if just my words had nearly made him come. His cock was angry and red already, the tip leaking precum on his flat belly. "Do you like it?" I asked as he continued to pluck at the nubs.

"I...yes...but I think it's more because you're telling me to do it...because you're watching me."

My dick throbbed behind the fly of my jeans. There was no denying what this precious boy did to me. I wanted to unleash myself on him, pleasure him and dominate him until he was writhing and crying, completely wrecked in his submission for me. But no matter how much it was what I desired, I knew the time wasn't right. Not for that, maybe not ever, because of all the reasons I'd thought about a hundred times, and also because of myself. A good Dom had to trust himself, had to be in the right frame of mind, and my thoughts and feelings were too chaotic where he was concerned. So this would have to do.

"Thank you for your honesty," I told him. "That's always what I expect from you. Now, I want you to stop and lube your hands, please."

"Yes, Sir." His hands were shaking as he opened the bottle and squirted the lubricant into his palms. He moved to wrap a hand around his cock, but one *tsk* from me and he paused. "I'm sorry. I forgot."

"It's okay, but if we continue doing this, you'll have

to do better, okay?"

"Yes, Sir."

"Now, you may wrap a hand around your erection and stroke, but don't come. You're not allowed to come until I give you permission—not ever. If you do, you'll be punished. Do you know why that is?"

"Because my orgasms are yours," Finley said breathlessly as he began stroking.

"Yes, good boy. Use your other hand to play with your balls."

He did as told, jacking himself as he tugged and fondled his heavy sac. His whole body was flushed and beautiful. He shook his head and closed his eyes, as if he couldn't handle it.

"It's hard…it's so hard. I already want to come."

"I know, but you can't until I say you can. Tell me how it feels."

"It's…amazing, the pressure and the movement on my cock, but the best part is knowing you're here, that you're in control of it. It's sort of like you're in my head and under my skin. I don't know if that makes sense, but that's what it feels like. And like it makes it better…you make it better…knowing you have the control and that I'm pleasing you when I do as you say. Usually I like something in my ass to make me come, but it's killing me to hold myself back already."

Damned if I didn't tremble. His words seeped inside me, making the need to own and possess swell until I struggled to breathe around it. "You please me very much. How about we get something in that little hole of yours?"

"Yes, please, Aidan, yes, please."

"Lower the hand from your balls and start with a finger."

I pressed down on my own erection as I watched him. Finley did exactly as told, still jerking his cock with one hand and pressing a finger in his ass with the other.

"Oh God!" He bucked off the bed.

"Stop," I commanded, and he stilled.

"I'm sorry. I'm trying. I'm so horny, and it feels so good."

"It's okay. Take a few deep breaths, and then go again. I enjoy tormenting you."

Finley inhaled, exhaled, inhaled, exhaled, slow, deep, steady breaths.

"Continue."

He did, fingering himself and jerking his dick. Every time he was close to losing his battle with his orgasm, I pulled him from the edge.

When I told him to push a second finger in, he almost lost it, shaking his head and writhing as if in pain.

"Please, Aidan. Please, I can't take it anymore."

"You can, because I want you to. You want to please me, right?"

His lust-hazy blue eyes held on to me. Some Doms didn't want to be looked at, but I very much did. I wanted his eye contact so I could see what I was doing to him, so I could see what he needed.

"Yes, Sir. I want it more than anything."

"Then hold out for just a little while longer for me, precious boy. I want to see your hole stretch around that dildo. Can you do that for me?"

"Yes." He nodded.

"Good boy. Lube it up."

Finley picked up the bottle and slicked the toy. It wasn't a large one, by any means. It was smaller than me.

"May I?" he asked, the question so beautiful, so perfect.

"You're doing so well. I'm so proud of you. Hold your legs back for me first."

His eyes flared, maybe because he believed I would touch him. I wanted to, but again, I wouldn't allow myself to. Instead I leaned in and spit on his opening. Finley gasped, his balls tightened, and his dick spasmed, more precum leaking. "You like that?"

"Yes, Sir!"

"Me too. I like seeing my spit coat your little hole, knowing you'll push it inside yourself."

"Oh God. Please let me come. I could do it right now."

"Soon," I replied. "Now fuck yourself on it, for me. Let me see how your hole stretches around the rubber."

"Yes, anything you say." Finley pushed at his rim with the toy. It took a moment, his opening adjusting as he slowly worked it inside. He took his time as he should, and when it popped in, he exhaled, then began to fuck.

Gasping noises pulled from the back of his throat as he let out panting breaths. He worked the toy in and out but didn't touch his cock again because I hadn't told him he could. "You're so beautiful like this, taking the pleasure I give you."

"Yes, yours. All yours." The muscles in his neck strained and his eyes rolled back as my named played on his tongue over and over and over again. "Aidan, Aidan, Aidan."

My hands twitched, I wanted to touch him so badly, but I did it with my words instead. "Such a pretty hole on a pretty boy. You're making me proud, taking the pleasure I give you, doing as I tell you to so magnificently. You're holding back because I command it even though your balls are painfully full, aren't they?"

"So full. Oh God, yes, Sir. Please let me come. I'll do anything."

I paused, watched, riveted, and then demanded, "Come."

Finley's back bowed off the bed as he cried out, his load shooting all over his stomach and chest, one pulse, two, three. Then he relaxed, limp and pliant against the bed, the dildo still in his ass. He looked properly debauched, and I fucking loved it.

"That's it…good boy. Your Sir is very proud of you."

"Thank you…thank you, thank you, thank you."

I scooped the cum from his skin. "Have you ever eaten your own?"

"No." Finley shook his head.

"You'll eat it all from now on unless I say otherwise. Open your mouth." He looked at me, his cheeks pink, and I wondered if it would give him pause, but then he spread his lips for me. "Good boy." His cum slid from my fingers into his mouth. Finley swallowed it, his eyes already drooping, this blissed-out smile on his face. I scooped the rest of it, and he licked it from my fingers. Then I pulled the dildo free and watched his hole begin to close.

"Thank you," he whispered again, dreamily, exhaustion hanging off every word. "I feel like I'm floating."

"That's normal. You're coming down. I'll keep you tethered." I set the supplies on the nightstand and lay beside him.

Finley rolled toward me, wrapped his arm and leg around me, burying his face in my armpit again as I kissed the top of his head and told him how good he was and how proud of him I was. The last thing he said before drifting off to sleep was, "Best birthday ever."

CHAPTER SEVENTEEN

Finley

IT WAS AMAZING, the fluttery, fuzzy feeling I'd had when Aidan had guided me through our…I wasn't sure what to even call it. Our scene? Me masturbating? Whatever it was, it had been fucking fabulous. Maybe the best thing that had ever happened to me.

He'd stayed with me for hours. At least, it had felt like hours. Eventually, I felt him slip out of bed. He kissed my temple and rubbed the back of his hand over my cheek as he so often did. He told me I was a good boy and that we would talk the next day.

It was Christmas, and Aidan had to work. I'd gotten up like always and made his coffee and breakfast, basically feeling like I was bursting out of my skin. I wanted to talk about last night. I wanted to know if we would do it again. I wanted to serve him well because he had treated me so very sweetly. He'd made me feel…worthy. Like he owned me, and there was nothing in the world I wanted more than to be owned by Aidan.

"It's tomorrow," I said when he finished his breakfast.

Aidan chuckled. "I'm aware."

"Remember you said—" He held up his hand, and I stopped immediately.

"When I get home from work. I'd like you to treat today as you would any other day. Take care of your responsibilities around the house, make the ham and scalloped potatoes for dinner, but I'd also like you to take a nap—just an hour. Set a clock. Last night was a big night, and you didn't get much sleep."

"Yes, Sir," I replied, but I really wanted to pout. Ugh. I hated waiting. I'd been waiting for Aidan for like nine months, and even waiting until tonight felt too long.

"Good boy." He made it all the way to the door before he stopped. "Merry Christmas."

A grin pulled at my cheeks. "Merry Christmas."

When Aidan left, I went straight into my day, cleaning and exercising. Afterward, I knew I should shower, but I didn't want to. Even though the only time Aidan had touched me was to scoop cum off my chest, it felt like I would be washing him and our night away.

And God, I couldn't believe he wanted me to eat all

my cum. I mean, it wasn't like I hadn't seen that in porn, and I knew people did it, but it was different to be commanded to eat all my loads. If we had as much sex as I wanted, I'd be eating enough to live off it.

And…now my dick was hard. I jumped in the bed and reached for my lube but then remembered that all my orgasms were Aidan's now. I grumbled, but I was smiling too. I picked up my phone, thought, and then just said fuck it and sent him a text.

Can I jack off?

No.

No? *No?*

Please? I'm dying. I'll think about you when I do it.

No. Do as you're told. It matters what I want and don't, correct? I control your orgasms, and I don't want you to come. You want to please me, which means you'll obey.

I trembled. Pleasing Aidan was the most important thing.

Yes, Sir.

Grumbling, I got in the shower and washed him off, partly because I was angry with him for not allowing me to jerk off. For a moment I thought about taking myself in hand or slipping my fingers in my ass because really, there was no way Aidan would know. I could blow my load all day and keep it from him…but I didn't. I wanted to make him happy. I wanted to serve him well, which meant I would obey him.

After the shower I lay down for my stupid nap, which I didn't really want, but fell asleep almost instantly. It was obvious I needed it, and of course he was right. Aidan was always right.

An hour later I woke up. I started the ham, cooking it with Sprite in the pan and brown sugar and pineapple the way my mom used to, which reminded me I'd talked to him about my mom last night, and how good it had felt to share her with Aidan. How had I not known I needed to speak about her, to remember her? But he knew. He always knew.

He was everything, and I so very much wanted to deserve him.

When it was almost time for Aidan to get home from work, I grabbed the cushion he'd gotten for me to kneel on in the kitchen and took it to the entryway. My knees kissed the fabric as I waited for him, my eyes down.

Heat skittered across my skin when I heard his key in the lock. The door pushed open, and I continued to wait.

"This is a surprise."

"I want to…serve you this way tonight. I want to be good for you. You treat me so well, and I want to be the same for you."

Aidan stepped closer. He cupped my cheeks and lifted my head. "You're very good to me. You serve me well, Finley. And I like it when your eyes are on me."

I opened my mouth, but no words came out. I cleared my throat. "Yes, Sir."

"Come. We'll eat, and then we need to talk."

"Can I eat at your feet?" It was my favorite place to be. I'd spend my life at Aidan's feet if I were allowed.

He nodded. "Make our plates and bring them to the living room. I'll wait for you there."

When he walked away, I rushed to the kitchen and got our food. I loved that he automatically knew it would be ready on time. It made me feel like a very good boy.

I set our plates on the coffee table before returning to the kitchen for drinks, water for me and a glass of wine for Aidan. He sat on the couch, waiting, and pointed to the rug on the floor, which I immediately dropped to.

"You love it, don't you? Being at my feet."

"Yes, more than anything."

He gave me another nod. "Eat."

I asked Aidan how his day was, and as usual, he didn't say much. I wondered why he didn't like to talk about what he did or if there was a reason he had decided to become a surgeon. There were so many things about him I didn't know, and I wanted to discover them all.

He told me dinner was good, and to be quiet and eat. He was so bossy, I loved it. We finished our meal in silence, and I took our plates, getting him another glass of wine before returning to my knees beside him.

"About last night—"

"It was wonderful! Even more than I could have dreamed!"

"Interrupt me again and I'll spank your ass. You won't enjoy it."

I wiggled before replying, "I'm sorry."

"Just don't let it happen again. Now, about last night. You were comfortable with everything we did, correct?"

Um...*duh*? I so wanted to say that, but of course I didn't. "Yes."

"You need it, don't you? Need your hungry little hole filled, but you also need to lose control, to give yourself to me."

My dick went hard in no time flat. Just his words had so much power over me. "Yes. I feel...empty so often. I like to be filled, but last night, with you guiding me, it was the best thing to ever happen to me. It made me feel like you..." I turned away, unsure if I should finish.

"Like what? And look at me when you reply."

I turned to face him again. "Like you own me."

A slow smile spread across his face, making me gasp. "Oh, but I do own you, don't I?"

"Yes, Sir."

"Good boy," Aidan replied. "The rules will change slightly. I'm still not fucking you, but your orgasms belong to me. We'll do what we did last night—you'll only touch yourself when and how I say you can. I'll control it all, every part of you."

But without touching me? I dropped my eyes.

"You're disappointed."

"Yes. I'm grateful for what you give me, but I want more. I want to serve *you*."

Aidan sighed. "You *are* serving me, Finley. You take care of my home, and your days are scheduled by me. You run my errands and cook my food and buy my groceries and kneel for me. You're giving me your orgasms, giving up control of them to me. It's my job to decide how I accept that control, and this is what I've decided." Again, he cupped my cheek, and I nuzzled into him. I loved it when he touched me. It made me feel like he tethered me to Earth. "You serve me well, precious boy. You are mine. I own you, and this is how I choose to use you, because I feel it's best. Do you trust me? If we're going to continue, you have to trust me. Remember, I expect honesty."

"Yes!" I rushed out. "God, yes. I trust you more than anyone in the world."

"Then accept what I offer with the understanding that it's what I feel is best for you right now."

Right now. He hadn't said *right now* before, which meant that later he might allow me to have more.

"Yes, Sir."

"And if there's anything I ever tell you to do that is a limit for you, that you're not comfortable with, you need to tell me, okay?"

"Okay."

"Now put your head on my lap."

I scurried closer and did as he said. This and in his armpit were my favorite places to have my face. I wished I could have it between his legs, but hopefully soon.

He played with my hair, petting and comforting me. "You're also going to enroll in college."

I froze. So that was why he got me a new laptop?

"You only have to take one class at first. I'll help you with the logistics. We'll make it work with your obligations to me, and before you get upset, remember what I told you—it's my responsibility as your Dom to do what's best for you. To help you reach your full potential in all aspects of your life. This is me doing that, okay?"

"I trust you." I was also really, really mad at him. Angry, in fact. My pulse thudded and my head suddenly felt like it would explode, but I did trust him.

"Good boy. Do you have more to say to me? Is there something you want to talk about?"

"No," I replied because regardless, if I wanted him to own me, this was what I had to do…and I wanted that, more than anything in the world. To belong to Aidan Kingsley.

"Okay. Did you obey me today? Take your nap and keep from touching yourself?"

"Yes."

"Very good. I'm proud of you." He maneuvered me so I looked up at him. "You're mine, Finley, and I promise I'll take good care of you."

I soared at his words, was literally afraid I would float away. "Thank you for…wanting me."

"I do, very much. More than I thought I would."

Oh, those were the best words.

"Now, why don't you lie on the couch. We'll watch one of your shows, and then I'll take you to your room and let you come again before bed. Would you like that?"

My heart jumped, and my dick throbbed. "Can we skip the show and go upstairs now?"

Aidan laughed. "Such a handful. No, precious boy. Patience."

I hated patience, but belonging to Aidan, I knew I would need a lot of it.

CHAPTER EIGHTEEN
Aidan

MY DAYS OFF had switched around this week because another surgeon was on vacation. It was a busy day for Finley. He'd taken care of his morning chores, then pouted and tried to stay home with me instead of going to school, which he'd started when the semester began in January, at one of the local community colleges. We were shocked everything wasn't full, but we'd gotten lucky. He was taking two classes, which was a surprise since I'd said he only had to take one. The boy had made sure his classes were late enough in the day that he could do his household duties on Tuesdays and Thursdays before going in. I'd tried to give him those mornings off, but he'd begged me to keep his schedule, and I'd allowed it. He had a way of getting what he wanted with me that I wasn't proud of. David teased me about it mercilessly.

But the truth was, I knew he needed it. While I

wanted Finley to have an education, a backup plan, as of yet, nothing fulfilled him the way serving did. It was in his bones, swam around deep in the marrow. It was as much a part of him as his DNA. The more time he spent with me, the more I saw it. He desired to serve and to be taken care of. There was no changing it, not that I wanted to. Changing him wasn't what going to school was about. He deserved options; I wanted him to have the opportunities my mother was never allowed to have.

And frankly, as the months passed, I saw that he liked attending his classes more than he wanted to admit. He'd tell me things he'd learned, and boast about scores on exams, and speak about his fellow students. So yes, I believed I was doing right by him, and I planned to continue on the same path, even if I wanted to possess him in every way.

Shaking those thoughts from my head, I glanced over to see it was almost time for Finley to get out of class. A smile pulled at my lips when I thought of the way he had been rushing around the house that morning, trying to clean, exercise, eat breakfast, and do all the things he was supposed to do before leaving. I couldn't say what made me do it exactly—whether I wanted to reward him, or just spent time with him, or show him off publicly, as we didn't often do—but I picked up my phone and sent him a text: **Come straight home today.**

There was a ten-minute delay, and I knew it was because his class was still in session. I forbade him to be on his cell phone when he was supposed to be learning.

Yes, Sir…but it's grocery shopping day.

Again, I smiled. The boy made me do that a lot. He was so beautifully submissive to me. He would come home because it pleased me, even though it warred with his set schedule in taking care of the home.

I know what day it is.

Yes, Aidan.

It took him a good forty-five minutes to get home, likely due to LA traffic. He came straight into my office and lingered in the door. "Can I come in?"

It was a rule—even when the door was open, he had to ask permission to come inside my office or bedroom. They were my spaces, and I liked having control over whether or when he could enter them. "You may," I replied, and Finley came inside.

"It feels weird, not doing the shopping today. You didn't order delivery, did you? I can do it. I promise. It's not too much." His voice was slightly panicked, his words rushing out too quickly. It hadn't occurred to me that he would think I was taking one of his responsibilities away because I didn't believe he could handle them.

"Come here," I told him, and he came. "Kneel."

A breath whooshed from his lungs, and his body relaxed in such a familiar way. I was reminding him he still had his place, and the boy very obviously needed that.

Finley went down to his knees and looked up at me. "Did I do something wrong?"

"No." I cupped his cheek, and he nuzzled into my hand. "I'm sorry. I didn't mean to worry you. I didn't realize you would think I was unhappy with you. I just wanted to reward you and give you a break because I'm so very proud of you. I thought we could go have a late lunch and then do the shopping together."

Finley's expressive eyes widened. "Really?"

"Yes, is that such a surprise?"

"Kind of. You know you, right?"

I tapped my finger against his cheek in warning. "Mind yourself or you'll be staying home."

"Please no! Sorry, Sir. I didn't mean to disrespect you."

"Don't do it again. Is there anything you need to do before we go?"

"No, Aidan."

"Then come on." He stood and moved back before I did.

Anytime we went places together, I drove the Audi.

When we got outside, he said, "I have to get the list. It's in my car." He stumbled a bit, and I reached out to catch him. "Your car, I mean."

I frowned. "You've been driving that car for the past year. I think it's safe to say it's yours." It was already the end of February, and he had moved in the March before.

"Oh my God. You can't give me a BMW!" he shrieked, and I tensed. Oh no. This wouldn't do at all.

"I can do what I want, yes? I'm the one in charge here. I was going to let you come tonight, but now I don't think I will. You've earned yourself a spanking instead."

"Noooo! That's not fair! I didn't mean it that way," Finley whined.

"And now you won't come tomorrow night either. Would you like to continue?"

I could see his annoyance. He wanted to argue back, but I knew he wouldn't. "No, Sir. I'm sorry." He crossed his arms, and I couldn't help but chuckle.

"Such a spoiled brat you are. Get the list." I peeked into the car as I walked by. "And I expect this cleaned this week."

"Yes, Aidan."

He was quiet as I drove to Santa Monica, to a Mexican restaurant I loved there. Traffic was brutal as always.

Finley tapped his finger restlessly against his leg, which meant he had things going on inside that head of his. I waited it out, knowing he would tell me.

We were pulling into the parking lot when he said, "I'm sorry I ruined our day."

"You've already apologized," I said as I parked. "There's no need to do it again. And you didn't ruin anything, boy. I quite enjoy punishing you."

Finley gasped.

"Why do you sound surprised? Do you think I don't enjoy turning that little ass red? Knowing I have control to do so? It's one of my favorite things."

The only times I touched him when he was naked was when I was giving him a discipline spanking or when I held him as he came down from his punishment or the high of an orgasm, as I talked him through it. It was always his hands when he jacked off or fingered himself, but they moved only on my command.

"I didn't know… I mean, I can tell you're hard when you do it, but I wasn't sure. Can I ask you something?" I nodded, and he continued. "Do you like hurting people? When you have scenes with someone, do you hurt them?"

"When I was active, yes, I did, but I haven't done that since I told you I wouldn't. And when I hurt someone, it's because it's not a hard limit for them. It's something they want or a limit they have allowed me to push."

The bulge in his pants was obvious. Finley squirmed in his seat, and I wanted to tell him to take himself out and make himself come…or shove his head between my legs and make him suck me until I shot down his throat.

"I hope you do that with me one day; not a lot…but some, and not just for punishment, but for pleasure."

"Finley," I warned, even though I wanted the very same thing.

"I know you won't, but I'm allowed to wish it, right?"

I sighed. "You're allowed. I'm going to go inside and get our table. Don't touch yourself, and stay out here until your erection is gone, then meet me inside."

"Yes, Sir," he replied without looking at me.

With maybe a little more pressure than I needed to, I gripped his chin and turned him so he was looking at me. He trembled, so I pressed just a little harder, giving him a taste of what he wanted. "You still didn't ruin our day, okay?"

"I… Thank you. I don't want to ruin this day. I love it."

"We haven't done anything yet."

"I still love it," he replied, and I nearly trembled myself. The things this little warrior did to me, and I didn't think he knew it. He'd captured me in ways I never thought myself capable of being captured. I wiped the tears under his right eye with my thumb, then pushed it into his mouth, and he dutifully sucked it. When I brushed the ones under his left eye, he opened his mouth again, but this time, I sucked them from my own finger.

He smiled at me as if I'd given him the damn sun, and I took that as my cue to go inside before I did something I couldn't take back.

CHAPTER NINETEEN

Finley

IT TOOK ALMOST ten minutes before my erection went down. It had killed me not to jack off. I was so turned on by the way Aidan spoke to me, the things he said, and the control he had over me. It was as if he'd cast some spell over me…which wasn't something he wanted, so maybe I'd cast an Aidan spell over myself? Whatever it was, it was there, and as I sat in the car and waited, I decided I was going to work hard to be better, to serve him and please him so well, that eventually he would want all of me. And in that I would be fulfilled because nothing made me feel as content as pleasing Aidan did.

He was waiting in a booth toward the back, with chips and salsa in front of him. I sat across from him.

"I ordered you a root beer. I know you like it, but only one. Soda isn't good for you."

I couldn't help but smile. Root beer was my favorite, and he knew. "Thank you."

"I didn't order food yet." He was browsing the menu, but I didn't pick mine up.

"Can I just get whatever you get?"

He looked over his menu and cocked a brow at me. "Yes," he answered simply.

The waiter approached, and Aidan ordered us each chicken fajitas with no guacamole or sour cream. The waiter took our menus and disappeared.

"How was class today?"

"Good. Well…not math. I hate it. I'm really bad at it. My English class is great, though. I love my professor. He told me I'm a good writer."

Aidan smiled proudly, which made me feel proud of myself.

"That's very good. I'd like to read something you wrote if you feel comfortable."

"Really?" I wasn't totally sure if I felt comfortable with it or not. I wanted Aidan to only see the best in me, and while my professor did say I was a good writer, I didn't know if I believed it.

"Of course, Finley. Think about it."

"Yes, Sir."

"And if you need help with your math, let me know."

"I will…but I want to try and do it all myself. You

know, to prove I can. If that's okay."

He cocked his head slightly and took a moment to reply. I felt his stare to my core, like he was looking for answers inside me. Aidan always did that, and he was very good at it. Finally, he replied, "Yes, it's okay. That's a noble goal, and I'm proud of you for it. But just know the offer is there, and it's brave to be able to ask for help if you need it."

"Yes, Sir."

We chatted more about my classes. He asked about the people I met and how I felt about what I was doing. He listened intently to every one of my answers. When I finished my root beer, the waiter asked if I'd like another. I declined and asked for water. When he left, Aidan said, "Good boy," and I felt it. My heart soared at the praise.

We continued to chat as we ate. Stupid thoughts flowed through my head. I wondered if the waiter thought Aidan and I were boyfriends, which obviously I wished he did. Aidan was my Sir, but I wanted him to be my lover and my boyfriend too. I wanted Aidan to claim me in every way it was possible to be claimed.

When we finished, Aidan drove to the grocery store. He walked with me but didn't do any of the shopping, letting me get items off my list and watching as I compared prices and used the calculator on my phone for amounts to get the best deals.

"I didn't know you did that," he told me. I had a credit card that was attached to an account Aidan kept for me to do the shopping and run his errands. It was separate from his main account and from the one he'd helped me set up when I first moved in with him, which was where he deposited my pay.

"Yeah. I remember my mom used to do it. Obviously, it was different for her. She had to, and I know you don't, but I guess…you never know. Just because you have money doesn't mean I want to waste it."

He smiled, and I could tell I'd pleased him. He reached over and cupped my cheek, brushing his thumb over the bone there. "That's a very good boy. I'm proud of you."

I blushed. "Thank you."

An older woman, a bit down the aisle from us, made a disapproving noise, and I looked over at her, embarrassed.

"Is there a problem?" Aidan asked her.

"You and your son are blocking the pasta sauce," she gritted out.

Oh God. She thought Aidan was my father? I didn't plan it, but I automatically took a step back. The moment I did, I wished I hadn't. There was no shame in who Aidan and I were. He was my world. I loved him. It was something I felt in my bones and not something I lied to myself about anymore.

Aidan placed his hand on my nape, strong and confident. He rubbed the back of my head, supportive and possessive. "I believe you're aware he isn't my son, because you've been watching the way I touch him and you listened to what I said to him. Quite nosy, hmm? If your intent was to shame us, you've failed."

She huffed, mumbling something about *sickos*, and walked away.

"Don't think twice about what she said, do you hear me?" Aidan said. He was like a god, and I wanted to bask in his strength and confidence. His care.

"Yes, Aidan. I'm proud to be yours."

He sucked in a sharp breath, then relaxed into a smile, dropping his hand away. "You never cease to amaze me. Now, finish teaching me how to bargain shop, please, not that I ever intend to do it for myself." He winked.

It was ridiculous, the idea that I could teach Aidan anything, but he listened as I spoke about my process and filled the cart with all our supplies.

When we got home, he stayed in the kitchen with me as I put the groceries away. We chatted about movies and planned dinners for the rest of the week—simple, everyday things.

Afterward, Aidan invited me into his office, where he sat working at his computer while I lay on the rug by his feet and did my homework. When I was done, we ended up in the living room, my head in his lap and his hand in my hair as we watched a movie.

The credits were rolling when he said, "Go upstairs, take off your clothes, then kneel by the chair and wait for me."

Oh God. My punishment. After the day we had, I'd forgotten about it...or hoped he'd changed his mind. The instinct to argue was there, but I didn't. I stood and said, "Yes, Sir," before going upstairs, stripping, and waiting by the chair he now kept in my room for when he spanked me. It hadn't happened a lot, but yeah, I wasn't perfect. There was a time when I'd thought something like this couldn't be a punishment, but it was, because it came from disappointing him. There was nothing worse than that.

My heart swooped, then thudded when Aidan came into the room with a brush in hand. He had never spanked me with anything other than his hand before, and I was filled with both curiosity and fear at the thought of it.

"I was upset with you before we left, for the way you spoke to me."

"I know. I'm sorry."

"But you also greatly pleased me after that—the shopping and your hard work at school—so I'm going to give you a choice. I can spank you with my hand, as I always do, but you won't get to come. Or I can spank you with the brush, which will hurt much more. You can't come while I'm spanking you, but I'll allow you to come afterward."

"The brush!" rushed out of my mouth before I could even think about it.

Aidan grinned. "How did I know you would choose that? Go to the bed. I've changed my mind about where we're doing this."

I crawled to the bed. I knew it pleased him, and I loved being at his feet. The carpet upstairs made that possible; he never allowed me to crawl on the harder floors downstairs.

Aidan sat on the bed and patted his lap. I lay across him and felt his erection, which made me shake. He shushed me and rubbed his hand over my bare ass. God, I loved it when he touched me this way, when he gave me the security of his touch. I wished he would slip his fingers between my cheeks and tease my hole before fucking me with them...and then I wanted him to hold me down and force his cock into me. I wanted to be fucked by Aidan so badly; not by the dildo I used when he allowed it, but by *him*.

I rutted against him, and a sharp, stinging slap came down on my left cheek. "Be good. Don't make me take away your reward already."

"Yes, Aidan. I'm sorry, Sir. I'll be good."

"I know you will. Now be as still as possible."

Another *smack* of the brush hit down on my other cheek, then the first again. The pain was more intense and sharp than that of his hand, but I knew he was going easy on me, I knew it would get worse.

He hit me in that pattern I knew was to protect me. Aidan would always keep me safe. The burn traveled around my ass, biting worse with each blow. It started out snappy and became severe. I did my best to be still. My cock was hard, and tears poured down my face. I was crying loudly, my sounds mixing with the *smack* of the brush against my skin.

"I'm sorry I was bad. I'll be good for you! Always want to be good for you!" I cried harder, and he spanked harder.

"You can do this, Finley. Take your punishment until I decide you've had enough. If you can't, if it's too much, use your colors—yellow and red—but I think you can take more."

I wanted to make him proud. Wanted to take exactly how much he thought I could, so I didn't tell him to stop. Tears mixed with snot, running down my face, getting on my arm and the bed, but as I hurt for him, as I lay there crying, something about my tears cleansed me. Made me feel less heavy and burdened, as if they were washing away pain I didn't know I had.

Then he wasn't spanking me anymore. He was lifting me, holding me as I straddled him, kissing my temple and telling me how proud he was of me, that I was his good boy. My ass rubbed against his jeans, more welcome pain from him.

"You did so well, precious boy. Sweet warrior boy. You have pleased me so very much."

Thank you, whispered through my mind, but I couldn't make the words come out. Couldn't form them or any others on my tongue, but they were there, in my head. *I love you. Thank you for caring about me. For punishing me.*

I cried until there were no tears left inside me. Aidan held me the whole time. He wiped them away, didn't seem to mind that snot was mixed with them. And when I finally settled down, he lifted my hand and spit in it.

"Jerk yourself off. You deserve it."

I was still on his lap, being held by him. He had never let me come this way. I did as he said and wrapped a hand around my cock. I hardly got three good strokes in before my balls emptied, shooting my load all over my chest and Aidan's shirt. I loved seeing my cum on him and wished he would mark me with his—all over my face, in my mouth, on my chest and ass. Every inch of me.

Aidan used his fingers to scoop my load from my skin. I opened my mouth, let him drop it inside, then licked my jizz from his fingers, smiling.

"You look proud of yourself," he whispered, petting my hair.

"I'm proud to be yours. Thank you, Sir. Thank you, thank you, thank you."

He kissed my temple again, my forehead, petted my hair. I felt weightless as he maneuvered me on the bed, as he checked my ass, his fingers dancing across the skin. I knew he would take care of me, which he did, and then he lay down with me and held me until my world went black…maybe even longer.

CHAPTER TWENTY

Aidan

MY HANDS WOULDN'T stop shaking.

Blood was all over the front of me, up to my elbows, the red mixing with the blue of my gloves and protective wear. I stood in front of the sink, willing my fucking hands to quit trembling, but they wouldn't. No matter what, I couldn't get them to fucking stop.

They had been rock steady during surgery. Precise. Urgent. Skilled.

It hadn't been enough.

I hadn't been enough.

"You did all you could, Dr. Kingsley," Lance, one of the trauma nurses, said.

Another was softly crying as she whispered to herself, "She was so young."

Eight years old. She had been eight years old, just like my sisters had been.

I cleared my throat. "Thank you, all of you. We did

all we could." The words felt empty; they *were* empty. They were true, yes. We had run a perfect trauma activation, had done all the right things, but again, it hadn't been enough.

From there it was a blur—cleaning up, speaking with the family—Christ, that always killed me—showering, driving home, sitting in the driveway.

Closing my eyes.

Imagining the wreck today that took eight-year-old Olivia's life.

Reliving the car accident that took Amy and Ari. That took my mom.

"*Fuck!*" My hands slapped down over and over against the steering wheel. Fuck, I'd wanted to save her. I'd wanted to save them.

It was dark out, almost eleven on a Friday night. The trauma call came in at 6:26 p.m. I was supposed to have gotten off at seven.

Forcing myself to calm down, I took a couple of deep, steadying breaths. The house was dark when I went inside, except for the lamp in the foyer. Finley always left it that way if he went to bed before I got in, and I found myself…disappointed. I didn't want to be alone. I wanted what he gave me, the parts I allowed myself to take—his submission, his servitude.

His company.

I'd never sought that out in a situation like this. I'd never had someone the day I lost a patient. I usually needed it a day or so afterward, the control, to know exactly what would happen because I willed it so. I didn't believe I had my desires because of what I'd lived through. It was too deeply sewn into who I was. And there were times it did help.

But tonight I just wanted *him*.

I went upstairs. He never slept with his door fully closed anymore, kept it open a sliver. I thought maybe because it made Finley feel closer to me, my sweet, precious boy.

I slipped into his room, leaving the hallway light on and the door open. I sat in the gray chair and looked at him as he lay on his side, curled up in a ball, the way he slept when I wasn't holding him.

I didn't know how long I sat there, watching him sleep. Rubbed my fingers together and imagined the softness of his hair, tightened my hand into a fist, wondering what it would be like to twine my fingers around the strands roughly as I fucked his throat.

It had been weeks since I spanked him, since he came on me and I felt him shudder against me. Since the heat of his ass was seared into my hand when I touched him, but it was there, so vividly ingrained into my senses. The way he sounded when he cried, and his scent, which was like strawberries from that bodywash he used and fresh sweat.

It had been a year since he'd moved in, and he'd given me more than he could ever know.

Finley rolled over, his eyes fluttered, and he sat up. "Aidan?" His voice trembled with uncertainty.

"Sorry. I didn't mean to wake you. I just..." Didn't want to be alone. Wanted him.

"You didn't wake me up. What time is it?" When I didn't answer, he plucked his cell phone from the nightstand. "It's after one in the morning. What's wrong? Did I do something wrong?"

Christ, the simple question made my pulse throb, made blood rush through my ears. The way he longed to serve me was exquisite. "No, my little warrior, you did not. I had a...bad night at work, is all. I lost a patient, and it reminded me of something else."

There was a quiet, sharp intake of breath. He was shocked at what I'd said. I never talked about what I did. It left me too raw, but tonight, the words had needed to fall from my lips.

"Can I...can I crawl to you?"

"Yes," I answered simply. There was nothing I wanted more.

Finley got out of the bed. He wore only a T-shirt and boxer trunks. He knelt, then went to his hands and knees, and slowly, so very slowly, crawled over to me. His instincts were so pure. He so naturally followed his impulses to serve.

"Sit between my thighs, with your head on my lap," I instructed, spreading my legs.

"Yes, Sir." Finley settled between them, facing away from me with his cheek on me. I touched his hair as I'd imagined earlier, watched it fall through my fingertips, twisted it around, and tugged lightly. Finley gasped…then settled against me further, rubbing his cheek on my jeans.

I didn't do anything more, just alternated between petting his cheek, his hair, and then tightening my hand in it and pulling gently. At one point he whimpered, and I let go. If I knew his limits, his desires, I wouldn't have. I would have tested him. I would have worked him hard so he gave all he was willing to me, but we had never had those discussions.

"Please don't stop, Sir," he murmured, making need rush through me. I tightened my hand in his hair again and pulled, sharper and harder than I had before. Finley squirmed, and I let go, before doing it again and again and again.

"Please," he whispered. "Please, let me serve you. Use me. I'm yours to use and command, if you want me."

It was my turn for a sharp intake of breath. My whole body sang, calmness and rightness working its way through me. "It's never been that I don't want you." Which I had told him more than once, but I knew he didn't believe me.

"It's not?" he asked, sweetness and eagerness on his tongue.

"No." My fist tightened in his hair, pulling harder than I had yet. I tugged him closer, until Finley was turning, where he was on his knees, facing me.

"Please," Finley begged again. "Use me. There's nothing I want more than to please you. For you to take whatever you want from me."

My resistance was about to snap, a rubber band pulled to the breaking point. It was likely to pop back against my skin, but I couldn't help it, couldn't hold myself back any longer. I wanted him too much, wanted to control him and hurt him and soothe him. "Unbutton and unzip my pants."

I felt a shiver rock through him. Finley's hands were urgent, working to open my pants as if he feared I would change my mind. Once they were open, he dived straight in, burying his nose in my underwear and inhaling my scent. With a tight fist in his hair, I pulled his head back, forcing him to look up at me. "Did I give you permission to do that?"

"No." He winced, and I loosened my hold slightly.

"Is that too tight? I don't know your limits."

"No. I just… I hate that I disappointed you already."

Oh, what would I do with this boy? He was incredible. "It's okay. You're learning, but I need you to work hard for me, to only do as I say, unless I go too far. If I do, you know what to say to get me to stop."

Finley nodded, looking up at me, his eyes wide open, taking me in, and not just physically. And letting me see inside *him* too. Letting me see how very much he truly wanted this. "Yes, Sir."

I made him wait then, just looked at him and caressed his cheek and pulled his hair. He waited patiently, like a good boy, but as the minutes went by, I noticed the panic and nerves in him escalate. "You like the way I smell, don't you?" I knew he did. He was always inhaling me. We'd spoken about it before, but I wanted to hear him say it again.

"Yes. God, I love it. It calms me down. Makes me feel like…I don't know, like no matter what, everything is going to be okay."

I hissed in response. How could I have waited so long to claim him in this way? He was so open, so honest in his needs in a way I'd never experienced. It was miraculous, really, especially for someone so young, but Finley was grounded in who he was and his desires. "You may."

He pushed his face between my legs sloppily. We'd have to work on his grace a bit. He nuzzled as deep as he could, especially since I was wearing my jeans, breathing me in. I let him root around there, let him engrave my scent in his memory so he would always know it, before I told him, "Use your mouth on me."

Finley grabbed for my underwear but stopped when I shook my head.

"No. I didn't say to take those off. Pull my pants down just a bit and suck and lick me through them."

"Oh…I'm sorry. Yes, Sir." I lifted my hips, and he tugged my jeans down to midthigh. His hot mouth went to my full balls first. He tried to take them both into his mouth, through the fabric. He was so hungry, so needy for what I had denied him for too long.

"Slow down, precious boy. It's okay. I'm not going anywhere."

"Yes, Aidan." He took his time then, sucking me, licking my shaft, wetting my underwear, and breathing me in. There was a wet spot from my precum, which he swiped his tongue at over and over.

"That's it. That's a good boy. Now pull me out."

He did. I lifted my ass slightly to make it easier, and he tucked the fabric beneath my balls.

"Can I take them all the way off?"

"No." I enjoyed telling him no, seeing him accept my answer even though it wasn't the one he wanted. Since it was my will, Finley didn't argue.

He went down on my cock, sucking and licking. It wasn't a great blowjob. It lacked finesse and experience, but those things didn't matter. What did was that it was Finley giving it to me, giving himself to me and my control. I wanted to use him hard, to snap my hips up and fuck into his mouth.

With my hand in his hair, I pulled him off me. Finley whined as if I'd taken his favorite treat from him. "Can you take it harder? Can you handle it if I fuck your throat? Not too much, but just more than I'm giving you now?" I knew he wouldn't be able to take it like other men I was used to. It was something we would have to work on, but I wanted everything he could give me tonight.

"God, yes. Anything you want. Everything." He was so beautiful, so passionate in his need to serve me, to please me, he stole my breath. I looked down at him for a moment, just taking him in. His blond hair in my fist. His gentle features and cheekbones. Those blue eyes that couldn't hide anything from me.

And I wanted to make him cry...to make him weep for me. "I might make you cry."

"Everything," he said again.

I nodded. "Tap three times on my right thigh if you need me to stop, like this." I did it to myself to show him. "And on my left if you need me to slow down. Do you understand?"

"Yes, Sir."

The second the words left his mouth, I shoved my cock inside. Finley choked instantly...then moaned around me. He was struggling some, and I didn't go as far as I could, but since he wasn't tapping, I trusted him that I could keep going. I used his mouth, choking him, savoring the gurgles, the mumbles, and his spit sloshing around in his throat.

When he tapped on my left thigh three times, I pulled back, stroked his face, rubbed my thumb over his red lips. "You're being such a good hole for me, giving yourself to me so wonderfully."

Finley grinned, his smile wide and bright and *proud*. Christ, it was awe-inspiring, the way he reveled in what he gave me. "Are you ready to go again?"

"Yes."

I continued using his mouth, making him gag and saliva run down his chin. Tears spilled from his eyes, and he looked up at me adoringly, as if I had given him the moon. It was the most incredible sight I had ever seen.

"I'm going to come, and I want you to swallow it all. Don't spill a drop or I won't be happy. Once it's in your belly, wrap your hand around your cock and stroke until you come."

He nodded, mouth full of dick, and I slammed in again. My balls emptied, my load shooting from them and spilling into his eager mouth. Finley swallowed every bit hungrily, then pushed his underwear down and got one good touch in before he shot his load too.

"What do you do with your cum?" I asked. He licked it from his hand, then bent and swiped his tongue across the cum that had gotten on my shoe. Christ, what an exquisite boy he was. "You were so good for me, Finley. Such a good boy. I'm very proud of you."

"Thank you."

"How do you feel?" I asked, dancing my fingers along his cheek.

He gave me another one of those pure, happy smiles, his eyes glassy. "Perfect. Like I'm finally where I'm supposed to be."

"Come here," I told him, and he crawled into my lap, wrapped his arms around me, and cried.

CHAPTER TWENTY-ONE

Finley

I HAD NO idea why I was crying, but there was something cathartic in it. I obviously needed it, and Aidan didn't seem to mind, so I just…let go. He held me and stroked my back and my hair, praising me over and over and telling me he was there, that he had me, and I knew he did. There was nowhere I felt safer, more cared for, than with him. I would never have to worry about anything as long as I had him.

I didn't know how long I cried. The world felt fuzzy and like time was running differently. I knew the chair couldn't be comfortable for him like this, but Aidan didn't complain, and I didn't want to ever leave this spot if I didn't have to.

Eventually my tears dried up, and we were just sitting there together, breathing together. His body tensed a bit, and I was afraid he was going to tell me to get off him, say we couldn't do this or that I hadn't been good enough for him, but then I remembered how he told me I was a good boy and said I did well for him, and there was no one in the world I believed like I did Aidan.

"I think I owe you an explanation for tonight." His voice was steady and calm as ever. He carried life on his shoulders, brave and strong, never wavering. It was why I'd been so shaken when I saw him tonight. Aidan had been in pain...hurting and lost, and I'd wanted to be there for him the way he was always there for me.

"You don't have to..." But I wanted him to. I wanted to know it all.

He chuckled humorlessly. "Well, yes, I never have to do what I don't want to, do I?"

No, he didn't.

"This is important, though." I nodded, held him tighter, and waited. A moment later Aidan continued. "My father...wasn't a very nice man. He met my mother when she was seventeen. He was ten years older. She got pregnant with me at eighteen. He was very...possessive of her."

"Dominant?"

"No, not like that. In an unhealthy way. She was young and insecure, and he took advantage of that. He didn't allow her to go to college or work. She never had a job outside of the home. He wasn't physically abusive, but he was verbally. He made her feel like she couldn't survive without him, like she was nothing, and she believed him."

Everything was beginning to click into place—why Aidan had been nervous about my age and why he insisted I be able to take care of myself; that I have my own income, even if he never let me use it, and why he wanted me to go to college. "You're not your father."

He kissed my temple, and it struck me then that we'd never properly kissed. Still, I enjoyed what he gave me.

"Thank you, precious boy. I appreciate that, but I've come to terms with who I am compared to who he is a long time ago. I know my dominance is nothing like his hateful control over her. She didn't feel like she had a choice. You or anyone else I play with always know there's a choice. Ultimately, you're in control, because you choose to give power to me. And if it's too much, you always have the power to end it, but yes, that's why I want you to go to school and to be able to take care of yourself. I don't want you to ever have to depend on me. I want you here because it's where you want to be."

"It is!" I nuzzled his neck. "It is the only place I will ever want to be."

"I don't know about that. You're only twenty. You

have a lot of life left to live, and I'm your only experience. You'll want and deserve more, but that's not what we're talking about right now. I'd like to get this out, and then I want the conversation to end. I don't want questions or to go into detail about it, okay?"

Well...no, it wasn't really okay. It was obvious Aidan tried not to allow himself to feel anything about whatever it was, but I was sure he needed to. Still, I said, "Yes, Sir."

"I was very close with my mother, much like you were with yours. She was...my world...along with my twin sisters, Amy and Arianna."

"You have sisters?"

"Not anymore. I got in an argument with my father one day. We didn't get along. I wasn't the kind of son he wanted. He believed me soft because of how I protected my mom."

Aidan soft? The man was crazy. "You're the strongest person I know."

"Don't put me on a pedestal, Finley. I'm just a man like any other."

There was no one like him, but I didn't tell him that either.

"So...he went to work. My mom knew I was upset and tried to make me feel better. She took us to the beach, my favorite one. She told me I didn't smile enough, and she wanted me to spend the whole day smiling, and…I did. It was a perfect day." He paused, took a deep breath, then continued, steady and almost without emotion. "On the way home, there was an accident on the Pacific Coast Highway. My mom and the girls…didn't make it. And tonight there was an accident, and I lost a patient the same age as my sisters were."

"Aidan…"

"Shh. I'm not finished. I said I want to get this out and be done with it. The trauma made tonight…difficult. Next time I use you, it'll be under different circumstances, and we'll have talked about it first. I also owe you a thank-you; you served me well tonight, Finley. You gave yourself to me beautifully, and it was exactly what I needed."

"Oh, Aidan." There were a million things I wanted to say, but I knew he wouldn't allow it. I knew he didn't want to hear them or speak them, so again, I cried. I cried for the boy he had been and the man who went into trauma surgery because of the people he'd loved most in the world. I cried because I didn't know if he had ever let himself cry over it, and maybe my tears would somehow soothe his aches.

He held me and kissed my head and rubbed my back.

What I had given him wasn't enough, didn't feel like it would ever be enough, so when my tears dried again, I asked, "Can I serve you more tonight?" I would give him everything if he wanted it. Always and forever.

Aidan nodded. "Stand up," he ordered, and I did. "Strip."

The single-word command made my body feel as if it was misfiring. Like there was electricity shooting around inside me.

I pulled my shirt over my head, dropped it to the floor, and stepped out of my underwear. I always felt so young next to him. He had hair on his chest, and I didn't. I was smaller boned, shorter, littler in every way, but he looked at me with lust and fire, and there was nothing I wanted more than to be consumed by him.

"Kneel and take off my shoes."

Oh God, yes! I went down and untied and removed his shoes.

"Now my socks."

I took those off too. Then...then I leaned in and kissed the top of one foot, then the other. I felt his eyes on me as I did so, but he didn't pull away or tell me not to.

Aidan stood, his soft cock hanging from his underwear. He had neatly trimmed dark hair there, the same midnight shade as what was on his head, only it was tighter, rougher. Jesus, it had been incredible having his cock in my mouth, filling it, fucking it, choking on it, having him steal my breath with it. He'd swelled so big for me, both longer and thicker than I was, but I didn't care about that. I liked that Aidan was bigger than me there too. He was gorgeous soft as well. I wondered if he would let me suck him when he wasn't hard, sleep between his legs. I would do it, and I would love it.

"Take off my clothes."

My fingers were shaky as I unbuttoned his shirt and took it off. I pushed his jeans and trunks down his legs next, and he stepped out of them. "You're...perfect," rushed out of my mouth, and Aidan chuckled softly.

"Come on. We're going to shower."

I followed Aidan to the bathroom, where he turned the water on. When he had it to temperature, he opened the glass doors and signaled for me to go inside. He plucked my sponge from where it hung, squirted my bodywash into it, and began to clean me.

"I thought I was supposed to be serving you?"

"You're supposed to do as I say. That's where the service is. If I want to wash you, I will. If I tell you to wash me, you will."

"Yes, Sir." I mean, it wasn't like I was going to argue. This was nice too.

Aidan slowly scrubbed my entire body—chest, back, arms, legs, avoiding my cock, which was already hard again, and my ass. He didn't have an erection, and I had to admit, that made mine deflate a bit.

Finally, he rubbed the rough sponge between my legs, over my cock and balls. I hissed, and he smacked my hip. "Remember, you're not allowed to come unless I say you can."

"Yes...yes, Sir." I really, really wanted to come.

"Turn around," he ordered, and I did so. Aidan washed my ass, rubbed my hole with the sponge. I trembled, my cock leaking. I wanted to beg him to do it more, to touch me and finger me and then fuck me until I couldn't breathe or move. I wanted to be ruined by Aidan so he would know that no one could ever fulfill me like him and I would never need anyone except him.

I cried out when he pulled away.

"Wash me," Aidan ordered. I felt weak, my knees like they didn't want to hold me up, but I took the sponge from him, added more bodywash, and smiled at the thought of my soap mixing with his scent.

"What has you grinning?"

"You...and smelling like both of us."

"Christ, you're a delight."

My mouth watered as I washed him. I wanted to lick him clean instead of using soap. I wanted to get on my knees and suck him until he got hard and then take his load again, even if he didn't allow me to come.

When I finished washing him, Aidan stepped under the spray and rinsed off. Then he put a hand on my shoulder and pushed me down. I went willingly, hungrily.

"Jack off while doing it, but don't come before I do. It's free game after that. If you disappoint me, you won't be coming for a very long time."

"Oh God." I licked the head of his cock. It tasted like soap and Aidan. I lapped at his balls next, hoping I was doing a good job, that I was what he wanted. I loved the feel of his sac against my tongue, wished he smelled more musky and like him.

I took his prick into my mouth next, sucked it and stroked it with one hand, the other working my own erection. My balls were tight and full, the pressure already starting to build. It might kill me not to come until he did, but I was determined to make my Sir proud.

His dick began to fatten and grow as I worked him,

FINDING FINLEY

and pride surged through me. I was getting him hard and serving him well.

This was a different blowjob than earlier. He wasn't fucking my face or pulling my hair, just standing there while I did all the work, like I was simply a means to an erection and then an orgasm for him, and damned if that didn't turn me on.

Finally, he swelled to full mast, his balls heavy and full. His breathing quickened, and that again made me proud. I loved having that effect on him. Being able to make Aidan feel anything was like flying.

I was *aching*, needy and wanting. I tried to take him deeper and choked. It made my dick jerk because it was hot as hell to choke on Aidan's prick.

"Don't come until I do. You can do it, Finley. Won't it feel better to have an orgasm after knowing you did as you were told? That you ate my load down before giving me yours?"

Yes, yes, yes! I wanted that. I worked him harder, faster, but his hand on my face stopped me.

"Slow down. It's not a race. Enjoy me. Savor me. Look me in the eyes while you serve me."

I looked up at him, at his intense gaze, and said, "Yes, Sir," with a mouth full of cock. It made him smile, and his dick twitched against my tongue, so I figured he'd liked that.

I did as Aidan said, watching him, opening up to him as I made love to his dick with my mouth, relishing, cherishing, enjoying him. He didn't turn away from me, or me him, as I sucked and licked and kissed, while tugging on my cock.

When the corded muscles in his neck tightened and his hand went to my hair, I soared. Aidan pushed into me, fucked into me as he came, filling my mouth with his salty seed that I really fucking loved. I wanted to eat it all day every day. As soon as I swallowed, my balls drew up and I pulsed streams of my own release onto the shower floor.

Immediately, I bent to try and lick it up, but the water washed it away too quickly. "I'm sorry." I felt as if I'd failed him. I was supposed to eat my own cum too.

"Don't be sorry for something that isn't your fault. We're in the shower. I'm not a cruel man, Finley. I don't expect the impossible. Lick up what's on your hand, and that's fine. I'm very proud of you. You did a good job."

Oh, how I loved to hear that. I was in the clouds, floating and flying on his words. "Thank you, Sir."

Aidan turned the water off, and we got out. He handed me a towel and took one for himself, and we dried off. My mind was spinning with a million questions. Would we keep doing this? Would he ever fuck me? What did it all mean? Would he sleep in my bed? Did he really, truly want me? "Will you sleep with me?" rushed out. I didn't plan on settling on that question, but it was the one that came out. "Please?"

"Yes, but that doesn't mean we'll share the same bed every night."

I dropped my head. "Okay."

"I'm not saying we never will. But there are a lot of things to figure out. It's been a long day for both of us. Tonight, we sleep. Tomorrow we'll figure out exactly where we go from here."

I nodded. "Yes, Sir." Really, I knew I should be happy with what I got, but I wanted it all. I was selfish that way.

Once we were dry, he climbed into bed. Aidan went to his back and pulled me to him, letting me nuzzle in one of my favorite spots, in his arm. I breathed him in, clean and fresh.

"Can I ask one thing?"

He sighed, obviously wanting to go to sleep. Still, he humored me. "Yes."

"This is great...I love it, but I want to sleep down there." I pointed under the blanket.

"Down where? If you can't even say it, you can't do it."

"Between your legs," I admitted, which made me feel like a pervy weirdo.

Aidan only kicked the blanket off and said, "Go."

So I did. I lay between his legs with my face on his thigh, his cock at my lips and his scent around me. "Can I suck it?"

"No," he said in a frustrated tone.

Ugh. "Can I say one more thing?"

"Yes, and then that's it. You're pushing your luck tonight."

"That was seriously awesome. Basically, the best thing that's ever happened to me. I mean, I know I've said that before, but *this* was really the best. I hope we do it all the time."

I jumped when a loud laugh fell from his lips. His chest vibrated, making the bed shake. A minute later, when he calmed down, Aidan pulled me toward him and kissed the top of my head, and then I went back to my spot. "I wouldn't have thought I'd be able to laugh tonight. You're a treasure, little warrior. I hope you know that."

I burrowed deeper into him, and because Aidan said it, I believed him.

I went to sleep between my Sir's legs, with a smile on my face.

CHAPTER TWENTY-TWO

Aidan

I HADN'T BEEN able to sleep. It wasn't anything Finley had done wrong. He'd done everything right. I was in awe of him, of his openness and eagerness to submit to me. He had given himself to me willingly and fervently, in a way that made me not only proud, but honored.

When I closed my eyes, though, I thought of the little girl I'd lost that night, of my sisters and my mom, who had been gone for so many years now. It was something I still wasn't over, even though I'd spent my entire adult life trying to save people because I couldn't save them.

And when I wasn't thinking about my past, I was thinking about the boy snuggled in the middle of my thighs. I'd spent a year fooling myself, telling myself that Finley and I wouldn't end up exactly where we were…and for what? Because of how my father treated my mother? I knew I wasn't him, but I still stood by my decision to let Finley have some kind of independence before I possessed him completely. He would always know he had a choice.

It was almost time for his alarm to ding, so I reached over, plucked his phone from the nightstand, and turned it off. It had been a long night for him. He needed the extra rest. At one point, I tried to slip from the bed, but he clung to me, whispered my name softly three times, and then promptly went silent again.

I continued to lie there because it was obviously where he needed me to be. I thought of our previous night and the things I shared with him, telling him about my family when I'd never shared that with another soul. And the way Finley had…cried for me—that was what it had felt like; as if some of his tears could absolve me from my pain. It was a beautiful thing I wouldn't soon forget.

At around nine I knew I couldn't stay in bed any longer. I ran my fingers through his hair, down the pretty arch of his spine. "Finley, it's time to wake up."

He moaned and snuggled into my groin. The boy really loved my scent.

"Finley." I lightly tapped his head. As if I'd somehow sent an electric current through him, he shot up to sitting, eyes wide.

"Oh my God. I'm so sorry! I slept in. I don't know how I did that." He almost tumbled out of bed, but I grabbed hold of him and kept him in place.

"You slept late because I turned off your alarm. You needed the rest, so there's nothing to apologize for."

"Oh. Thank you."

"You're welcome. Come on. We'll go downstairs, make breakfast, then talk."

I helped him from the bed and walked to the bathroom. Finley followed behind. His eyes didn't leave me the whole time I took a piss. They weren't on my face either. When I moved to wash my hands, he seemed to snap out of it and went to the restroom himself and washed. "Put on a pair of sweats or pajama pants, a T-shirt, and no underwear. I'll meet you in the kitchen."

"Yes, Sir. Can I brush my teeth first?"

"Yes." I went to the en suite in my bedroom, brushed, then slipped on a tee and a pair of basketball shorts.

Finley was already in the kitchen making coffee when I arrived. "We'll make breakfast together, something simple like eggs and toast."

"I..." he began as if he was going to argue, but settled on, "Yes, Aidan."

So we did. I allowed Finley to make the scrambled

eggs, and I handled the toast. A few minutes later we sat at the table, with food, coffee, and orange juice.

"Can we talk about last night yet?" he asked eagerly, and I chuckled.

"After we eat."

He hurriedly scooped a bit of eggs into his mouth.

"How's your throat? Is it tender? I used you pretty roughly for your first time."

"It's a bit tender but not bad at all."

"We'll work on it, more slowly. We can also get you another dildo that you can use to practice deep-throating."

His face flushed a pretty pink. "Okay. I'd like that."

I nodded, and we ate our breakfast. Then I waited for him to do the dishes because I knew it would stress him out not to. As much as Finley wanted to talk about last night, he also deeply worried about disappointing me and not taking care of his responsibilities, so I made sure he was able to.

I led him to the living room afterward, where there was a rug beneath the couch because I knew being at my feet would be where he was most comfortable for this conversation, and I wanted to protect his knees.

I sat on the sofa, pointing to the floor, and he immediately went down to it. "Last night—"

"Was amazing and I want to do it again!"

I cocked a brow at him. "Then maybe don't interrupt me so you don't find yourself in trouble already."

"Oh, yes, Sir. I'm just so excited!"

A swell of joy bloomed in my chest. He made me feel…light in a way I wasn't sure I ever had. "Back to last night. Is there anything we did that made you feel uncomfortable?"

"No."

"And you've made it quite obvious you want to keep going."

"God, yes. More than anything."

I nodded. "That means the rules will change a bit. We'll have a sexual relationship. I'd rather you experience it with me before you go on to play with other Doms so you know what to expect and how you should be treated."

He flinched, then asked, "What if I never want to be with anyone else?"

"Never is a long time, Finley. There will be no expectations here. You'll always have a choice on whether this is where you want to be or not, and it will be good for you to know new men and experiences so you can figure out exactly who you are and what you want." The truth was, while I cared for him, I didn't know how to give him more outside of sexual pleasure. I was thirty-nine years old and had never truly given myself to another person, had never let anyone else in. And there were almost twenty years between us, which was unfathomable. I would never hold him to any promises, because eventually I would be an old man and he wouldn't be.

"I already know who and what I want."

I let his comment go. There was no doubt in my mind that Finley wanted me and I him, but I still believed forever a long time, especially for someone his age. "There are two main points we need to discuss…well, outside of limits and desires, that is. The first is that I'm always in charge. I think we both know and want that, yes?"

"Absolutely," Finley replied.

"The second is that your household responsibilities are completely separate from the sex. I'm paying you to take care of the house and run errands, not to fuck. If you decided to step away from working for me, sex can still be on the table if we both want it. If you decide you don't want to play together anymore, you can still keep your job. One has no bearing on the other. Do you understand that?"

He smiled up at me as if in awe, as if I had given him the world. "You're a good man, and I don't think you even know it."

I waved off his compliment but still replied, "Thank you, boy. I'm not sure about that, but thank you for believing it," because I wanted him to know he was appreciated.

"Now, to scenes. What are your desires? Limits?"

"I don't think I have any limits. I want to do everything," he answered, and I tensed up. This was definitely why it was good I was his first.

"So, if I told you to go get a knife and I wanted to use it on you, that would be okay?"

His eyes widened, a moment of fear there as if he didn't know what to say or how to respond.

"Does shit interest you?"

He shook his head frantically.

"See? So you don't want to try everything. Luckily, I'm not interested in those things either."

"But I don't know all there is to do, so how can I know all my limits and what I'd like?" he asked, and I nodded.

"We'll go through some things, and you tell me if it's something you're interested in or not. And if there's anything I miss that you know you want to try, we'll discuss it."

"That sounds like a good idea."

"Throat fucking and choking you with my cock are obviously something you enjoy."

"Yes."

"Anal sex?"

"Oh my God, yes! I've wanted you to fuck me forever, but I've never…"

"I know. I'm honored to be your first," I replied because I wanted him to know he was giving me a gift and I would do right by him. "And you're interested in some pain? At least curious about it?"

He blushed again, but like the brave boy he was, Finley didn't allow his fear to hold him back. He truly was a warrior. "Yeah. I'd like to be spanked sometime when I'm not in trouble. And like, maybe some other stuff too? I'd like to try crops and floggers or maybe a belt. Oh, and smacking! I really want to try that. I don't know if I'll like it, but the thought of it gets me hard, so I think I might. Do you do those things?"

"I do, yes."

"And you like it when I cry?"

I cupped his cheek, brushed my thumb beneath his eye. "Yes, I enjoy that too. Knowing you're open enough to me to do so, that I'm laying you bare is… It's a beautiful gift, Finley."

"I like it too."

"Good boy. And bondage?"

"I'd be interested in that as well."

"I don't do a lot of rope work. If that's what you're interested in, we'll have to find someone else. David maybe…"

"You're going to let other people use me?"

"Is that something you want? Something that's a possibility? It doesn't have to be sexual, but if you have a need I don't have the experience to provide, I'd like to be in control in how you get it."

"I…I don't know."

"We'll put it on the back burner for now and readdress it later. But cuffs and things I can give you."

"Yes, Sir."

"Do you have an issue with fluids? I don't do blood play, but what about spit?"

"I like that."

"Just on your hole? What if I want to spit on your face or in your mouth?"

He grinned and shifted. "I, um…I think I would like that."

"I enjoy cum play too—obviously, since I make you eat it—but I might do other things with it."

"Yes, I'm good with that."

"Watersports?"

His eyes darted down, and his face brightened like a tomato.

"There's no shame here, Finley, remember that. Don't ever be ashamed of what you desire."

His eyes met mine again. "I guess it depends on what we're doing with it? I want…I want to like, hold your cock when you pee. The thought of that does all sorts of things to my head. Like I'm there to serve your every need that way. You're too powerful to even be bothered to handle your own dick to take a leak. I want to serve you that way, but I don't think I want to drink it or anything…but it would be hot if maybe you wanted to do it on me sometime? Just to see if I like it? I mean, as a sort of marking your territory thing. That makes my brain go crazy in a good way too."

His gaze fell, so I petted his head, rubbed my fingers through his hair. "You're doing so well. You're being very good, so open and honest like a good boy should be."

"Thank you, Sir."

"You're welcome. What about orgasm denial and chastity?"

"Yeah, I'd like that. Not all the time, but sometimes."

"I enjoy orgasm denial too, and some chastity play,

but I don't do that long term either. You have a beautiful cock, and I don't plan to shrink it."

His eyes went wide, as if that surprised him. He likely hadn't known that was a thing.

From there we went through toys and a few other things before I asked, "Is there anything else you want to share with me? Something I didn't mention that's important to you?"

"I, um…I want to have your cock in my mouth more. Even when I'm not sucking it. Like if we're watching TV, I want to be told to hold it in my mouth…or in bed and stuff too? Like when I slept between your legs last night. I'd love to be able to nurse your cock while I did that."

My dick twitched behind my shorts, definitely liking that idea. "Okay. You can be my little cock warmer—oh, that reminds me, what about name-calling and humiliation?"

He nodded. "Not all the time, but sometimes. I want to feel like I'm your slut or your cock warmer."

"Good. I think we have a strong list to start with." I chuckled. "You are an absolute treat, precious boy. Thank you for all you give me."

"There's nothing I wouldn't give you. You're my Sir, and I want to belong to you."

"You do," I replied, my voice rough.

"There's one more thing…" I signaled for him to continue, and he did. "I want to crawl more for you. When we're home and I'm not cleaning or cooking and such. I want to be on my knees more often, outside of just kneeling. It's like…I almost feel the strongest when I'm on my knees. Do you think that's weird?"

"No, definitely not weird." I brushed the back of my hand across his cheek. "I would like that very much, but I'm going to give you a job to do, then. You're to schedule someone to come in and carpet the downstairs, all except for the kitchen and dining room. We'll get more rugs for those. I want a high-quality carpet, something thick and comfortable that won't be as hard on your knees."

"What? You can't carpet your downstairs just for me!"

My hand shot out, and I slapped him. Finley gasped, reaching up and touching his cheek. I hadn't hit him hard, but it was definitely enough to catch his attention.

"Is it your place to tell me what I can and can't do to my own home?"

"No, Sir. I'm sorry. I didn't mean to disrespect you. I just…don't feel like my stupid knees are worth spending all that money."

"It's my job to decide what's worth it and what isn't. It's your job to obey."

"Yes, Sir. That's what I want."

"Good boy." I lowered his hand from his face and caressed him. "That was okay?" I asked, since it was the first time I'd done something like that to him. It was important that he be completely honest with me as we figured out his limits.

"Yeah…it, um…it got my dick hard."

"The slap?" It was something that sounded sexy in theory but wasn't always something people liked.

"Yes."

"Go upstairs to my room. Take off your clothes, kneel beside the bed, and wait for me."

"Yes, Sir!" Finley practically sang before shoving to his feet and running eagerly for the stairs.

I took a couple of deep breaths, acknowledging that this boy was going to change everything.

CHAPTER TWENTY-THREE

Finley

I WAS SO excited, I worried my heart might bust its way straight out of my chest. I had no idea what Aidan had planned, but whatever it was, I knew I wanted it. And he was having me in *his* room, not mine, which made me soar just thinking about it.

I stripped out of my clothes and threw them in the corner before kneeling on the side of the bed, closest to the door. His bed was on the same wall as the entrance, with large windows and the door to the balcony across from it, and his bathroom to the side.

My cock was hard…so hard and red. Precum dripped from my slit and ran down my shaft.

It was likely only about two minutes until Aidan came upstairs, but it felt like an eternity. He was still dressed, and even in something as casual as basketball shorts and a T-shirt, he still looked like some kind of god. His very presence was so dominant, so commanding, but there was always kindness in his eyes, which didn't take away from the strength in him. When I watched scenes in porn, I never saw the gentle nature in the Dom's eyes that my Sir had.

"Look at how wet you are. Your cock is leaking all over," he said as he approached me.

"Is that okay? I thought maybe it was weird."

He frowned. "It's very okay, precious boy. It shows me how much you want me."

My heart was thundering again, excitement and nerves zipping through me, making it hard to sit still. I shifted. It was like my body was buzzing and I didn't quite know how to control it.

"Hey…it's okay. You're doing fine. Focus on me, on pleasing me. You don't have to be scared, because I'll always take care of you. And you don't have to worry about what to do, because I'll always instruct you. The only thing you need to focus on is doing as your Sir says." Aidan wrapped his hand around the back of my head and pushed my face into his groin.

I breathed him in, rooting my nose around, wished he were naked so I could smell him better and feel the rough hair of his pubes against my face, but this helped. Just being controlled by him and sniffing him helped.

"Better?"

"Yes, Sir."

"Good," he replied, then slapped me. I gasped, shocked, desperate. I wanted to ask him to do it again but knew I shouldn't. "Take off my shorts and underwear. And next time you remove your clothes, I want them folded. Set them on the chair if we're in my room or yours. If we're somewhere else, you may improvise, but I want them folded."

"Yes, Sir."

He removed his shirt, folded it, and tossed it to the chair. I slid his shorts down his legs, doing the same with them and trying not to allow myself to get hypnotized by his cock. It was… I thought maybe it was the most beautiful dick in the world.

"We're going to do this slowly. I want you to take your time, to focus on my pleasure…on taking me deep because it's what I desire. You'll need to work hard to relax your throat, and I promise, I'll only give you as much as you can handle, even if you feel like you can't—trust me. If your mouth is full of cock and you can't speak, tap my right thigh three times to stop, left thigh to slow down. If you can speak, use red and yellow, like we discussed before. Do you understand?"

"Yes, Sir," I replied, my voice trembling slightly. God, why was I freaking out? This was exactly what I'd always wanted.

"I'll pay attention to your reactions as well. If I notice you struggling in the wrong way, I'll stop. Are you okay? Still with me?"

"Yes, I just... I want to be good for you. I want to serve you well." As soon as the words left my mouth, I realized that was the root of my fear. Not Aidan or this. Never this. It was only that I wouldn't be good enough for him or that I wouldn't do this well. I wanted so very badly to please him.

"You already are good for me, and you already serve me well. There's no shame in struggling, and as long as you try, that's what matters."

That helped. When Aidan said something, it was impossible not to believe him. "Thank you."

"This will be slightly different from when I used you the first night. I'm not just fucking; we're going slow, working on how deep you can take me. It probably felt rough to you before, but eventually you'll be able to take me harder. Open," he said, and I stretched my lips. Aidan used his hand to angle his cock toward my mouth. He pushed in slowly, his eyes never leaving mine as he gently worked his way to the back of my throat.

I gagged...tried not to cry, but was soothed when he said, "It's okay. You can do this, precious boy. Focus on what I want." His dick was still on my tongue but not as deep as it had been. He slipped it slowly to the back of my throat again before pulling out some. He worked with me patiently, taking his time and learning where my gag reflex lay, testing it in a way that wasn't too overwhelming. The whole time he spoke words of encouragement, reminding me to relax, telling me to look him in the eyes, saying I was good and beautiful and looked so perfect with my mouth full of his cock.

And like always, Aidan's words opened something in my head, unlocked this door that only he had the key to, this place where I could just let go and *be*. Where he was waiting for me, protecting me, guiding me, and suddenly I realized my eyes were blurred. I was crying and he was fucking my throat, gloriously, dominantly taking what he wanted from me, what I so longed to give him.

I still gagged several times but not as much. I knew he wasn't fully letting loose on me, that he was still working me into it, but I was in that place in my head where I could just let go and be a vessel for his pleasure.

It was everything I wanted it to be, and I felt proud, like I was doing well for him, because I was trying and I was giving him my tears and he told me I was serving him well.

I cried harder when he pulled his cock free. I wanted

it back, wanted it jammed down my throat until I couldn't breathe unless Aidan chose to give me breath.

"Close your eyes, and remember, don't come."

My eyes fell shut, and I was kind of like...oh, I have a dick and it aches with need. All I'd thought about was Aidan, of his pleasure and his cock, until he'd reminded me.

I heard him working his erection, then felt the splatter of his cum on my face—my cheek, my lips, my forehead.

"Look at me," he ordered, and I did. He was still kind of blurry from tears, but I could see him staring down at me...and smiling. "I love this. I wish I could make you walk around all the time with my cum on your face. Everyone would know you belong to me, that you're my toy, my cocksucker. Would you like that?"

I shuddered. "Yes, Aidan. God, yes."

He rubbed the cum on my forehead into my skin, smeared it in. Then he pushed what hung from my lips into my mouth. "Don't swallow. Keep your mouth open." The jizz from my cheek was added to my mouth, mixing with my saliva that pooled there. Aidan tilted my head higher, bent, and let a drop of his spit land on my tongue.

Yes, yes, yes! It was dirty and primal and I loved it.

"Swallow," he told me, and I did, gulped it all down. "Good boy," Aidan said, skyrocketing me to the sun.

He pulled me to my feet and pushed me to the bed. "Do you want my hand on your cock or my fingers in your hole?"

Oh…he was asking me? I didn't think he would do that. It made my brain spin again, so I answered with the most honest reply I had. "I want whatever pleases you."

He moaned, this deep, throaty, possessive sound that made it obvious I'd made him happy.

"Christ, the things you do to me," he said, digging in his nightstand drawer and pulling out a bottle of lube. "Get on the bed. Open your legs."

I did so, holding them wide for him. When his lubed fingers circled my rim, I melted into the mattress. Yes, this was what I'd wanted. What I'd needed. Aidan knew. He would always know.

He started with one finger, which quickly became two. He fucked me with them, then slapped me. "Aidan, yes! God, yes!" I rushed out, and he did it again, finger-fucked me and slapped me. My dick hurt, my balls fuller and tighter than they had ever been as I leaked all over my stomach.

I was crying again. Was that okay? I wondered hazily. I knew he liked my tears, but I cried a lot. I didn't realize

I had so many of them in me until Aidan unlocked them.

I arched off the bed when two fingers became three and he smacked me again. "Come, precious boy. Come for me," he said, and I did. I screamed and spasmed, my whole body vibrating as my orgasm ripped through me and I was catapulted into the secret place Aidan's dominance led me to. Where the world was fuzzy yet righted and I didn't feel like I was on Earth.

"Christ, you are incredible. I'm so proud of you. You're such a good boy, Finley. My precious warrior boy." He was holding me and stroking me. When his fingers touched my lips, I didn't have to think about it; I opened for him, took my load from him as he praised me and comforted me and led me back to the ground again.

When I came out of it, we were lying the right way in the bed, our heads on the pillows and my face in Aidan's sweaty arm. I loved that he was always there when I needed him, giving me the care and encouraging words so I knew I did well.

"Can I lick it?" I asked, surprising myself.

Aidan seemed to hesitate...then raised his arm and nodded. Maybe it was weird, and maybe it was supposed to be gross, but it wasn't to me because it was Aidan...my Sir. The hairs there were rough against my tongue. I savored each lick, the salty, musky taste of him going to my head. When I was finished, he held my face, and I looked at his lips. "You've never kissed me."

"Do you want to be kissed?"

"Yes, Sir."

He pulled me over so I straddled him. His hands were still on my cheeks, and he lowered my lips to his, not seeming to care I'd eaten our cum and licked up his sweat. His tongue swept my mouth possessively, owning me, commanding me as I kissed him back and savored this gift he was giving me.

Afterward, he pulled away and asked, "Everything we did…it was all okay? Nothing that you realize you don't want to do again? Did I test limits you didn't know you had?"

"No." I shook my head. "It was perfect, and I loved it all. I would do it again right now if you'd let me."

He chuckled. "I'm nearly twenty years older than you. It takes me a bit longer."

"I can wait." I would wait for Aidan forever if I had to.

Something changed in his eyes. They darkened for a moment, but not in anger, before the look was gone. He nodded. "I won't ask you that every time, but I'm telling you now—never worry about using red or yellow. For this to work, I have to know your limits. I'll push them, I'll push you, yes, but if you can't handle something or if I go too far, you have to tell me. If we do something and you later realize you would rather not do it again, tell me and we won't. If you're not honest with me that way, we can't do this."

"Yes, Sir. I'll tell you. I promise."

"Good boy," he said, and God, I loved it. There was nothing like being Aidan's good boy. "Just so you know, I get checked regularly. I have my latest results on my computer, which I can show you later. I'm STI-free. And you had the physical I told you to have earlier this year."

I had. He'd made me go to the doctor, which I thought was lame, but I'd done it. I hadn't ever fucked anyone in my life, but Aidan said it was important to have everything—not just my sexual head—checked yearly.

"You're safe with me, and when I fuck you, it'll be bare. Do you understand?"

A smile split my face. I couldn't help it. I was dying to have my ass filled with Aidan's load.

He could obviously see my joy at the thought because he grinned. "You're incorrigible, you dirty boy. What am I going to do with you?"

Dominate me. Love me. Own me.

He kissed my forehead, pressed my face down until my cheek lay against his chest, and I let the beat of his heart lull me to sleep.

CHAPTER TWENTY-FOUR

Aidan

"I HEARD ABOUT what happened. Are you okay?" David asked as we went for a jog a couple of days later. His question didn't surprise me. Although he didn't know my past, he saw how I reacted when I lost a patient, and David was good at reading people. It was one of the things that made him a good Dominant.

"Yeah, I'm fine." Fine was overselling it, but I was okay. She wasn't the first patient I'd lost, and unfortunately, she likely wouldn't be the last. I didn't mean that in a callous way; it was the truth. There was no getting around it. Plus...Finley had helped. He had beautifully given me what I needed, and in that gift of submission, he had also found what he needed.

"Holy shit. You're fucking him now, aren't you?"

I whipped my head around and looked at him. "What?" How the hell had he known that? "We haven't said one thing about Finley, and you've drawn that conclusion."

David rolled his eyes, slowed his jog, then began to walk.

"You're using this as an excuse for a break," I teased.

"You're trying to change the subject. And good for you. There's no reason you shouldn't have been playing with him all along. You're crazy if you think I don't see how much you want him. Even from the start. Taking some random boy home and moving him in? That's not you, Aidan."

I groaned because there wasn't a thing he'd said that wasn't true. From the moment I saw Finley in the restaurant that first night, everything I'd done was out of the ordinary for me. And I *had* wanted him from the very first moment I'd seen him. "I still don't understand how *I'm fine* brought you to the conclusion that I'm fucking him."

"Because I know you," he replied simply. And he did, as much as anyone really knew me, at least. The only one who knew me better was the very boy we were discussing. I wasn't sure how I felt about that still, but it was done. Finley had deserved to know, and there was no going back.

"We are…mutually fulfilling needs for one another. That's all it is; just like any scene, really."

"Yeah, except the boy is head over heels in love with you, lives with you, and you've basically been in a relationship for a year. You know, just like with all your other random boys," he said sarcastically.

He was right. It wasn't something I did often, but I took a deep breath and let myself be honest, let David in. "I don't know how to be all that he'll need." I could be his Dominant, his employer, the man who put him on his knees, but there wasn't a doubt in my mind that Finley would want more. He always seemed to want more, and eventually, I found myself giving it to him. It pleased me to provide for him, but outside of sex, dominance, and care, I feared I was empty. That wasn't easy for me to admit, even to myself—that there were things I couldn't do.

"I think you're doing a good job of it so far, Aidan. You've cared for that boy for a year now. You've provided for him and have been good to him. That's all there is to it. You just keep doing that."

"You make it sound simple," I replied as we weaved our way through the wooded path.

"Oh, God no." David chuckled. "But you overthink things sometimes, and by sometimes, I mean all the time. Just do what you're doing, and it'll be fine. I have faith in you."

David was a good friend. I was lucky to have him, and I knew that if I allowed myself, I could fully let him in as well. He wouldn't judge me. Still, it wasn't something I could do, not yet, so I said, "Thank you. For always being there. I know I'm not always…"

"The most fun guy around?" David teased.

"Fuck you," I replied with a grin.

"You're welcome. Now come on. My break is over, so I'd like to get back to showing you up."

This time, I couldn't hold back the loud boom of laughter. "You wish," I replied as we began to run.

FINLEY HADN'T BEEN home when I got there. I knew he wouldn't be. He had class and then a couple of errands to run for me, things I could do myself but allowed him to do because it was something he needed.

I showered and dressed, then made a quick trip to the adult store. There were a few things I needed to purchase.

While I hadn't fucked him yet, Finley had had his mouth on my cock every day since this all began. He was getting better, but he had an easily triggered gag reflex, unless he was blissed out of his mind enough to let go.

When he did, when he got to that place where the world around him was all fuzzy except for me and what I demanded of him, the boy stole my breath. He quite honestly always did, which was something I was able to ignore sometimes better than others.

Despite what David said, I knew there were parts of me I couldn't give, doors that were locked, and as far as I was aware, there were no keys. But what we were doing now, I would gladly continue, because Christ, what the boy did to me.

After grabbing what I needed from the adult store, I paid and went home. I put some of the items in Finley's room and others in mine. I knew he would be home any moment now, so I stood at the top of the stairs and waited. When he closed the door behind him, I said, "Stop."

Finley immediately obeyed, standing in the foyer and looking up at me.

"Set your bag down."

He leaned it against the wall.

"Take your clothes and shoes off."

His eyes brightened. Christ, the boy always seemed to have sex on the brain and was thrilled anytime he was going to do it.

Finley swiftly took off his clothes, his cock already

hard and tall against his belly. He folded them as he was supposed to, then waited as if unsure where to put them.

"Set them on the table for now. Walk over to the stairs, and when you get there, crawl up to me."

We really needed to hurry and get the downstairs carpeted. At least the stairs and upstairs were good for his knees.

"Yes, Sir."

Finley obeyed beautifully. He was…fuck, he was exquisite on his knees, as he obviously tried to seductively crawl up the stairs.

I cocked a brow. "Is someone trying to seduce me?" I teased.

"I'm trying to be sexy. Is it working?" He grinned, and I felt this…fullness in my chest. It was such a foreign feeling, I nearly stumbled backward with the pressure of it.

"You're always sexy, precious boy."

He shined so brightly at the compliment, it was as if the sun lived inside him. Hell, maybe it did.

Finley knelt at my feet when he got to the top of the stairs. I rubbed a hand over his head and praised, "Good boy," and the light in him shined even more intensely. "Come on." I led him to his room, Finley crawling behind me. I considered having him undress me but decided to torture him a little instead.

He waited, looking up at me, as I slowly began to unbutton my shirt. I could see the excitement and questions skating around in his eyes. He was hungry for me, needy, wanted to know what I would do with him, to him.

When I reached the last button, I slipped the shirt off my shoulders and laid it across the chair.

"Can I do your pants?" Finley asked.

"No."

He whimpered.

"Be good or you won't get anything at all."

"Yes, Sir."

His eyes were riveted on me as I finished undressing. My cock was hard, a stone pole between my legs. I ignored it, sitting on the bed and patting my lap. "I'm going to spank you. This is for pleasure, so you'll be allowed to come, but remember, only when and how I say you can."

"Yes, Sir," he replied before frantically scrambling onto the bed and over my lap. I chuckled at his eagerness. He was so fresh and pure and hungry for life in a way I wasn't sure I had ever been. It gave me something, seeing him this way, that I'd never had in a submissive before.

I rubbed my hand over his ass and felt him tremble against me, his cock pressing against my leg. Goose bumps chased my hand when I did it again, just petting him, caressing the plump globes of his smooth, pale ass.

"Oh God," he whispered.

"I haven't done anything yet."

"You're touching me. I love your touch. It makes me feel connected to…well, you, obviously, but like, to the world. To myself. Does that make sense?"

My pulse thudded against my skin as fire lit a trail inside me, blooming into an inferno. Christ, he was magnificent, and he didn't even know it. "Yes, that makes sense."

"Plus, I'm just so eager for you to spank me, I feel like I'm going to burst out of my skin. It's killing me to keep still."

I lifted my hand and smacked down on his right cheek. Finley tensed, then released a shaky breath. I didn't give him time between before I did the same to his left cheek, then lower on the right, pink blooming in my wake. He was rutting against me with each smack, begging and pleading, "Please, Sir. *More.*"

I painted his ass red with smack after smack, the color darkening with each one. He was crying then—he cried so easily and beautifully for me but kept begging for more.

I reached over and plucked the brush I'd placed on the nightstand, then rubbed the bristles across his skin. Finley cried out, his hands fisting in the blanket as he looked over his shoulder at me. His eyes were red, his face wet, his chin trembling. It was the most intense spanking I'd given him, with more heat behind my swats than I'd allowed myself in the past, but it wasn't enough. I wanted to keep going, to test him, to bring him to the edge and watch him soar.

"Remember your colors—yellow to slow down, red to stop. Use them if you need them."

He nodded.

"Say it," I pushed.

"Yes, Sir."

There was a loud *smack* when I slapped the smooth side of the brush down on his ass. Finley spasmed, cried out…then hissed a quiet, "*Yessss.*"

It was one of the most incredible sounds I'd ever heard.

I alternated between his cheeks and areas on his ass, not giving him more than I thought he could handle, but again, testing him, taking him further than he'd gone before, and when he couldn't stop shaking and mumbling, "Please…yes…I need to come," I tossed the brush down and pulled him up so he knelt beside me.

"Jerk off on me—my cock and stomach."

Surprise flashed in his teary eyes. I spit in his hand, and he wrapped it around his dick and did as told. It was less than ten strokes later that his head fell back and he shot his load, landing on me just as I'd ordered him to do.

Finley reached for me to finish me off, but I smacked his hands away. "I didn't say you could touch me."

With my fist around my dick, I jerked until my balls drew up and I spurted on my own chest and stomach, my cum mixing with his. "Clean it off," I ordered.

Finley licked his lips, hunger sparking in his gaze before he leaned over and ate our cum from my body.

"Come here," I told him. I took his mouth, remembering how he'd asked for a kiss before. I tasted us both there, and he moaned as our tongues tangled. When I pulled away, he lay against me, and I held him, caressed him, as he relaxed against me.

"God, that was the best. It's going to hurt to sit down."

"You'll think of me each time you do."

"I always think of you," he replied softly.

I couldn't find the words to reply, so instead I nudged him. "Let's go into the bathroom."

Finley's brows pulled together in confusion, but he easily stood up and went. His gaze landed on the dildo, suction-cupped to the shower. "I want you to use this daily—not on your ass, but your mouth. Practice deep-throating it, testing your gag reflex, and then pushing past it. Just a few minutes, every morning or evening. It's your choice when, but keep it the same every day."

"Yes…yes, Sir," he replied, looking almost…sad.

"It's not because you don't please me. You satisfy me very much, but remember, I'll always test you and push you to be the best you can be at everything, and that includes being a cocksucker."

Finley smiled, apparently quite happy being called a cocksucker.

"Now come here. I need to take a piss, and I don't want to do it myself."

"I… Yes, Sir!" Finley walked over and stood behind me. He wrapped his arms around me and grabbed my cock, aiming it at the toilet. This wasn't something I had ever done with a sub before, but I already felt excited at the thought of using him as someone who held my dick when I needed to pee.

I let loose and it splashed on the rim, Finley adjusting my aim so it landed in the toilet. He peeked around me, watching as I went, his heart thumping madly against my back, and if I wasn't mistaken, he was getting hard again. When my stream finished, he shook me off, then grabbed toilet paper and cleaned what we had spilled along the seat.

"Thank you...God, thank you." He reached for me, then stopped. "Can I hug you?"

That question twisted me up in such unfamiliar ways. I always provided aftercare, obviously. It was one of my favorite parts, but I had never been asked for permission to just hug me before. I don't think I would have wanted it from anyone but him.

I nodded, and Finley wrapped his arms around me. He rubbed his cheek against the hair on my chest and continued to thank me over and over and over again.

"Thank *you*, precious boy. You serve me well."

We parted and washed our hands. I examined his ass to make sure it was okay, before having him put on loose flannels and nothing else. We ordered dinner, and he lay on his stomach on the floor, doing homework, while I sat beside him with my laptop.

"Can I ask you something?" he questioned a little while later. When I nodded, he continued. "Why do I cry?"

"I think it's a combination of everything. The emotions and endorphins and being laid bare. It's a lot to take in."

He nodded, looking satisfied with that answer.

I'd never been a fan of kissing. It wasn't that I hated it, but I didn't get the draw. Suddenly, though...I did. I teased his lips open and took his mouth again. His taste was familiar, comfortable, and yes, it was abundantly clear I did enjoy kissing now. He smiled when I pulled away, likely knowing it.

When it was time to sleep, I went up with him, watched him as he crawled into bed, before going to my own.

CHAPTER TWENTY-FIVE

Finley

THE SUN WARMED my skin the moment I stepped outside. It was a gorgeous day, and I was suddenly super thankful to be meeting Ian at an outdoor café, just down the street from campus.

I wondered how people lived in other parts of the country. Southern California was the best. I mean, sure, the traffic sucked and it was expensive as hell, but the weather, God, I loved the weather.

Or maybe I just saw everything differently now; maybe the sun felt better against my skin because I felt better inside of it.

I felt fulfilled.

Whole.

Well, mostly. I still wanted Aidan to love me, wanted to tell him I loved him, but I was scared. Plus, I was pretty sure he already knew.

I hefted my backpack on my shoulders as I started

the short walk to the Campus Café. It wasn't really part of the college, but I knew a lot of the students used it to eat, study, and for the free internet access. I'd heard about it plenty, but this would be my first time there.

As I walked, my jeans rubbed against my ass, making me wish it were still sore from Aidan's spanking last week. It was…well, it was everything. I basically said that about every sexual encounter we had, but it was true. Each time I was with him, he seemed to bring me to higher places. He still hadn't fucked me, and I was *dying* for that, but I loved to cry for him, to be spanked by him, and the few times he'd let me hold him while he pissed, because being used by Aidan gave me something that most people wouldn't understand.

I glanced up and saw Ian already sitting at a table on the patio. There was water in front of him and another for me at one of the two empty seats. "Hey, you," I said as I approached. He stood, and we hugged.

"Lunch is my treat today," he said quickly.

"Ian…" He knew I liked to pay. I had an account that had more money than I ever thought I would have. Sure, it wasn't much to some people, but it was to people like me and Ian. Why shouldn't I pay when it was so much easier for me?

"You always get it. This time I want to do something

for you."

Honestly, I understood that. I would feel the same, so I nodded. "Fine. Whatever."

"So, how is Cinderella doing in her castle?" he teased.

"Perfect," I replied. It was truly how I felt sometimes—like Aidan was a king, and I was the boy he'd saved and turned into a prince. His prince.

"Oh, but the real question is, has he taken the maiden's virginity yet? Or are you still intact?"

"Oh my God." I laughed. If there had been something handy to throw at him, I would have done it.

"Did he do it? Are you with child!" Ian joked, making me laugh even harder. God, I loved him. He was the best. I was so very thankful to have him.

"I hate you," I said when I settled down.

"You don't hate me. You're jelly that I've had dick and you haven't."

And maybe I was. "We've done so many other things that would probably scandalize you, my little vanilla friend. I might not have had Aidan in my ass, but I'm satisfied." Not that I didn't want him to fuck me, because I did, but yeah, he still rocked my world in every way.

Ian sobered, taking a drink of his water before saying, "Seriously, Fin. It's great to see you happy. I might not understand your form of happiness, but it's clear that you are."

It was one of the things I adored about him. Ian might not get wanting to submit to someone, wanting to hurt or be made to cry or feel used. I was sure as shit positive he wouldn't understand when I did things for Aidan like revel at the chance to be at his feet or hold his dick when he peed, but those things filled all the empty places inside me, and Aidan saw that.

"Thank you," I replied. I wanted to tell Ian that I loved Aidan, loved him more with every breath I took, but I was scared to. If he knew, he would ask if Aidan loved me, and when I told him I didn't know, he would worry.

I was saved from spilling it out when the waiter approached our table. He looked to be in his early twenties. He had brown hair and green eyes, scruff along his jaw, and…shit, he was hot. It wasn't the first time I'd thought that about him. I wasn't blind.

"Hi. I'm Jordan. I'm taking over for Phil. Are you ready to order?" He looked over at me, and there was a spark in his eyes. "Oh, hey—Finley, right? You're in my English class."

"Hi. Yeah, I think so." Which I already knew, but I wasn't going to make it sound like that.

"You wrote that killer essay Professor Adams was raving about. I'm shit in this class. You're a really good writer."

I felt my cheeks heat because I was a bit of a slut for compliments. "Thanks. And I'm sure you're not that bad."

"No, no. I assure you I am," he replied, and I chuckled. Jordan smiled at me, and I looked away.

"I think I'll have the chef salad with ranch," I told him.

Ian ordered fish and chips, and then Jordan took our menus. When he did, he looked at me again and gave me another grin before slipping away.

"Well, shit. If Aidan won't fuck you, Jordan sure as hell will. He wants you."

I rolled my eyes. "He doesn't want me." The words came out automatically. I was sometimes in this weird place where I was caught between my insecurities and like…having eyes in my head. Part of me struggled to feel like anyone would really want me, but then, I'd seen how he'd looked at me. Jordan definitely found me attractive.

"Liar, liar, pants on fire," Ian teased.

"It doesn't matter if he wants me or not. I belong to Aidan."

"Sweetheart, you're a person. You don't belong to anyone."

This was one of those moments that reminded me that no matter how supportive Ian was and how happy he was for me, he still didn't get it. "I *want* to belong to Aidan. I've given myself to him, and he's taken me, so yes, I belong to him."

"I'm just saying…you're twenty. Remember that there's a whole world out there, okay?"

It wasn't something I needed to remember because I didn't care who or what was out there. Still, I replied, "I know," to keep the peace.

"And even if Aidan is your boyfriend or whatever, that doesn't mean you can't have friends besides me."

"I know. Aidan would never tell me I can't have friends. He always asks me about people from class and says I should go hang out with them."

"Good." Ian smiled. "So…is Aidan your boyfriend? Is that what you guys call it?"

The truth was, I didn't know. I just knew he was my Sir and I was his boy, but I did want to be his boyfriend too. I wanted to be able to tell people that I belonged to Dr. Aidan Kingsley. "I don't need to be Aidan's boyfriend," I lied. Ian cocked a brow at me but didn't argue.

We chatted about random stuff, laughing and enjoying ourselves, and soon Jordan was back with our meals. He handed Ian his and then me mine, saying, "I know it's just a salad, but ours are really good. The dressing is homemade, and it's to die for."

"Oh…thanks," I replied. "I'm sure I'll love it."

"Let me know," Jordan said. "Did you guys need anything else?"

"No, we're good. Thanks."

As he walked away, he looked over his shoulder at me again. I gave my attention to my food. It *did* look like a good salad.

"Oh, Finley, taste my ranch. See how thick and creamy it is," Ian teased, and this time, I did throw something at him, my balled-up napkin, and we both laughed.

"He was putting it on thick, wasn't he?" But it did feel good. It was okay to think that, right? Even though I loved Aidan.

"He really was. I might be a little jelly."

"You can have him. I just want Aidan."

"Yes, but Jordan with the thick and creamy ranch wants *you*. He'll fuck you."

"I hate you," I said again, before changing the subject. We finished our meal, Jordan forgotten. I just enjoyed the time with my friend.

When we were done, Ian went to the restroom. While he was gone, Jordan brought the bill, set it on the table, and then handed me a piece of paper. "You know…if you ever want to study together sometime…which basically means helping me not suck at English…"

I laughed uncomfortably but took it. I was twenty years old, and this was the first time a guy had ever given me his phone number. "I, um…thank you. But just so you know, I have a…" Sir? Dominant? I wasn't sure what to even call Aidan to someone else.

"Boyfriend?" Jordan filled in the blank for me, and I nodded. "Shit. Just my luck. But we can still study together sometime, if you want. If not, that's okay too." Then he slipped away, and I looked down at the paper with his phone number on it.

A year ago, I would have thrown it away. I wouldn't have been able to trust anyone or open myself up to a friendship outside of Ian, but now I just thought, I deserved this, right? Friends? Serving Aidan had changed me so much, I was beginning to realize there were things I wanted for myself. I never thought I cared about having friends, and I sure as shit hadn't wanted school before him, but now? Now, the thought of studying with someone seemed…like something I deserved, something that could be fun. Something that everyone did, and why shouldn't I do that too?

I paper-cut my finger when I folded it up. "Shit." I shoved it into my pocket and sucked on the injury. Ian came back, paid, and we said our goodbyes.

I felt the paper, like a weight in my pocket, the whole drive home.

CHAPTER TWENTY-SIX

Aidan

I SMELLED COFFEE and had a feeling someone had slipped into the room with me this morning.

I rolled over and looked up. It wasn't until Finley smiled at me, wearing nothing but a pair of boxer trunks, coffee in hand, that I realized I was smiling too. That I had been smiling from the moment I'd smelled the beverage and known he had come in.

"Good morning," he said. "I woke up early, practiced my deep-throating, and made coffee. Is it okay that I woke you?"

I chuckled, sitting up. "When someone comes into the room with coffee and tells you they sucked a dildo for you, it's impossible for it not to be okay. Sit." I patted the bed.

Finley handed me the mug, and I took a sip as he settled on the bed beside me.

"Why couldn't you sleep?" It was the weekend, and

he was allowed to get out of bed later then.

"I don't know. My mind was buzzing, so I thought I'd get up and start the day."

It was something I was fairly familiar with—trouble sleeping, that is. With my schedule and being on call sometimes, it was hard to get my body to rest when it should. "What do you want to do today?"

Finley shrugged. "Whatever you want. I just want to spend the day with you. Is David still coming over for dinner tonight?"

"Yes, he is. Do you have homework?"

Finley shook his head.

I glanced at the clock to see it was only eight. It wasn't often that Finley and I went out together. It wasn't often that he went out at all, unless it was for school, to run errands, or to have the occasional meet-up with Ian. That wasn't my doing. I wanted the boy to have a life outside of me, but I likely hadn't done a good enough job commanding him to do things. The truth was, I liked to spend time with him, and when we had it, I preferred to be in the house with him, allowing him to serve me. That wasn't fair to him. "What would you like to do?"

He thought for a moment. "We could maybe go to the beach?" My muscles immediately tensed up. Finley didn't seem to notice as he continued. "It's always been relaxing for me."

My stomach twisted, and I set the coffee down, suddenly not feeling like drinking. He looked at me with those big, curious, eager eyes of his, excitement dancing around in him, and I knew I wouldn't deny him. It wasn't as if I never went to the beach. Sometimes social functions were held there, or I ate at a restaurant near the water. It wasn't something I could avoid, but it always did things to my head, made my thoughts go places I didn't want them to go, made me hear Amy's and Ari's laughter and see my mom's smile. "Then we'll go to the beach." The words were heavy on my tongue, but I forced them free.

"Oh my God! Yay!" He clapped his hands adorably. It reminded me that not many people had done nice things for Finley in his life, that he had spent it feeling alone and unloved after losing his mom.

I leaned over and kissed him. He gasped into my mouth, then smiled against my lips as I swept my tongue inside. Kissing wasn't something we did often. I spanked him and fucked his throat, but kissing was much rarer.

Finley whimpered when I pulled away. "I changed my mind. Let's stay in bed all day." He reached for me, but I grabbed his wrists, holding his hands over his head, my grip on him tight. I hadn't gotten around to using restraints on him yet, which was something I needed to remedy soon.

"Be good. You wanted to go to the beach, and now that's what we're doing." I got up, and he pouted as he followed me to the bathroom.

"Can you use me a little before we go?" he asked, and even though my dick perked up at the thought, I shook my head.

"No." As much as I loved using him to get off, I equally enjoyed tormenting him. Making Finley needy for me, knowing that he couldn't have what he wanted until I said he could, checked all my boxes.

"You like to make me miserable." He stood in the doorway.

"Yes. Are you surprised? You like it too, like knowing I'm in charge of you, that I own you…don't you?"

He flushed that pretty, pretty pink I loved on his cheeks. "Yes, Sir. I love belonging to you."

"Good boy." I nodded toward my cock, and Finley rushed over. He pulled my dick free, held it, and aimed it at the toilet for me, the way he loved to do. Afterward, we showered together, and I made him wash me. He whimpered when he washed my hardening prick, begging me again to fuck his mouth. He was hard and leaking, and there was nothing I wanted more than to push down into his throat and take what was mine, but I still denied him. It was fun to make him suffer.

Finley made smoothies for breakfast, and I packed the few beach supplies I had—towels and sunscreen and a few cold drinks in a cooler, before we drove to Santa Monica. It was still early, so parking wasn't as horrible as it could have been. An hour or so later and we would have been screwed. I purchased two beach chairs at a little shop there, and then we found a spot on the sand and set up.

He was wearing board shorts, and though I was too, that definitely wouldn't do. "Next time we need to get you a Speedo. I want to see more skin."

Finley gave me that smile that lit up my chest. "Yes, Sir."

My limbs were still too tight, my head sort of a mess. I saw families and children, little girls running and moms and dads laughing, and all I could think about was them. If I hadn't fought with my father that day, if I hadn't angered him, they would be alive. It was devastating how one small choice could change so many lives, only you never knew it ahead of time.

"Aidan?" Finley asked, and by the crease of his brow, I could tell it wasn't the first time he'd tried to get my attention.

"I'm sorry, what?"

"Sunscreen…can I put it on you?"

I nodded.

He knelt behind me, squirted lotion into his hands, and began to rub it into my shoulders. My eyes fell closed as I tried to focus on him, on this boy who had come into my life and, with nothing more than being himself, had turned my world on its axis. I knew he didn't realize how incredible he was, the things he was doing to me, but I also knew I wouldn't tell him.

"Aidan, what's the matter?"

"Nothing."

He crawled over me until he sat between my legs, then rubbed sunscreen on my chest. "Did I do something wrong? If you tell me, I can fix it. I'll try and be better."

His words snatched the air from my lungs. He was so eager to please, to serve, to be good for *me*. It also broke my heart how quick he was to assume he'd messed up. "You didn't do anything wrong. It's just…the beach. It's hard for me because of the day I lost my family."

His mouth dropped open. "Oh my God. I'm so sorry! I wasn't thinking. We can go right now." He began to stand, but I grabbed his waist, holding him in place.

"We're not going anywhere."

"But, Aidan—"

"No!" I cut him off. "I'm fine. I want to give this to you, and you want what I want, yes?"

He nodded slowly.

"Giving you this will please me very much. And when you give me what I want, it gives you what you need, doesn't it?"

"Yes, Sir."

"It's settled, then. Now continue lotioning me before you give me a reason to punish you."

"I…" he started, then said, "Yes, Sir," and did as told.

When he finished with me, I made sure to slather his body as well. He was so pale, I would have to watch him to make sure he didn't get burned.

We sunbathed for a little while, but I could tell he still felt unsure. I didn't want him to feel guilty or as if he was causing me pain, so I told him, "Come," and he snuggled closer to me, my arm around him and his head on my chest. "How are your classes going?"

"Good. I got an A on a math exam, and my English teacher has used my papers for examples three times."

"Good boy." I kissed the top of his head. "Is that

something you think you might want to do?"

"No…I just want to serve you."

I sighed. "Finley…"

"What? It's what I want," he snapped, and I smacked his ass, making him squeak. "Oh my God. What if someone saw?"

"So?" I asked. "You belong to me. I can do as I wish with you, and you can serve me and still want a degree and have a career. I *am* capable of cleaning my own house, you know."

He chuckled. "Hiring someone, you mean."

"Or that." I stroked his chest as I forced myself to say the words that needed to be said. "You won't serve me forever. What happens when I'm not around?"

"I don't want to think about that," he replied, burrowing into my arm deeper and inhaling, taking his comfort in my scent and knowing I was there.

"But you need to, precious boy."

"I'm going to school, and I'll admit I like it. Can't that be enough?"

No… I knew I should tell him no. It was selfish not to; it was binding him to me when logically I knew he needed to have the means to take care of himself. Still, I said, "For now."

"Thank you, Sir."

As I lay there, feeling the sun kiss my skin and taking in the blue sky, which rivaled Finley's eyes, I wondered if there was anything I wouldn't give him if I could.

CHAPTER TWENTY-SEVEN

Finley

I FELL ASLEEP. I didn't know how long I'd been out, but the sun and being in Aidan's arms just made me feel so safe, so loved, that I'd drifted off.

And when I did, I'd dreamed of my mom. She had always loved the beach. She smiled brighter there, said it made her feel invincible. Her problems looked a whole lot smaller when she compared them to the vastness of the ocean.

I felt horrible that I'd suggested we come here. That I didn't even think about Aidan's loss or the fact that his mother had taken him to the ocean before she died.

But he'd stayed because I wanted it. Maybe it was selfish of me, but all I could think was, *Maybe that means he loves me*. It was one thing to order someone around and take your pleasure from them, but another to make a sacrifice like this.

"Thank you, Sir," I said against his skin.

"Oh, you're awake. I was going to get you up soon so you didn't burn. And what are you thanking me for now?"

"For this...bringing me here. It was her favorite place. It reminds me of her." Could Aidan and I have ever been at the beach together? Probably not, since he was so much older than me, but I'd like to think we had.

He cleared his throat. "You're welcome. Would you like to go in the water now?"

I shot up into a sitting position. "Can we?"

Aidan snickered, then sat up and cupped my cheek. "You are so easy to make happy. I love that about you. No matter what has happened to you, you're still able to find joy in the smallest things. Don't ever lose that."

Love... He'd used the word *love*. God, I wanted to climb on his lap and tell him I love him, to beg him to love me too because that would make me happier than anything in the world. Instead, I said, "You make me happy. No one has before you," then pushed to my feet. "Now come on!"

I began to run, and I couldn't have been more shocked when Aidan ran too. He chased me into the water, where he tackled me, keeping his arms around me to hold me up. I was laughing and then he was too, this loud, passionate laugh I knew began deep in his chest. I felt it radiate out, vibrate through me, and it made me laugh more. I wasn't sure I'd ever heard this sound from him before, this pure, joyous, almost glee. I wanted to do everything in my power to make Aidan do this every day for the rest of my life, because I didn't think he took delight in many things.

We played in the water together, splashing and swimming and dunking each other. He was never out of arm's length, holding me and protecting me as if I really was precious to him and he truly did own me. I was Aidan's, meant to take care of him, and he took such beautiful care of me. Every now and again he would kiss me, sometimes with tongue, others just a press of his lips to mine. Strangely, those felt even more intimate.

When my limbs were tired and I'd laughed more than I ever had in my life, Aidan pulled me close and pushed my wet hair off my forehead. "Are you ready to go home?"

Home. Living with him was the only home I'd felt was mine since my mom died. "Yes."

"We'll pick up dinner on the way. It's been a long day."

"No!" jumped from my mouth, and when he cocked a brow at me, I said, "Sorry, Sir. I just… I want to cook for you and David. Can I serve you?"

He looked at me for what felt like an eternity, like he had this special way of seeing beneath my skin, deep inside me, before nodding. "You may."

Aidan held my hand as we walked out of the water. We packed up together, dried off, and once we were finished, walked to the car. When everything was closed in the trunk, I went to walk to the passenger side, but Aidan's hand wrapped tightly around my wrist. "Thank you, for today."

"What did I do?" I asked, my heart pounding against my chest.

"You gave me this back—the beach." And then he simply let go, turned, and got in the car as if he hadn't just rocked my whole world. As if he hadn't just made me truly feel like the precious boy he so often told me I was.

WHEN WE GOT home, we showered together for the second time that day. From there I went to the kitchen and began making dinner. I'd decided on baked salmon, roasted potatoes, and salad. David arrived, and he and Aidan sat in the living room while I cooked. This would be the first time I'd serve someone other than Aidan in this way, and I was ridiculously excited about it. I wanted the evening to be perfect so Aidan would be proud of me, so he would be honored that I belonged to him.

I enjoyed being in the kitchen, cooking for them as they visited. It made me feel...like I had a purpose, a responsibility, a way to care for Aidan when he did so very much for me.

Still, my mind was a bit of a mess. I was thinking about what he'd asked me about school and wanting to do something with English or writing. I liked it, yes. Thought I could enjoy it, for sure, but I loved this too. I wanted to belong to him.

Added to that were random thoughts about Jordan and the phone number he'd given me. Not that I wanted him, because all I needed was Aidan, but I still had the number and was still wondering what it would be like to have him as a friend.

Then there was today—Aidan taking me to the beach despite his history. His laughter, and how he held me, and when he told me I gave him something. It made my brain spin in the best way and wish for things I was scared to wish for.

So yes, I was a bit of a mess.

Still, my dinner looked fabulous. I plated the food and opened the wine before walking into the living room, where nowadays I often crawled and knelt on the new, comfortable carpet. "Dinner is ready," I told them. They both looked up at me, and Aidan smiled.

"Thanks," Aidan said as they stood.

"It smells great," David told me, and damned if the praise and appreciation didn't light me up inside. "Oh, he likes that," David added.

"Yes. He's a bit of a praise slut." Aidan winked, and I trembled.

We sat at the table together, the three of us. They spoke about medical stuff that was over my head, before David asked me about school. I felt...a little stupid, having the conversation go from what they did—saving lives—to me, who took two stupid college courses. "It's good," I replied.

"I'm very proud of him. He's excelling in his classes, and his English teacher is quite fond of his work," Aidan said, and his compliments filled me up until I feared I might burst. Suddenly, I didn't feel stupid anymore.

They both raved about the meal, which only made me feel better. Aidan was right. I was definitely a bit of a praise slut.

After we ate, Aidan asked, "Would you like to come to the living room with us?"

I definitely intended to, but leaving the kitchen made

me feel like I was going to panic, so I asked, "Can I clean up first?"

"Of course." He kissed my forehead.

"He's precious, Aidan. A very good boy," David said, and my blood pumped through me a little faster. It wasn't the same as getting compliments from Aidan, but I still enjoyed it.

"Thank you," I replied.

They left the room, and I quickly cleaned up before joining them. David was laughing at something Aidan said. Aidan sat where he always did on the couch, and I lingered a bit, unsure if I was allowed to kneel for him when David was there, but really wanting to. My thoughts began to spin a bit, and my stomach tightened.

"On your knees, please," Aidan directed, answering my silent question. I exhaled a breath, feeling at ease again. I knelt on the floor between Aidan's legs. He pressed my head down against his thigh and began running his fingers through my hair. David didn't look twice, the two of them continuing their conversation as if this was completely normal…and I guess it was. It was our normal.

They included me in the conversation, asking my opinion on topics, and I realized I really liked David. He cared for my Sir and treated me with respect, making me so glad Aidan had him.

It was close to an hour later, Aidan's hand still in my hair, when David asked, "Did you get the invite to the play party?"

That piqued my interest.

"I did," Aidan replied, tugging on my hair gently.

"I'm thinking of going. Are you bringing your boy?"

"No, I think we'll sit this one out," Aidan replied.

"Play party?" I asked. I mean...that sounded fun to me.

"Private events," Aidan answered. "Where people can play together, or can play with your partner and be watched, that kind of thing."

My head popped up, and my cock began to fill with blood. I couldn't imagine getting to see others together, to compare myself to them, and for everyone to know I belonged to Aidan. "Can we go?"

David chuckled.

Aidan frowned. "I just said we weren't."

"But I really want to!"

"And I said no," he replied, his voice tight. I could tell he was upset, but I was upset too. I wanted this, wanted to proudly serve him in front of others.

"On that note, I think it's time for me to go." David stood.

"I'll walk you out." Aidan threw his leg over me and stood as well.

"Good night, Finley. Thank you for dinner," David said. I mumbled a goodbye at him, my arms crossed.

Couldn't we at least talk about this? Was he ashamed of me? Did he think I wouldn't serve him well? It reminded me of that moment with Jordan when I hadn't known how to explain who Aidan was to me.

It felt like Aidan was outside forever with David. I sat on the carpet for a while, then stood and paced the room. My thoughts were getting out of control. I kept wondering why he didn't want to go with me, if this was something he used to do—and obviously it was, since he'd been invited and David asked if he was going.

The second Aidan came back inside, closing and locking the door behind him, I said, "I want to go!"

"You've made that obvious, as I've made my response obvious. Watch your attitude. We'll talk about this when you've calmed down."

Then, without another word, Aidan went upstairs to his room.

CHAPTER TWENTY-EIGHT

Aidan

I DIDN'T KNOW what was wrong with me, why I'd reacted the way I had about the party. I'd played at events like that many times. It wasn't something Finley and I had discussed before, and there was a part of me that didn't want to share him, that didn't want what we had to be for anyone else. It was a selfish desire. He obviously wanted it. Wasn't it me who'd said Finley deserved all the experiences he wanted? To know more than just me? But now that I had the chance, I'd shut it down without having a conversation with him, maybe partly because I knew he would want to go.

He was changing me, tying me up, putting me in his own form of bondage, when I had never been bound before.

With a sigh, I opened the door and sent him a one-word text. **Come.**

A moment later his door creaked open. When he

reached the hallway, he stopped, looked at me. "May I crawl to you?"

Those words made an earthquake go off inside me. Oh, the way this boy served me. "You may."

He knelt, crawled over as I went to sit on the bed, and laid his head against my thigh. "I'm sorry for disrespecting you."

"I know. You'll still be punished, but we'll figure that out later. I apologize for walking out and not listening to you. I shouldn't have done that."

"It's okay."

"No, it's not. Can you explain to me why it's important to you to go?"

Finley nodded against my thigh, but it still took him a moment to reply. "I just… Are you ashamed of me?"

"What? No. Do you really think that?"

Another pause, then, "Not really? I mean, I know you, and you're so very good to me, take the best care of me, so part of me knows you're not. But then my thoughts do funny things to me sometimes, and I question it. Do you think I won't serve you well in front of others?"

My heart ached. I was letting him down, failing him. I was his Dominant. I was supposed to make him feel secure. "No, precious boy. That's not it. I don't care what anyone thinks. I care about taking good care of you."

He pushed closer to me, putting his face between my legs. My dick hardened, plumped against his face as he breathed me in. I continued. "I don't quite know why I decided we wouldn't go. Then, when you spoke to me the way you did, I dug my heels in on principle."

"I'm sorry," he said again, pushing his nose against my sac. "There's something else I need to tell you. I, um… There's a guy…he's in my English class. He was hitting on me, I think."

I sucked in a sharp breath, my chest aching in an unfamiliar way. "Did you want him to be hitting on you?" It was something we should discuss so I knew how to move forward with him. If one of his desires was to be shared or to be allowed with other men, I needed to know.

"I don't know. It felt good, obviously. I don't want him the way I want you, though. He gave me his number, and I took it. But I told him…I told him I had someone, but I didn't know what to say. I didn't know if I should say *I have a boyfriend* because you're not that to me. You're my Sir, but what else does that mean? I didn't like not having the answer to that. I think that weighed on me with the party too, like…what do I mean to you?

Is this a secret? It made me feel insecure and like maybe you really are ashamed."

I had definitely failed him in this, and I hated that. I should have seen it coming. He should have had answers to these questions long ago. But the truth was, I didn't know how to reply. "This is something we need to break apart, I think. First, you need to figure out if you want that boy." The words were hard to push out, but I needed to. And Finley deserved that, if that's what he wanted. I had always known this day would come.

"Not like I want you…never like I want you. I don't think he could give me what I need anyway. But maybe as a friend? We can like, study together or hang out the way I do with Ian. I've never had that…not with anyone else. I've never even studied with a friend before."

I'd told myself I was giving him what he needed, that I was making sure he had a life outside of me, but in that moment, I realized I was doing a shit job of it. Why hadn't I pushed Finley to make friends? "Invite him over. Or go out with him. That's an order. And if you decide you want to sleep with him, or anyone else, you come to me."

He nodded. "But what do I tell him about us?"

That was harder to answer. I thought maybe…a part of me wanted to tell him that whatever he needed, I would give him. Whatever he desired was his. Still, old habits die hard, and the thought of giving myself to someone enough that they had the power to hurt me…I wasn't sure I could do that. "I've never had a boyfriend, Finley." Christ, even the word felt weird on my tongue. I was a thirty-nine-year-old man having this conversation with a twenty-year-old boy.

"Neither have I," he replied, the feisty little thing.

"Good point, but I think there's a difference between you and me. I don't know that I can be what you want."

"And I do? I didn't know if I could be the submissive you desired, and sometimes I still don't. I don't know if I know how to be a boyfriend either, but I'm willing to try. Does anyone ever know these things? Isn't that what relationships are? Trying?"

He was right, of course, to the extent that I felt it hard to breathe. I was nearly forty years old, and he understood this better than I did.

"I want to really belong to you," Finley added.

"You do."

He looked up at me then, his eyes watery with tears and so much fucking want and heartbreak that I felt it to the marrow of my bones, deep down in my soul. It was different seeing him cry now than when I wanted his tears. Then they were cleansing; now they were debilitating. "Does that mean you don't want to try?"

"I..." Shit, I did want to try, didn't I? It wasn't something I had ever considered—that I would have someone permanently, that I would be someone's *partner*, because I still wasn't sure how I felt about the word *boyfriend*.

Even thinking it made my heart kick up and my palms sweaty, but when I looked at this sweet, strong warrior of a boy, it helped. He soothed something inside me I hadn't known ailed me, which was why I opened my mouth and took a risk. "We can try, yes." I almost told him I couldn't make any promises, but as he'd said, that's what relationships were. Who ever knew if they would last when they went into them?

"Really?" Finley asked, with heart and hope on his tongue.

"Don't get too excited. I'm not sure it'll be much different than what we're doing now," I teased, which was another dose of reality I hadn't let myself swallow before.

"It matters to me, Sir...*my* Sir." The way he said *my* made me realize how much he'd needed something to hold on to. Finley had spent his life feeling like he didn't belong to the world around him, without any sense of security. Even when his mother was alive, they'd struggled to make ends meet. This, what we had, gave him something to hold on to. Made him feel secure and tethered to something in a way he truly needed.

This wild feeling of possession surged through me. I had dominated many men, *had* many men, but none gave me the satisfaction I found in him, and through the gift he gave me—his submission and his loyalty—I felt more whole than I ever had. "Take off my pants."

Finley's blue eyes zeroed in on me, a smile on those sweet lips of his. "Yes, Sir."

I removed my shirt as he began opening my pants. Once my shirt was on the floor, I lifted my hips and he pulled my jeans down. He stopped when he got to my shoes, removing them and my socks. When I was naked, he leaned over and kissed the tops of my feet. It was such a simple thing, but it made me feel worshipped in a way I hadn't known I needed.

"Can I suck you?"

"Lick my balls first. Tell me why you like it there."

Finley leaned in and immediately began lapping at my sac with long strokes of his tongue. "It's where I belong—at your feet, between your legs. Like, I feel so close to you, you're surrounding me, and I breathe you in and know everything will be okay."

My hand knotted tightly in his hair as he began

tonguing my balls again. He put so much faith in me, gave himself to me the way he should, and I wouldn't allow myself to let him down again.

"More...please," Finley begged, and I pulled his head back by his hair, made him look up at me before smacking him. His eyes rolled back, not from the strength of the slap, but in obvious pleasure that rushed through him and made him twitch.

"God, yes, Aidan. I—" I pushed my cock between his lips before he could say more. Fucked into his mouth with long, deep strokes, pushing back toward the spot that made him gag. He was getting much better at this.

I pulled out and slipped in again. "Relax your throat, precious boy. Breathe through your nose. You can do this. Make your Sir proud."

I felt the tension ease out of him. He nodded, eyes firmly on me, dick stretching his lips. We didn't turn away from each other as I fucked his mouth, pushing past that point, testing him, using him, the way we both needed.

His hands were on my thighs, where he could tap if it was too much. When he didn't, I pushed him down, felt his throat loosen as I slowly worked my way as deep as I could. I held him there, in control of him, then pulled him off again. "Good?"

"Perfect."

I used his mouth like it was a hole for me to fuck, taking my pleasure and making him soar. Each time I thought I would come, I pulled his hair back, leaned over, and licked his tears, or kissed the tip of his nose, or spit in his mouth—nasty, dirty things, and sweet, caring things, though in a lot of ways, for us they were all the same. Maybe not for some, but that didn't matter.

The last time I pulled him off, something in my movements must have told him I was done with him. Finley tried to go for me again, his pupils wide. "Please, Sir. Please, I want your load."

"And I plan to give it to you, when and how I wish."

CHAPTER TWENTY-NINE

Finley

"TAKE OFF YOUR clothes," Aidan ordered, and I shoved to my feet. My brain was already spinning, like I was too open and taking everything in—the feel of the carpet, soft beneath my feet, the cool air against my skin, the scent of Aidan's musk and woodsy bodywash in my nose. I was overly stimulated, tugging at my clothes, my eyes unable to focus, while I was working through the fact that Aidan had agreed to be my boyfriend, and wondering if he could possibly love me the way I loved him, and *oh God*, was he finally going to fuck me?

Suddenly his hand was on my face. I hadn't even seen him stand, but he was there, in front of me, and my thoughts began to settle with the feel of his skin against mine, smooth with a couple of rough spots. That easily, Aidan could center me. That was the extent of his power over me, the power I gave him, which made me feel both strong and utterly raw at the same time.

He backed me toward the dresser, then lifted me and set me on it. I realized I still had my socks and underwear on.

"Focus on me." His voice was steady as always. "Take a couple of deep breaths."

I breathed as I bowed my head, resting my hands on the surface between my legs.

"Christ, you are so beautiful." He touched my face again, ran his hand down my neck, wrapped an arm around me and traced my spine with a finger.

There I went. Now I was grounded again. He stepped away, and I hopped down. I kept my gaze locked on him as I took off my underwear and socks, then stood before him, naked and wanting, my cock tall and hard against my belly.

"On your knees."

"Yes, Sir." I fell down to them.

"Come to the bathroom with me."

I crawled behind Aidan, loving the view of his long legs, muscular, hairy thighs, and his firm ass. I watched as he reached under the counter and—*oh my God*—pulled out an enema kit. Was he going to do this to me? Was Aidan going to stay while I cleaned myself out?

As if he heard my silent questions, he said, "I'm

going to get you ready for me. I'll be here the whole time, unless you tell me red."

"I...yes, Sir." Just the thought of it had my face flaming. Heat scorched from my cheeks down my neck and beyond. This was Aidan. There was nothing I couldn't do in front of him. Nothing I couldn't take from him.

Nerves tickled at the base of my spine as I watched him prepare it. He ordered me to get into the shower before attaching the enema nozzle. He pushed the tip inside me, and I tensed. It wasn't large, obviously, but I felt it.

"Relax," he said gently. "I'm here." And then he was filling me with water. It felt...weird. This pressure and fullness. My breathing sped up, but when I focused on Aidan, his hand on my stomach, it helped.

I didn't know how long he made me hold it, maybe one minute and maybe a lifetime, but then he was directing me to sit on the toilet and telling me to let it out, and holy shit, how could I be doing this in front of him? How could he want me after hearing me release myself?

"Good boy. You're doing so well."

His pride made me proud. It was amazing how he could strip me down, put me in situations that should be humiliating, but what they did was build me up, widen the lines of trust between us.

Suddenly I was in the shower, and he was cleaning me, then drying me off and leading me to the bed. Somewhere along the way, my dick had gone soft. Aidan seemed to notice and told me to lie over the side of the bed.

"Yes, Aidan," I replied and panicked slightly when he walked away. He went to his closet and came back with a flogger.

"Feel this," Aidan said as he let the strands dance along my back, my ass, my thighs. "Do you know what it is?"

"A flogger."

"Yes. It's suede. See how soft it is? This is a good one to start with because it's fairly gentle, and how much it hurts hinges on me. It won't give you too much pain, but depending on how hard I hit you with it, enough. Use your safe words if you need them."

Then…oh God, then he leaned forward and pressed a soft kiss right above my ass. It was so sweet, yet somehow possessive, that I nearly melted into the bed.

A second later the flogger snapped against my back. It was obvious Aidan wasn't hitting me very hard. This little sting zipped through my skin and made me want more. The soft strands danced along my skin—back, sides, ass, just touching and tickling until I thought I would go insane. Then they were gone before landing on me with a *snap*, again and again and again, on my ass, on my back. I writhed against the bed, my dick hard and aching, my balls full enough to burst.

"Stay still," he commanded.

"Yes, Sir. I'm trying." I bit down on my arm, trying to focus on not moving. Aidan continued to paint my skin with the most perfect, subtle pain, in increasing little shots, but not too much, not even close.

My eyes went blurry, and I began to cry. Not because of the hurt, but because he was giving me this beautiful moment where my brain and body surrendered to him as he did with me as he pleased. And *yes*, did I revel in it.

"Please, Sir. Can I have more?"

Aidan hissed, then swung the flogger again, making the most perfect sensation bloom beneath my skin. I could feel the difference, the strength with which he rained the swats down on me, and I wanted to lie there in that moment forever, beneath Aidan's flogger, under his command, but I also wanted him inside me, to fuck me and complete me and mark my insides as his, the same as he was doing against my flesh.

I was shaking, like my skin would crack open and I'd

spill myself all over the bed. It was as if Aidan had the ability to take me apart but also put me together. How he could do both simultaneously, I didn't know, but he could.

There was a soft *thud*, and I knew it was the flogger hitting the floor.

"Still with me?" Aidan asked.

"Yes…God, yes."

"Look at me," he demanded, and I turned, doing just that. He was trying to read me, see if I was okay. I knew it without him telling me, and I tried to show him I was ready for more, that I didn't need a break. I just needed him. My Sir nodded, knowing me, always knowing me.

"Up on your hands and knees."

"Yes, Sir." I did as told, trembling with need and love and the endorphins shooting through me. He pulled lube from the nightstand, and that easily my eyes rolled back and my cock flexed, dripping precum.

"You're hungry for it."

"For you…always you."

"My little warrior slut," he said, his voice husky.

Yes, yes, yes! I was a slut for him, now and always.

"Such a pretty little hole," he said as wet fingers danced around my rim. My legs and arms were shaking. I was afraid I wouldn't be able to hold myself up.

"Be still for me if you want me to fuck you," Aidan said, and I knew he would follow through, so I closed my eyes and took deep breaths, fighting to keep my limbs steady.

He pushed a finger inside, and I gasped. He tortured me, slowly sliding it in and out. "Can I beg?"

"Yes. That doesn't mean I'll give it to you, though."

"Please, Sir, more!" I cried out, and Aidan didn't give it to me, just slowly pumped that one finger in and out.

He smacked my ass with his other hand. My balls were so full, so very full, and I knew I couldn't come until he gave me permission, but I was already there, teetering on the edge. I didn't know if I could handle it.

I arched my back when Aidan pushed another finger in me, sliding it in and out, over my prostate, delivering smacks against my ass at random moments.

"This hole is mine to do what I want with it."

"Yours," I replied, tightening my hands in the blanket. "*Oh, Sir,*" I purred when another finger pushed in. Three. Aidan was fucking me with three fingers, stretching me for his cock. He would be the first man inside me, and I suddenly found myself so glad that I hadn't been able to give my body to the other men I'd sought out. I was his to command, to own, and this right belonged to him as well.

Aidan spanked me and finger-fucked me until I thought I could die. He was going easy on me, I knew that, and I was thankful while also wanting him to let loose, to wreck me for anyone other than him.

"I'm going to come," I gritted out.

"Don't. Not if you want my cock."

My head began to spin again. I nearly crumbled when he pulled his fingers out, then rose from the ashes when he slowly pushed inside.

My tears hit me, running in waves down my face, but I didn't know why I was crying. It was loud, sobbing cries, as Aidan gave me what I'd so longed for, slowly and perfectly, his hand sliding down my back.

"Shh. Let go. I'm here. I have you, precious boy."

I was in that place only Aidan could send me, in my head but also in the clouds. Flying yet grounded by him. He pulled me up so I knelt, his knees on the bed, my back against his chest as he slowly, so very, very slowly fucked into me.

"My good boy. You are so perfect. The way you give yourself to me, such a treasure. Let go, you can do it."

White light flashed behind my eyes, and I was pretty sure I shot myself to the stars. My orgasm ripped through me; spasm after spasm, he milked it from my balls. I didn't know it was possible to have that much cum inside me, and it was soon, so fucking soon. He'd just gotten inside me, and he hadn't come. That thought made me cry harder because I felt like I'd failed him, like I hadn't given him what he deserved.

"Shh. It's okay." He wiped my tears, held me close, his cock still deep inside me. "You did good, precious boy. You served me well."

"Keep going," I begged. "Please, please keep going. I want you inside me."

He pushed up and into me, making me gasp. His arms were still around me, his nails slightly digging into me.

Aidan licked the side of my face, likely taking a combination of tears and sweat. He did it again and again as he took me in long strokes. My body was tender, my hole aching, but it would hurt worse, hurt in my soul if he pulled out.

"Such a good hole for your Sir. Tell me. Tell me you're mine."

"I'm yours," I gasped. "Your hole, your toy, your boy."

"My needy little boyfriend, apparently." He chuckled softly in my ear.

"Yes!" I called out, finding my way through this weightless fog I was in. He had called me his boyfriend, and I knew he did it for me, but I didn't care.

"A place for me to deposit my load too." Then his teeth bit into my shoulder, and he shoved in deep. His cock jerked inside me, swelled, and I felt the first burst of warmth. His cum…was *inside* me, and I began to cry as he shot again, filling me, licking the painful bite mark.

It was so weird, this empty, achy feeling when he pulled out. I let go, just collapsed, but Aidan held me up. He whispered in my ear words I couldn't make out. I was too far gone, lost in subspace, but just hearing the echo of his voice and feeling his breath against me, his body as he held me close to him, was all I needed. I knew I could let go, that I could get lost in it because my Sir was there, holding me and caring for me. Taking care of me.

So I let myself stay adrift, knowing Aidan's arms were the life preserver I needed.

CHAPTER THIRTY

Aidan

FINLEY SLEPT THROUGH the night. I wasn't able to, but that was okay. I wanted to watch over him. I examined his back and ass, kissed the mark my teeth had made on his skin. Ran my fingers through his hair and massaged his nape, so even in sleep he would know he wasn't alone. The boy clung to me, and anytime I moved, his grip on me tightened as though he was afraid I would disappear.

He was stunning, the way he gave himself to me, the way he yielded to me. He gave me a gift, and I wasn't sure he realized the extent of how precious it was.

I'd called him precious boy from the start, and he truly was, more and more every day, and it was truths like that, gnawing at my thoughts, that kept me awake.

I had agreed to be his partner. It made me feel double the need to do right by him. Having a submissive, taking that gift someone gave, was a monumental responsibility. One I thrived on and needed, but now it was twined with the fact that Finley still worked for me, and he was my boyfriend, and still young, so very young. The waters were murky. I wanted him, there was no doubt about that, and I knew that what we did fulfilled us both. Finley needed this, but what about other experiences I was robbing him of?

There was a choice, always a choice, of course, but how would he know what he was missing if he'd never had it? Just like the situation with the boy from school—Finley hadn't known what it was like to truly be wanted by someone outside of me.

Yes, my thoughts weighed heavily on me. Doing right by him was the most important thing, and I guessed only time would tell exactly what that was.

So I continued to take my comfort in him, in holding him and caring for him.

Before I knew it, the sun was rising, peeking through the blinds, creating lines across his skin.

More time passed, and then his eyes fluttered open and he looked at me, sweetly, softly, so open and brave, showing me all he felt inside. "Did last night really happen? All of it?"

I chuckled, kissed his forehead. Oh, the way he tangled me up. "If you can't feel me, then I must not have debauched you enough."

"I can," he whispered. "My skin feels a little achy, and my hole is tender." His cheeks colored pink. "I just wanted to hear you say it."

I sighed, questioning my sanity because I thought maybe there wasn't anything I wouldn't at least attempt to give him. "It all happened."

"I have a boyfriend." He grinned.

"You have a Sir, who is also that, yes."

Finley nodded, looking at me with adoration I wasn't sure I deserved. Hell, that I wasn't sure anyone deserved. Leaning in, I kissed him gently, licking at his lips before pulling away.

"I'll cook you breakfast," he said, rolling over and wincing.

"No. I think I'll spoil you today." He deserved it, and needed it, even if he didn't realize it. "Do you need to eat now, or can you wait a little while?"

"I can wait."

"Stay." I rose, went to the bathroom, and turned on the faucets of my Jacuzzi tub. As it ran, I plucked the bubble bath from beneath the sink. It wasn't something I used, but he did, so I'd purchased some for in here too. I added it to the water before going back to him.

"Lie on your stomach."

"Yes, Sir." Finley rolled over. The marks on him were fading quickly, as I assumed they would. I hadn't given him nearly as much as I was used to. Then I spread his ass cheeks and looked at his hole.

"*Oh my God.*" He buried his face in the pillow, obviously embarrassed.

"I gave you an enema and fucked you, and this has you shy?"

"That did too! The first part. It's different now, though. We're not like, doing anything or whatever."

"Yes, but your body is mine, and I can look at it anytime I want to."

"Yours," he replied, thrusting against the mattress. I swatted his ass.

"None of that. Come on."

"Yes, Sir," Finley grumbled, but he came, following me into the en suite.

"I need to piss."

He gave me that happy little grin before holding my cock as I let loose. I thought about what he'd said before, about marking him that way, and damned if my whole body didn't light up at the thought. When I finished, he shook me off, and I climbed into the tub.

"You're going to take a bath with me?" he asked.

"Yes." I wasn't a bath person, but he was. "Hurry

and go so you can join me."

His dick was hard, so he sat down to piss, angling his cock into the toilet. He washed his hands afterward before climbing between my legs, his back against my chest.

"How are you feeling about last night?" I asked as I ran a washcloth over his chest.

"I'm feeling like the luckiest boy in the world."

"Give me more than that."

He nodded, thought, then said, "I didn't know it was possible to feel this much. It's like you open me up, let all my deepest desires, fears, wants, and emotions free. Does that make sense?"

"Yes," I replied, my blood singing at the response.

"You take my mind to this place that only you can find, and you…bring me this peace. These things I knew I needed, but it's even more because it's you."

His words pierced my chest, dug into my skin and bones, down to my soul. "Good boy. That's what I want to hear. Nothing we did was too much?"

"I want *more*, Aidan."

I couldn't help but chuckle. The response wasn't surprising. "Slutty little sub, aren't you?"

"For you, yes."

We didn't speak for a while then, just enjoyed the

bath. Eventually, I washed him, then made him stand as I jerked him off and allowed him to come on my chest. I made him lick it away before drying him and dressing him in comfortable flannels and a tee.

When we got downstairs, I put a pillow on the kitchen chair. "Sit."

"Yes, Sir."

I made coffee and cooked breakfast. I made one large plate and gave him the mugs of coffee before leading us to the living room.

"On the floor, please."

"Yes, Aidan."

He knelt, and I sat on the couch. I scooped a bite of potatoes on the fork and held it out for him. Finley gasped, then shivered, looking at me adoringly. "Thank you."

We ate that way, me feeding him a bite before taking one of my own—potatoes, eggs, and bacon. I'd never fed a submissive this way, but I liked doing it for this boy, my boy.

When we finished, he said, "Thank you. I've wanted that, for you to feed me. Can I do the dishes?"

"Do you need to?"

He nodded.

"You may."

Finley cleaned the kitchen, and then we went into my office. He lay on the floor and studied while I checked emails and took care of a few things. Later we had lunch and sunbathed by the pool.

After dinner, I took him to the living room with me. He looked surprised when I unbuttoned and unzipped my jeans, pulling myself out. I plucked the towel I'd set on the table and laid it out on the couch. "Find a movie to watch."

"Yes, Sir." Finley licked his lips. Such a hungry boy for me. He flipped through the options, choosing an action movie.

My dick was soft as I sat down and told him to lie beside me. "I want your mouth on me. You'll be my cock warmer while we watch the movie. You'll hold it there as much as you can. Take a break if you need to. I don't want your jaw to get too sore, but your job isn't to get me off; it's just to be a hole for my dick to rest in."

"Yes, Aidan," he replied, eyes wild with desire and the need to please me.

I ran my hand through his hair as he kept his mouth on me, both of us reveling in the way I was using him and his gift of giving himself to me.

It wasn't long until he began drooling, saliva running down his chin and my balls. I'd let him suckle me every now and again, and he did so with hunger. He rarely let me out of his mouth, obviously wanting to excel at this. When the movie was over, I said, "Get me hard."

It took him no time to get me there, and then I was holding his head down and fucking into his mouth until I spilled my load down his greedy little throat, and all I could do was bask in the treasure that was my precious little warrior.

CHAPTER THIRTY-ONE

Finley

IT WAS HEAVEN to sleep in Aidan's bed. He held me tightly. Sometimes he would get sweaty and pull away, but when I snuggled up to him again, he would sigh and wrap his arms around me. I didn't care if I got his sweat on me. I loved every part of him.

When my phone buzzed, telling me it was time to get out of bed, I was surprised when Aidan went with me into the bathroom. He usually waited until I went downstairs to cook before he got into the shower.

He let me help him pee, then told me to wait and disappeared into his large walk-in closet. "I got something for you," he said as he walked out. He held open his hand, and I gasped.

"A cock cage?" My brows knitted together.

"Yes. Is that a hard limit for you?"

I thought for about one point two seconds before shaking my head. Hell no, it wasn't a hard limit. It was… "It's kind of hot, knowing I'll be caged for you. Wearing that when no one will know."

His lips pulled into a grin that made me weak in the knees. "I thought so as well."

"It's not going to fit right now." I pointed to my erection. I felt like I was always hard in Aidan's presence.

"Oh, to be young again," he teased.

"You don't seem to have a problem getting there either, and how could I not be when you always turn me on?"

He chuckled playfully, before his hand shot out and he grabbed my balls.

"Holy *fuck*," leaped out of my mouth. I hadn't been expecting the tight fist that squeezed around my sac. But then my eyes rolled back at the look of power and torment to come in his eyes, and my skin began to prickle with the best kind of heat. Ugh. God, I always wanted him, loved to hurt for him.

Aidan used his other hand to grab my nipple and twist, making a sharp panting sound escape me. "Such language from that sweet mouth of yours."

"Oh God…I just…didn't expect it. You hurt me so good."

Something flashed in his eyes that I couldn't decipher, but then he leaned in and kissed me. Aidan's tongue swept my mouth, possessed it, until I had to hold on to the counter so I didn't fall. Aidan's kisses were the best, and I loved when he gave them to me.

"There we go." He let go of me, and my dick was, in fact, soft. "Problem solved." Aidan winked, and this giddy sort of excitement rushed through me. This was one of my favorite Aidans—the one who let go and was playful. But I loved the tormenting Aidan too, which was what he turned into next as he knelt, put a plastic ring around my balls, and then fit the cock cage on me.

"How long do I have to wear it?" I asked when he stood. I looked down at myself, at my dick tucked away and unable to get hard unless Aidan allowed it.

"As long as I want you to."

I nodded. "Yes, Sir."

"Now, you're going to wear it at least all day. Every time you feel it there, I want you to remember who owns you. I want you to think about the fact that you're caged because it's what I want, and to wonder what others around you would think if they knew. It will be our dirty little secret."

"Oh God, that's so hot."

He shook his head, but a smile teased the right side of his mouth. "Focus, boy."

"It's hard."

"And you're not."

"That was bad...like such a bad joke." But it was also the best joke because he made it, showing that side of himself to me.

"Eh, I'm an old man. My jokes aren't the best. We're getting off track here. You're going to wear that because I want you to and because you're mine. You're also going to have your cock caged when you speak to that boy today. You'll make sure he knows you have a partner, but let him know that playing with others is something we're considering."

Heat flared in my cheeks as my thoughts warred with each other. I wanted to tell him no, that I didn't want or need anyone other than him. But I also liked the idea of…feeling wanted by two men? Having them both? Knowing what it was like to be with someone other than Aidan? That didn't mean he wasn't enough for me or that I didn't love him, but it was a fantasy.

"Yes, Sir."

"Make plans with him to study and hang out. You can do it here or somewhere else, and while you do this, remember that you're only doing it because I allow it. Remember who owns you, Finley."

"You," I whispered. "Always you."

"Always is a very long time. And one more thing—

the party. We have time for that one, so it's something we will think about and discuss again. If not that party, we can go to another."

Oh God…it was really a possibility?

Aidan didn't give me much time to think about it. He leaned in and pressed a kiss to my lips. "Now go downstairs and start breakfast. I'm behind."

"Yes, Aidan."

It was…weird to walk around with my dick in a cage. I felt it there as I pulled on some sweats, as I walked downstairs and cooked Aidan breakfast.

We ate together, and he kissed me at the door—he was kissing me a lot more today—then grabbed my cock and said, "Remember what I said."

"Yes, Sir."

I was distinctly aware of the cage with every move I made, as I cleaned and exercised and deep-throated the dildo suctioned to my shower. He'd never told me to stop practicing, so I hadn't.

It felt odd washing myself in the shower and then taking a piss for the first time, but all it did was remind me of Aidan and that I belonged to him, and that was…that was everything.

Nerves tickled at the base of my spine as I sat through my English lesson. My professor rambled on, and for the first time I found it hard to focus. All I could think about was the cage on my cock. I kept wondering if anyone could possibly know. They couldn't, of course, and that was both a comfort and disappointing. It would be hot if people knew Aidan controlled me that way.

Which made me glance at Jordan, who looked over at me and smiled. He was cute, that was for sure, in this boyish sort of way. Well, a way I supposed people thought when they looked at me. That had never been my type, not really. I could appreciate Jordan's looks, but I'd always wanted a man like Aidan. There were things he could give me that I didn't think someone like Jordan could, which was probably stereotyping. Jordan could be dominant as fuck in the bedroom for all I knew.

When my professor dismissed class, my hands shook slightly as I put my stuff away. I knew without looking that Jordan would come over. I wasn't sure how, but I did, and then he was there.

"Hey, you. How have you been?"

"Good," I replied as we walked out. The cage felt heavier suddenly. My brain imagined this sign over my head that pointed to me and said something like *Dirty little freak who can't come until his Sir allows it.*

"You're smiling. Why are you smiling?" Jordan asked.

Oh...I hadn't realized I was. I guess I really did like being a dirty little freak who belonged to Aidan.

"Nothing. Wanna sit down for a minute?"

"Sure," he replied. We went over to one of the picnic tables under a tree. Jordan nodded for me to sit down first, which was sweet. "How are you feeling about the upcoming exam? Good?"

"Yeah, you?"

"That would be a no, Mr. Teacher's Pet." He winked.

"Hey! Whatever!" I playfully shoved him, then jerked my hand back, surprised I'd done it. It was such a normal thing to do, but I had never allowed myself to have friendships like this outside of Ian.

"I'm giving you shit."

We were both quiet for a moment. I didn't know what to say. All I could think about was the chastity I was wearing and how nervous I was to actually invite Jordan to do something. What if I wanted to play around with him? Would it ruin what I had with Aidan? What if Jordan turned on me or just wanted to laugh at me like so many other people in my life? What if he found out what kind of relationship I had with Aidan, and what if, what if, what if—

"You okay?" Jordan asked, with a hand on my shoulder.

"Yeah, sorry. I'm fine. Just...have a lot on my mind. Can you stay here for just a second? Don't go anywhere...please, and I'll be right back."

Jordan frowned in what was likely confusion, but then he nodded. I left my bag with him before jogging over to the building and leaning against it. No one was around me, and my heart was going crazy as I called Aidan. I didn't ever interrupt him at work, and I knew there was a possibility that he couldn't answer, but I suddenly needed him. Needed to hear his voice and work through this with him.

"What's wrong?" he asked instead of hello.

"Nothing. I... I don't know? Is it okay that I called?"

"Of course it is. Take a couple of deep breaths and calm down, and then I want you to tell me exactly what's on your mind. Don't think of it as what's wrong; just share your thoughts."

Wow...that was a good way to put it. I hadn't thought of that, so I did as Aidan said. I took a couple of deep breaths and then just...opened myself up to him as he was so good at making me do. There wasn't anything Aidan couldn't give me. "I'm a little nervous. About the friend thing. I want it, but I'm scared he'll like, reject me or whatever? And then I'm also scared I might want him and it'll make you not want me, or that he'll figure out I'm submissive and think I'm weird, and I can't stop thinking about the cage and being both excited by it, about belonging to you, but also weird about wearing it and talking to Jordan like…I don't know. That's it. That's what I'm thinking."

There was a soft sigh on the other end of the line. Not one that sounded angry or frustrated, but just…unsure. "I'm sorry. I should have checked in with you before I had you do this."

"What? No. This isn't your fault."

"It's certainly not yours," Aidan replied. "Maybe it's no one's fault, and it's just something that happened, but I still feel responsible because you're mine, are you not?"

Well…that helped. My thoughts quieted some, and my heart slowed.

"Do you want to take the cage off? If it's a limit for you, or you're reacting in a way we hadn't anticipated, you can."

"No," rushed from my mouth. I hadn't realized how much that wasn't what I wanted until Aidan asked.

"Okay, so we have that piece figured out. And the second, which I should have started with, is no matter what happens or what you decide you want, you're still mine, Finley. You will still serve me and still belong to me. If we have to adjust rules, we will, but your desires won't make me turn away from you. Do you understand that?"

I leaned against the wall, and suddenly...suddenly it was all okay. I could breathe, and my pulse didn't race. "Thank you, Sir. I needed to hear that."

"I'm sorry I didn't tell you this morning, then. You're being a very good boy right now—doing as I say and calling me when you're struggling. That's what I'm here for."

"Thank you." And now, that easily, I was starting to feel...confident. Strong. Sure.

"Do you want to spend time with Jordan? Get to know him? When we first spoke about it, you did."

My eyes locked on the brown-haired boy sitting at the picnic table, waiting for me. The one who teased me about being good at English. "I do."

"Then do it. You *can* do this, Finley. Do it and make me proud. And if it doesn't work out, that's okay. If he doesn't turn out to be what you think, that's okay. If he uses who you are against you in any way, or if that makes him decide he doesn't want to be friends with you, that's *his* loss and not yours. You are...you are incredible, my precious warrior."

Oh God. My eyes were cloudy, and it felt like my

heart was so big, it was going to make me burst. Aidan thinking me incredible made me feel that way. I wanted nothing more than to make him proud and to do what he said. "Thank you. I'm better now. I…" *I love you. I love you, I love you, I love you.* "I miss you."

"You just saw me this morning."

"I miss you still."

He chuckled softly, but it sounded weird. "Silly boy. Now go make your Sir proud, and if you need me again, call me. And remember, his loss, okay?"

"Yes, Sir," I replied, then ended the call. I felt stronger, stood taller, reveled in the weight between my legs as I walked back to Jordan.

He looked up at me and gave me a grin again. "Is everything okay?"

"It is now. That was…my boyfriend. I had to call him and talk to him real quick. I also wanted to see if we could hang out sometime. You can come to our place—mine and Aidan's—and we can like, study or whatever."

Jordan clutched his chest playfully. "Oh, you're breaking my heart. I forgot you had a boyfriend."

"I do. But we're not like other couples. I mean, God, this is weird. I'm not saying I want to screw around with you. Oh fuck, I probably shouldn't have said that. I just want to be friends, but we've considered…you know, but that's not what this is about. I just want to study with you and get to know you and maybe be friends with you."

A loud laugh jumped out of Jordan's mouth, and I immediately took a step backward.

"No, no!" His eyes widened, looking panicked. "I wasn't laughing at you. You're just cute as hell, that's all. I would love to be your friend, and I've also had threesomes and played around with other couples before, so I wouldn't be opposed to that either. Or you know, if it was just you and me and your man doesn't care. But if not, friends it is. I don't think I can pass English without you."

I smiled, feeling…good. Happy. Like this was something I needed outside of Aidan. That didn't diminish who Aidan was for me and how much I needed him, but it was good to have this too. "Cool. That sounds good."

"Put your number in my phone. And you're sure your man doesn't care?"

I shook my head. "He just wants me to be happy." In a way, no one in my life ever had. All of this—Jordan, school, everything—was because of Aidan. I gave Jordan my number, and then he sent me a text saying hi.

"That way you can save mine if you didn't already. Come on, I'll walk you to your car, and then I have to go to work."

I nodded, grabbed my bag, and we headed for the lot.

"Do you work this weekend?" I asked.

"Sunday but not Saturday."

"Maybe we can do something then. I'll talk to Aidan."

His forehead wrinkled as if he was a little confused, but he nodded. "That's your boyfriend?"

"Yeah."

"Oh, you got it bad. You're all red, and you have a dopey smile on your face."

"Shut up!" I nudged him. This was…nice. Fun. "I do have it bad, though."

"Lucky guy," Jordan replied as I led us to the car. "Are you shitting me? This is your car?"

"It's Aidan's, but I drive it."

"Wow…okay. This is getting more and more interesting." I was surprised when Jordan reached over and gave me a hug. "I hate to cut this short, but I really do have to go. We'll talk soon, okay?"

"Yeah." I nodded. "Okay."

Jordan turned and walked away, and I stood there, watching him go. When he disappeared, I climbed into the car, fumbled with my phone, and sent Aidan a text.

I did it!

Good boy. I'm very proud of you. I'll give you a surprise tonight to celebrate.

Then he sent me the squash emoji and the one that looked like splashes of water. A laugh jumped out of my mouth. That definitely hadn't been expected, but I loved it.

I can't wait. Thank you, Aidan. Not just for this, but for everything.

You're welcome.

And then…then he sent me another emoji. A heart.

CHAPTER THIRTY-TWO

Aidan

WHEN I GOT home, the house smelled like roast and potatoes, and Finley was on his knees, waiting. He had his pretty little head bowed, his hands on his thighs. His hair was wet and floppy as if he'd just gotten out of a shower. He didn't move, didn't look up, simply…waited.

He stole my breath, ripped it straight from my lungs. I wondered if he knew the power he had over me. That I wasn't sure there was anything I wouldn't do for him, and how different I was with him than I'd ever been with any other man.

"You are lovely." I stroked his head, and he leaned into my touch, chased it as though it was what he sought above all else.

"Thank you, Sir."

He obviously needed me after the day he'd had. Maybe wearing the cage and speaking with Jordan had been too much. I knelt beside him and turned his head so he looked at me. "I want to remind you how proud I am of you for today. You called me when you needed me, like you should always do. There's no shame in leaning on me."

"It helped…center me."

I brushed his hair from his forehead. "Are you still wearing it?"

"Of course. I would never take it off without asking you."

"And you like it?"

His lashes fluttered in that adorable way they sometimes did when he was embarrassed. "Yes. It's scary, makes me feel dirty, which is sort of exciting, but it also reminds me that I am yours."

"Good boy." My hand slid down, and I loosely wrapped it around his neck. A vision flashed through my head of Finley wearing my collar. I'd never collared anyone, never thought of it, but I was positive I wanted to do it to him. The boy enchanted me, made me feel like I was someone else. "You had a big day. You need me to take care of you tonight, don't you?" I said, dropping my hand.

"Yes, please. So much."

"Do you need to tend to the food first?"

He shook his head. "It's done. I have it out on the counter. It'll get cold, so if you want to eat first…"

I clicked my tongue. "No, no. I don't need food. I want to devour *you* instead."

"Oh God," he replied. Those words always made me smile.

"Crawl for me," I instructed, pushing to my feet. Finley heeled at my side, across the carpet, and toward the stairs. "I'd like to put you on a leash, keep you from getting too far away from me. Maybe go to one of the parties and parade you around as mine. Would you like that?" He would. I knew he would.

"Yes, Aidan." His voice held that floaty quality, like he was already slipping to that place in his head where he thrived so beautifully.

We took the stairs, and Finley followed me to the bedroom—my room…our room, it was beginning to feel like. "Take off my shoes."

"Yes, Sir." He did one, then the other, and then took care of my socks.

"Pants and underwear."

He grinned up at me with hooded, lust-filled eyes as he obeyed beautifully. My dick, achingly hard, sprang free as he tugged my jeans and boxer trunks down.

"You may leave them on the floor." I jerked my shirt

over my head and dropped it to the pile with the rest of my clothes.

"Can I..."

He didn't have to finish the sentence for me to know what he wanted. "Nuzzle."

He moaned, leaning in and doing just that. He buried his nose in my groin, dipped down under my sac, taking what he needed from me—my scent, my comfort. I played with his hair, soft brushes with my fingers, then tugs, before rubbing the sting away.

"Enough." My grip in his hair tightened. Finley whimpered when I pulled his head back. "Stand up."

"But, Aidan—"

"Shh." I held my hand over his mouth. "Do as you're told."

Finley nodded and stood.

"Take off your clothes. Leave them with mine."

He scrambled quickly, yanking on his pants and pulling on his shirt in this eager, frantic way that made my dick throb, before folding them and setting them aside. Then he was standing in front of me, gloriously naked, his prick tucked away in chastity. "You're incredible." I walked around him, danced my fingers over his chest, his shoulder, his back, down to his ass, which I squeezed. Goose bumps ran after my touch. He shivered and let out a sharp breath.

"Please," Finley begged.

"Please what?"

"Touch me, Sir. Fuck me. God, I crave your cock. It doesn't feel right when it's not inside me now. Like I'm empty."

The words were potent, almost enough to crack my resolve, to make me just push inside him, keep him in this house, in my bed, so I could use him anytime I pleased. Instead, I said, "Patience. Because you were so good today, I'm giving you the choice of keeping the cage on or taking it off."

Finley surprised me by shaking his head. "I don't want to decide. I want you to do what you want with me."

My cock jerked against my stomach, my body hot with the overwhelming feeling of possession. "Stay." I went to the closet to grab a few supplies, then came back to the room. I set all but one on the bed. "Give me your wrists."

Without question, he held his hands out to me. The cuffs were new, soft black leather, with a chain between them. He wasn't used to being bound, and though it was something he said he was interested in, I still wanted to start easy on him in case he struggled with it.

He looked so innocent, standing there with a cage on his cock and cuffs on his wrists, his blond hair a perfect halo around his head as he took me in with those big, expressive eyes of his. I wasn't sure there was anything he wouldn't give me, and that made me feel both powerful and afraid. Invincible and unworthy. There was nothing in my life that was more important than doing right by him.

I fisted a hand in his hair, and he whimpered beautifully.

"More," Finley begged.

"Only when I wish it." My hand fell away, skating down his body. "Who does this belong to?"

"You, Sir."

"Tell me."

"My body belongs to you."

I pushed my fingers between his ass cheeks and pressed against his rim. "Whose hole is this?"

"Yours, Aidan. Yours, please."

He was shaking, his whole body almost convulsing with need and the endorphins shooting through him. I smacked his ass, and he fell against me, his legs unable to hold him up. He was so far gone already, so blissed-out. My arm snaked around him, and I held him up, raining more swats down on his ass. "You're such a slut for it.

You'd stay locked up in this house to be my sex slave if I wanted it, wouldn't you?"

"Yes, yes, yes," he mumbled over and over.

Keeping him against me, I pulled him to the bed. "On your knees, ass in the air with your arms out in front of you. Hold on to the bottom part of the headboard and don't let go."

"Yes, Sir."

I traced my hand down his spine. "You arch beautifully."

His ass was a slight pink, but it wasn't enough for me. I wanted him red, wanted him to feel me there for days and know he was mine. "Remember your colors—yellow and red."

I plucked the flogger from the bed. This one wasn't suede and had thinner strips than what I had used on him before. It would give slightly more sting if I put enough power into the swing, which I intended to do.

He jerked when the first *splat* hit his ass. I kept going, painting his cheeks as I hit him—his thighs, his ass cheeks, his back, watching the color burst to the surface of his pale skin.

Finley would press his ass toward me, wiggle and cry out. His hands fell from the headboard once, so I held off, pulled away because I knew ending the pain would be more punishment than anything else. "What did you forget?"

"Oh no. Sorry, I'm so sorry," he said through his tears, gripping it again, and I resumed giving him what we both wanted. Left cheek, right cheek, left thigh, right. Over and over, putting more into each swat until his skin was an angry red.

"How are you feeling? You still with me?" I asked, dropping the flogger to the floor.

Finley looked at me over his shoulder, tears streaming down his face, his eyes red and his lips curled into a small smile. "I'm perfect." His voice was hoarse, rough from crying and calling out, but damned if it wasn't the most beautiful sound I had ever heard.

I spread his cheeks, looked at his tight, pink hole, then leaned in and brushed my tongue over it. Finley nearly lurched off the bed.

"Fuck…holy fuck… I had no idea…"

I smiled against his crack, nibbling his cheeks, then giving him my tongue again. He continued to push back against me, tried to ride my mouth as I ate his hole.

"*Yours, yours, yours,*" he kept saying over and over, as if he was on repeat. Each time I heard the word, it went straight to my heart, to my head, to all the parts inside me, the dominant parts that had always been there, but also the depths I hadn't known I had before him. My boy. My Finley. My precious warrior.

"How's your cock feeling?" I rubbed my thumb against his rim.

"Weird…like I'm so turned on and want to get hard, but I can't. I'm leaking a ton, though."

"Just how I like it." His balls were tight orbs. I cupped them, played with them as I grabbed the lube. I worked him open with one finger, then two, then three, taking my time with him.

"I want you. Please, Sir."

"We have all night." But truthfully, Christ, I wanted him too. I lifted him and turned him so he lay on his back. Finley opened his legs for me beautifully, then reached back and grabbed the headboard again.

"Like this?"

There was a pull between us, this electric charge I couldn't control, and before I knew it, I was leaning over him, my tongue in his mouth, needing a taste. His lips were flavored with salt from his tears, and I sucked it off him, kissing and rutting against him. He was so eager to please me, so open and raw, never hiding anything from me. "You honor me so well. You're mine." I'd claimed him a hundred times before, but this was different. I felt him, in that place in my chest, the one reserved for him.

There was no denying it. In many ways, he was a master to me as much as I was to him.

I pulled back, looked down at his cock, saw it strain against the plastic of his cage. I wanted to see him hard for me, so I fumbled to take it off, then finger-fucked his hole and watched it grow, long, thick, needy.

When I ran my tongue from root to tip, Finley jolted off the bed. "Oh my God." I sucked the tip, and he began shaking. It was like he couldn't keep still, as if his skin would crack open and he'd break apart.

I lubed my cock and replaced my fingers with it, shoving inside him in one swift, rough push. A tremor raced through him, radiating into me as his body squeezed me tightly.

"Please, Sir. I need to come."

"When I say."

I fucked into him ruthlessly. His body jerked, pushed higher on the bed each time I did. Still, he didn't let go of the headboard. His eyes rolled back, and his body arched toward me. Muscles strained in his arms, his neck, his stomach. I pulled his legs up and over my shoulders, jackhammering into him furiously. It was like I was possessed, this need to ravage him, to have my scent, my cock, my body all over him so I would always be a part of him.

My orgasm was right there, teasing at the fringes. Finley shook his head, pleading, begging. I slammed into him and let loose, my cock spasming, my body trembling as I shot my load deep inside him. "Let go. You can come," I said as I continued taking him, feeling my cock slide inside him with my cum.

Finley's body bowed. He cried out as he shot long, thick ropes of cum along his torso. He was mumbling incoherently as I slowed down but still slid in and pulled out, watching my dick push my load inside him.

His hole was stretched when I pulled out. I grabbed the small plug and wet it with lube. "I'm going to plug you, keep my cum inside you."

He nodded, smiled, and I could tell I pleased him. Finley's ass took the plug as I tucked it between his cheeks, and then I kissed his chest, his lips. "Good?"

"I love you," he whispered and started to cry. "I love you, I love you, I love you."

Of course he did, and I'd known that, but I'd thought hearing it would strangle me. Instead, it gave me breath. He filled my lungs with air and my body with blood.

He was deep, so deep under, and kept saying it, those three words, like they were the only ones he knew.

"I love you too," I said softly, but he didn't respond,

likely couldn't. Hell, I didn't know if he even heard me, he was floating so high.

I had to pry his clenched hands from where they clutched the bed. After I removed the cuffs, I lay beside him and pulled him over. Finley went easily, lying on top of me, his head on my chest. I held him, stroked him, kissed his sweaty hair as he came down and drifted to sleep.

CHAPTER THIRTY-THREE

Finley

I EASED SLOWLY from sleep to being awake. Aidan's arms were around me, his heart beating against my cheek, his hands stroking my back.

It was heaven. Seriously, I didn't know how anything could be better than where I was right then, in his arms after he took care of me. After he flogged me and fucked me and soothed me. After he fulfilled the needs that lived so deep inside me, they were a part of me I knew I could never ever live without. Not now. Not after having them.

I had a feeling he hadn't slept at all, but he had lain there, giving me what I needed, and I knew he would do it all night if that's what I needed.

I shifted, felt the plug in my hole, felt my ass, back, and thighs still sore from the flogging. Feeling it, remembering what he'd done to me, was almost enough to make me fly again. "Hi," I said lamely, without looking at him.

Aidan's answering chuckle pulsed through me. He tilted my head up, his eyes pinning me. "Hi yourself."

"What time is it?" I asked.

"About ten."

"Holy shit. I'm sorry! You haven't eaten dinner. You could have woken me."

He frowned. "I know I could have. I don't need you to tell me that, remember? You needed the rest. Now, lie on your stomach so I can look at your ass."

"I don't want to move from this spot. I would like to live right here. Can I do that? Do you think it would work?" I teased, and he snickered. I felt invincible every time I made Aidan laugh.

"Unfortunately, I don't think that's possible. They might frown upon it at the hospital. Now, do as I say, please."

"Yes, Sir." I slid off him and lay on the bed. His fingers tingled over my skin, studying it.

"Still marked a bit. You have a couple of bruises. Does it feel okay?"

"There's a bit of a pounding ache to it."

"Let me rub some cream on it." Aidan plucked a bottle from the drawer, squirted some on me, and rubbed it in. "Perfect." He kissed my lower back.

I didn't know what it was about that gesture, about

what he said. Maybe it was the…hell, what sounded like reverence in his voice, but it made my thoughts spin and pieces of memories float to the surface.

I love you. I love you. I love you.

I'd told Aidan I loved him. My eyes snapped to him, and his brow furrowed, as if he could sense something was wrong.

I'd told him I loved him, and he was still there. Could that mean he loved me too?

"What's wrong?"

"Nothing," I lied. "I'm hungry." Well, I *was* hungry, so that wasn't untrue, but I was also freaking out a little because of what I'd said, and what it meant, and wondering if Aidan loved me back.

"Stay in bed. I'll go get dinner."

I opened my mouth to argue with him, but he cocked a brow as if he knew. "Yes, Sir."

Aidan chuckled, kissed the tip of my nose, and got out of bed. And that…that stupid nose kiss made my eyes tear up.

He might love me too. I felt it in that simple press of his lips. If he didn't now, maybe he would grow to. He wasn't kicking me to the curb or telling me not to love him, at least. The thing was, Aidan made me feel loved, each and every day. Whether it was forcing me to go to school or giving me a schedule or allowing me to serve him. Whether it was orgasms or spanking me the way I craved and holding me for hours afterward. All those things made me feel loved. For over a year he had made me feel this way, even before we were fucking.

Before Aidan, I hadn't felt loved since my mother died, and that made me cry more, which made me feel really fucking stupid. Why was I so damn emotional? It was as if Aidan opened this door inside me and gave me permission to *feel*, when I hadn't felt in so long, and now I couldn't turn it off.

A few minutes later he came back in with a large plate and a bottle of water. He frowned when he saw me crying. "Hey, what is it? What's wrong?" He set the food on the nightstand.

"I don't know. Nothing. Just…why does this make me feel so much? What we do?"

He sat beside me and petted my hair. "Because it strips you down. It opens you up to this place where you can't help but feel. It's like there's this door in your brain, this place that stays locked up, and what we do opens you up so you can acknowledge it. It's setting you free. You have to be open to me to do what we do, and it's safe here and your brain knows it."

I needed closer to him, wanted to crawl inside his

skin and live there. Wanted us to always be a part of each other. "Can I..."

"Hold on." Aidan changed positions on the bed, leaned against the headboard, and opened his legs. I crawled between them, lying on my stomach with my cheek on his groin. His cock was flaccid, lying in a thatch of dark, curly hair.

"Can I tell you something?"

"You can tell me anything, but afterward, I'm feeding you."

"I..." It was weird because I wasn't even sure what I was going to say. I knew there was something there, something that had always been there, but I hadn't allowed myself to acknowledge it. "When I was younger, I used to be angry with my mom."

"I think most kids feel that way at some point." He stroked my head.

"Yeah, but...I was angry with her for things that weren't her fault. I was angry she had to work so much, angry that we didn't have enough. I was mad that she got pregnant with me when she did, and I felt like...like it was her fault we didn't have family. I was angry that she had me so young and made them turn us away. I wanted a family so bad, Aidan, to be like other people and to have more than just her." I held my breath, waiting for him to shove me away, to tell me I was spoiled and ungrateful and a horrible son.

"Finley." When I didn't move or reply, he said my name again, more sternly this time. "Finley."

"Yes, Sir?" I looked up at him from where I lay between his legs.

"You were just a child."

"So? I was a kid who knew how much my mom loved me, that she would do anything for me. That she felt just as lonely as I did, but that she felt it because of *me*, and I was still angry with her because of it."

"And you still loved her too. We all feel emotions that seem selfish or wrong sometimes, but they're not. You loved your mom, and she knew you loved her. You were young and confused. Feelings are...well, they're a clusterfuck sometimes. There are times I blame myself for what happened to my mom and the girls, when logically, I know it wasn't my fault. It was a thing that happened. A terrible, horrible accident. But no matter how much I know that, I still use it as an excuse not to get close to people or to be angry with myself. We're human, and we're flawed, but don't think for one moment that those things make you a bad person. You loved her, and she loved you."

"You think she would understand?" He didn't know

her, and maybe it made me immature, but if he said she would, I'd believe him.

"She would."

"She loved me...so much. I still feel it sometimes. Does that sound crazy?"

"No." He shook his head. "It sounds very much like you. I wish I could allow myself to feel it—my mom and the girls. Sometimes I don't feel worthy of it, even though, again, I logically know that's not the case."

"There's no one in the world more worthy than you!"

He chuckled, cupped my cheek, and smiled sadly. "You are so precious. So strong. I wish I could see the world through your eyes."

"You are...everything. And I know that sounds childish, but to me, you are. I love you, and I know you don't want to hear that. You think I'm too young, but I know how I feel."

There was sadness in his eyes, a deep despair I'd never seen the depths of. It made my chest ache.

"I love you," I said again.

"You're quite fond of saying that tonight."

My cheeks heated, and I had no doubt they were redder than my ass. "It's true."

Aidan sighed. "I know. I won't tell you how you feel.

And I…I'm struggling with the fact that I very much feel the same."

I tried to sit up and cheer that Aidan loved me, but he held me in place and shook his head. If I continued, the moment would be over, so I held my breath and waited.

"I didn't expect to feel this. Ever. Not for you or anyone. And I do struggle with the fact that you're only twenty. I don't ever want to take advantage of you or, again, for you to feel like you have no choice other than me. I worry that I don't have it in me to love you the way you deserve. That I'll hold on too tight because I don't want to lose you, or that I'll keep myself closed off so I don't lose you. It's been too long since I allowed myself to love someone, and I don't know that I'm very good at it."

"Are you kidding me?" How could he feel that way? How could he not know how wonderful he was? "You show me every day. From the moment you brought me home, you've made me feel protected and cared for. Hell, since the first moment I saw you when I was a kid, you made me feel that way."

"That's different from love."

"No, Aidan. It's really not. It's an extension of that. No one could ever love me as well as you do." I wrapped my arms around him and rested my head against his groin again.

"Such a precious boy," he said, and I knew he didn't believe me. I would have to believe it enough for the both of us.

My stomach growled, breaking the moment, and Aidan chuckled. "You need to eat. Sit up."

"Yes, Sir." It felt weird as hell to sit with a plug up my ass, but I also loved it because Aidan had placed it there. Because it kept me full of his cum for as long as possible.

He scooped a bit of roast onto a fork and fed me, a bite for me and one for him, until we were both full.

When we were finished, he made me roll over so he could remove the plug. I didn't want to, but Aidan didn't want me to wear it too long, since it was my first time.

We cuddled in bed after that, the room dark, my head on his chest. His arm was wrapped around me, his breath in my hair. "I love you," I told him, giddy I could say that now.

Aidan paused, breathed, "You too."

I went to sleep with a smile on my face.

CHAPTER THIRTY-FOUR

Aidan

I'D HAD TWO scheduled surgeries that day, and I was beat.

It had been two days since…Christ, since Finley told me he loved me, and I couldn't stop thinking about it. I was like a lovesick kid, thinking about our relationship all the time and grinning like a fool when I thought of things he said or did. The irony of it didn't escape me. I worried so often about Finley's age, but when it came to emotions, the boy had it together better than I did. I was crazy about him but afraid of it too. He truly was a fair-haired warrior. He had little fear, and when he did, he kept going, pushed past it to fight for what he wanted. I could take lessons from him.

I sighed as I got dressed after cleaning up at the hospital. David and I were having dinner, and Finley was having Ian over. There was nothing I wanted more than to go home to him, but I wanted him to have time with his friends, and I always tried to keep my dinner plans with David, as it had been him who'd kept me social for years.

He hadn't worked today, so I met him at the restaurant—Japanese tonight. I sent a quick text to Finley to see if he wanted me to bring dinner home for him, and he replied almost instantly.

No, Sir. Ian and I made food.

See you soon. Be good.

I'm a very good boy! :) Love you!

Another sigh. Those words came so easily, so frequently for him already. Each time I heard them, I wanted to ask for them again, while also wanting to beg him to refrain. It was difficult, experiencing things you never expected to feel, and I was positive I would be shit at it.

I texted back: **I'll be home in a couple of hours.**

pouts

I chuckled and got out of the car. David was inside, waiting for me. He grinned when our eyes caught, and I made my way over and sat down.

"How was today?" he asked.

"Long but successful, and that's what matters."

We chatted about random things—work, Southern California traffic, a new boy he'd played with.

"Are you guys going to the party?" he asked. "Finley

seemed to want to."

"He did." It wasn't something Finley and I had spoken about since, and while what we did was ultimately up to me, I wanted to discuss it with him. There were experiences he shouldn't be robbed of and parts of himself he had a right to explore. "I'm not sure. I'm going to talk to him about it."

David laughed, this hearty, rich sound that started deep in his chest.

"What's so funny?"

"You. It's crazy seeing you this way. It's good, of course. It's nice to see you happy, and I hope you know the boy makes you that way."

"Of course I know," I snapped, a little on edge, then added, "Sorry."

He shook his head. "No worries. You adore him, Aidan. He adores you. You fulfill each other's needs. Just focus on those things and not…" He waved his hands in the air. "Whatever it is you always focus on."

It was a reminder that though David and I had been friends for years, he didn't know much about me. He knew more than anyone except Finley, but still, not much. I was shitty at friendship too, apparently.

I groaned, rested my elbows on the table, and ran my hands over my face. I could do this. It really wasn't that hard. "I'm in love with him," I admitted. See? I'd said it, and the earth hadn't opened up and swallowed me whole.

"Um…no shit?"

"Fuck you."

He laughed again. "Sorry. I should be more supportive. I'm guessing this information is newer to you than to me."

"Remind me why I'm friends with you again?"

"Because I understand you and once in a while let you beat me and fuck me?" he teased, but no, it wasn't those things at all. It was that David had always been a good friend. He had never pushed me unless I needed to be pushed, but still never too far. Maybe it was the Dom in him that knew how far to test me. "Are you still afraid you don't know how to love him? Because you do, Aidan. That boy adores you, and you love him and take care of him every single day."

"It's…difficult." The truth was there, at the tip of my tongue, and I thought maybe I was going to set it free. I needed to do that. I understood it. I needed to be able to trust. I'd done that with Finley, and I should do it more with David as well. And I thought maybe it would make me better for Finley, and that made it all worthwhile. "I don't want to get into a lot of details, but my childhood wasn't the best. My father was mean, possessive. He liked to have my mother under his thumb, and not in a good way. I wasn't what he wanted in a son, but she…she and my sisters. I loved them. I lost all three of them in a car accident. I'm the only one who survived."

"Jesus Christ, Aidan. How am I just hearing about this?" He leaned forward and put a hand on my arm.

"Because I'm emotionally stunted?" I tried to make light of it, but he didn't take the bait. He gave me a sad look, like he felt sorry for me, and I hated pity. "Anyway, I stopped caring about anyone or anything after that."

David frowned. "You really believe that, don't you? Jesus, these fucking Doms."

"You're a Dom."

"Yeah, but I'm not an idiot one. You care. If you didn't, you never would have intervened at the restaurant that night. You never would have taken Finley home and given him more than that boy has probably ever had. Patients love you. It amazes me how much. You are so good to them, even though you're often a stoic asshole outside of the hospital."

I couldn't argue with that last statement. It was a fair assessment of me.

"I could name a thousand other ways I see you, and

have seen you, care and love people over the years. Hell, you keep these dinners with me, even on days you'd rather not. Don't sell yourself short, Aidan. That's an order." He winked.

"Did you mistake me for a switch?"

He chuckled. "I'm serious. Get out of your head and open your eyes."

"I'm trying," I admitted. "Fin makes me want to try."

"That's the first time I've heard you call him that."

I frowned. I hadn't even realized I'd said it. He was right. If I used his name, I always called him Finley.

"He's a very lucky boy, Aidan. Any man would be to belong to you."

I nodded, feeling like I was going to bust out of my skin. "Thank you…but can we stop now? I think I'm getting hives."

David laughed again, and a second later I joined him.

"Yep. Definitely happier now. He even has jokes."

I rolled my eyes, but I was smiling.

We didn't speak about anything of consequence for the rest of the meal. I really couldn't believe what I had shared with him, but a part of me was glad I had.

I spent the drive home thinking about Finley, of what he had shared with me about his mom and his wish for a family. That wasn't something I could give him. Mine were all dead, except for my father, whom I had nothing to do with. I didn't want children of my own. I didn't know if he did either. The more I thought about it, the more I considered his blood relatives. His mother was gone, and apparently his grandparents wanted nothing to do with him. But there was a possibility he had more people out there than he knew about.

It was still on my mind when I got home. Ian was already gone, and Finley was sitting on the floor at the coffee table, doing homework. He moved to come to me, but I shook my head. "Stay."

He nodded and smiled. "Yes, Sir."

I made my way over and sat on the couch. He gave me those cute puppy-dog eyes that I was nearly powerless against. I playfully rolled my eyes, but honestly, I loved that he always wanted to be close to me, that my touch meant so much to him. "Come here."

Finley climbed onto my lap, straddling me. He was wearing a pair of basketball shorts and no shirt. I pushed my hands under the waistband of his shorts and held his ass. "I need to speak with you."

"That doesn't sound good at all. Can't you just fuck my throat or something?"

This bloom of happiness expanded in my chest.

Christ, I truly did love him. He made me feel like a different man. "Later, horny boy. This is important. First, did you have fun with Ian today?"

"Yeah, it was nice. We just hung out."

"Good." I nodded. "Second…that party David and I discussed is Friday, and I need to know if you want to go and why, so I can make a decision."

He frowned, which surprised me, as he'd been so eager to go before.

"I love you and you love me, even though the words get stuck more often than not, when I just want to tell you all the time. But…since we both feel that way, I shouldn't want to go to a play party and…well, whatever would happen there."

It was a reminder of how green he was, how inexperienced. "There is no *shouldn't*. You want what you want. It's okay if you don't, but it's also okay if you do. It's something we need to talk about together and set rules for, if that's the case. Like…would you only want others to watch? Would you want me to share you with someone? Would you want to be with someone without me? If so, I would need it to be someone I trusted, like David."

"What? No, not without you. Never without you. It's just…" He shook his head. "It feels wrong."

"Oh, precious boy. You are such a treasure." I cupped his face. "It's not wrong unless we decide it's wrong for us. I know plenty of people who are in loving, committed relationships and who are open, or have rules when they play with others, and I know others who aren't. All that matters is what is right for *us*, what you need. I was quick to make a decision without you last time, and that wasn't fair. Yes, I'm your Dominant, but these are things we should discuss and come to an agreement about."

I honestly wasn't sure what I wanted. Did I get a thrill about parading him around as mine? Letting others look or even touch, as long as they knew he belonged to me? Yes. But there was also a part of me that wanted to keep him to myself.

"Do these parties happen often?"

"Fairly, yes. There are a few more coming up."

"Can we wait for one of those and think about it?"

"That's a very good idea." Now for the hard part. "I want to bring up something else, and I want you to know that whatever you decide, I'll support you. Whatever you need from me, I'll give you."

He frowned. "Okay…"

"I wanted to see if you'd like me to do some research into your family, to see if I can find out who your father is or if any family on your mom's side might be interested in a relationship with you." I wanted to give him that. If it was something he wanted, I needed him to have it. "But before you answer, I need to make sure you know that no matter what we find, that doesn't change how remarkable you are and how much I…how much I love you."

"I love you too, Sir. So much."

"I know."

"Do you think you'll be able to find something?"

"I don't know. I can't make any promises, but I can try."

"What if we find them and they don't want me?"

"Then that's their loss. But there's also the possibility that they do." I didn't want him to spend his life alone the way I had, without family, not if there was something I could do about it.

"Yes…but don't tell me, okay? Don't tell me if you find anything, unless you talk to them and it's good news. Otherwise, I'll keep on pretending they don't exist."

I smiled. "Good boy." Then pulled him forward and kissed him.

CHAPTER THIRTY-FIVE

Finley

"HOLY FUCK. I can't believe this is your house," Jordan said as he stood on the porch. My stomach was a little woozy because this was so damn new for me. I just wanted it to go well, and I'd had no idea how much until I was getting ready for today.

"This is Aidan's house. I'm just lucky enough to live here. Come in." He did, and I closed the door behind him.

"I think I misjudged you, dear, sweet Finley. Do you have a sugar daddy?"

My eyes snapped to his. "What? No. It's not like that." Or maybe it was? No, Aidan paid me, but I worked for him. I'd worked for him before there was anything sexual between us.

"Oh my God! You do have a sugar daddy!" Jordan practically screeched. "I was giving you shit, but I can see it on your face! Also, your head looks like it might explode. Wow, I didn't know people could get that red."

My chest tightened, and I suddenly felt like I couldn't breathe.

"Hey, I'm sorry. No worries. I swear you'll get no judgment from me." Jordan began rubbing my back. It was crazy how easy it was for him to give affection, to treat me like I was a friend he'd known for years, when really we knew nothing about each other. "Do you think you can find me a sugar daddy?"

I didn't know why, but the question made me bark out a laugh. Once I started laughing, I couldn't stop. A second later Jordan was laughing too. We were just standing there, in front of the door, giggling like a couple of idiots, and I knew right then that Jordan and I would be good friends.

When we settled down, I said, "He's not my sugar daddy, but I am kind of his…houseboy? Well, I used to just work for him, but now we're…"

"Boyfriends," he finished for me. We were that; obviously, we were. We'd talked about it, but I wanted to share more with Jordan. I wasn't ashamed of the relationship Aidan and I had, despite my earlier freak-out.

"Yeah, that, but he's also my Dom. I'm…submissive, or whatever?"

"Damn, boy. Go you!" Jordan teased. "So we probably wouldn't have been much of a match, but you're still cute as fuck, and I still totally want a sugar daddy. Do you think your man can hook me up?" Jordan waggled his eyebrows at me playfully.

"I'll see what I can do," I joked back. "Should we go into the dining room?"

"Sure." Jordan shrugged. "I'm sort of afraid to touch anything."

"Oh my God! I was the same way! I swear I felt like I'd walked into a magazine or something." I led Jordan to the dining table, where he unpacked his bag. I already had paper, my laptop, and the course book on the table. "It's funny, though, because Aidan really isn't materialistic. He has all these nice things, and he appreciates them, of course, but he's also so…modest."

Jordan nodded. "Yeah, I think I know what you mean. I was raised by my grandma, and we've never had much. I mean, we are your everyday, lower-middle-class family trying to make it in Southern California."

"Are your parents not around?"

"My mom is. She doesn't live here, though. We don't get along well."

"Oh," I said, unsure if I should ask why. The last thing I wanted was to make this a downer of a day.

"Her loss." Jordan smiled. "I'm basically fabulous."

"Obviously!"

"You're a smart boy, Finley. Flattery will get you everywhere!" We dissolved into laughter again, and then we began studying.

I enjoyed working with him. He had a great memory, and though he wasn't much of a writer, he definitely had drive. We stayed at it for an hour or so, until we both got tired of working on school things.

"Do you want to hang out a bit more?" Jordan asked.

"Yeah, absolutely," I replied, happy that he wanted to stay. "I was going to make Aidan's favorite cookies, which I know is sort of lame, but…"

"I don't mind helping. Gotta please your man." He winked.

Jordan and I made double-chocolate-chip, then did the dishes together. We talked about movies and music. Apparently, Jordan loved going to the Pantages and watching plays.

"I've never been," I admitted.

"We can go sometimes. I'll take you if your man doesn't mind. It's pricey, so I don't do it often."

I loved the idea of that—of hanging out with Jordan more. "I can pay," I replied.

Jordan winked. "We'll go Dutch, sugar baby."

"Whatever," I teased just as the oven timer went off.

"Oh my God. I can't wait to eat them!"

"We have to let them cool," I told him.

"Why do we have to do that? Is it in the cookie handbook?"

"Yeah, I'm pretty sure it is."

"Have a little fun, Fin. We'll have one ooey-gooey, too-hot cookie and let the others cool."

I grinned back at him. "Okay." And that was exactly what we did.

CHAPTER THIRTY-SIX

Aidan

I JUGGLED TWO pizzas in my hands as I unlocked the door. I'd come home earlier than expected and thought it would be nice to bring dinner so Finley didn't have to cook.

The second I stepped into the house, I heard the laughter. It was similar to Finley with Ian, but something was a little different about hearing him laugh with Jordan. Maybe it was because Jordan wanted him and Finley wasn't sure if he wanted Jordan, or maybe it was because it was new, but I felt it, and I couldn't stop the smile pulling at my lips.

He needed this, and it was so damn good to hear him laugh and chat with a friend. In some ways, Finley was so serious, older than his years because of what he'd lived through, and it was so rare that he could just let go. He was able to when he served me. I wasn't a fool not to know it or admit it, but he needed more than me. It was then that I knew I'd done the right thing. Finley put so much faith in me as his Dom, and he was supposed to, of course. But the truth was, regardless, I was just a man, one who made mistakes and questioned myself like everyone else.

I stepped around the corner and into the living room, where I'd heard the laughter come from.

"Aidan, you're home early!" Finley stumbled off the couch.

"Sit. You're fine. You don't have to get up. I brought pizza for dinner if you guys are hungry."

"I don't know about Finley, but I'm always hungry," Jordan teased, and Finley pushed him playfully.

"We had cookies not that long ago."

"Are you hunger-shaming me?" Jordan asked as I stood back and watched them together. There was an ease to how they interacted with each other already.

"Oh my God. No, I'm not. Come on."

When they reached me, I cocked a brow at Finley, and he said, "Oh. Aidan, this is my friend Jordan." He turned to his guest. "This is my Sir, Aidan."

"Your Sir, huh?" I hadn't been expecting that.

"Yeah, I told him. My Sir/boyfriend, Aidan." He grinned up at me, and damned if my pulse didn't accelerate.

I turned to Jordan. "Nice to meet you." We shook hands.

"You too," he replied.

"Here, I'll take these." Finley plucked the pizzas from my hand, and the two of them headed to the kitchen.

I was pretty sure I heard, "Holy fuck, your boyfriend is gorgeous. *Rawr*," followed by Finley's laughter.

I kept my distance, giving them space. Eventually, Finley came to my office to tell me he was taking Jordan home.

When he came back about an hour later, I was still sitting at my desk.

He knocked, and at my nod, he came into the room, slowly went to his knees, and put his head on my lap. "Thank you, Sir."

"I didn't do anything, sweet boy."

"You did more than you'll ever know," he replied, and somehow, I knew he didn't want anything more than friendship from Jordan, but he was incredibly happy to have that.

CHAPTER THIRTY-SEVEN
Finley

"OH MY GOD. Stop!" I shouted to Ian and Jordan as they continued to splash me. "I hate you guys." I ducked under the water, swam over to Ian, and jerked him under. When we both came up again, the three of us were laughing, and it struck me then—which, after everything, was a weird place for it to happen—how much my life had changed.

It was summer, and I'd finished my first semester of college. I was swimming in the pool of the house I shared with my boyfriend, who was also my Sir, while I laughed with my friends. Real friends. It made my heart race suddenly, thinking about it all.

Ian frowned, as though he could tell. "Is everything okay?"

"Yeah, I'm just…happy." I had been happy for a long time by then, and it was because of Aidan.

"No shit. I'd be happy if I lived here too," Jordan

teased, and this time, Ian splashed him. "I'm giving you shit, Fin. You know that." He hugged me and gave me a loud kiss on the cheek. Even though it hadn't been long, Jordan and I had gotten extremely close, and I felt lucky to have him.

"Come on. I need a tan," I said, and the three of us went to lie on the chairs by the pool. Ian turned on music on his phone, and we listened and talked and just…were.

Eventually we went inside, changed, and ordered pizza. Aidan and David were out, doing whatever it was they did. The pizza came, we ate, and then Ian went to his bag and got out a bottle of tequila. "Oh, oops. How did that get there?" he teased.

"Fuck yes," Jordan replied. "Do you think Aidan will care if we crash here?"

Ian pulled out margarita mix next. I was twenty years old, and I'd never done this—never gotten drunk and just hung out with friends. Which was ridiculous, really. That was a rite of passage…and I wanted that. Hanging out with them reminded me of things I'd missed. It went back to what I'd been thinking before, about how happy I was, and feeling that way made me want to soak up even more experiences. "I'll ask him."

Giddy excitement buzzed beneath my skin as I texted

Aidan.

I love you!

Uh-oh. What do you want?

Hey! That's not fair. I say I love you all the time. *pouts* But...I wanted to ask if Ian and Jordan can sleep here.

Sure. That's fine.

Thank you! <3

I tossed the phone to the coffee table. "He said it's cool."

"Did you ask your daddy if you can drink?" Ian teased, but almost in a mocking way. I knew he didn't get it, but he didn't usually make me feel weird about my relationship.

"Fuck off. He's not my daddy, not that I would be opposed to that. It's hot." I played it off, but I was slightly irritated.

Ian rolled his eyes.

"Ugh. I'm still jelly," Jordan replied.

"Tell him. He doesn't understand kink. He's judgy."

"I'm not judgy," Ian replied. "You're happy, so I'm happy. I'm sorry for being an asshole. Can we drink now? And if you don't drink with us, I'm going to be annoyed."

The truth was, I should have mentioned it to Aidan. He liked to be in control of most aspects of my life, and I was perfectly fine with that. More than fine with it. I loved it, but Ian's comment made me want to prove that I could do what I wanted…even though I didn't really want to do what I wanted. I wanted to do what Aidan said. This shit was confusing sometimes.

Still, I didn't call him before we went into the kitchen and made our first drinks…or when we made our second or third round. I was feeling light and buzzy, like there was all this laughter inside me that I couldn't let out quickly enough. Everything was funny. Ian put on Gaga, and the three of us began dancing around the living room. These were moments I should have had over and over by now, and I hadn't, but I loved that I could now.

Ian and I began to dance. He rubbed his ass against my crotch, and that buzzing just got louder and faster and more intense. Jordan was singing along with the song, using the almost empty tequila bottle as a microphone, when his eyes went wide and he suddenly stilled.

My pulse shot up because I knew, fucking knew, what that look was about. I turned around to see Aidan and David standing at the edge of the living room, David with a huge smile on his face and Aidan with an eyebrow raised.

"Aidan, you're home!" I ran to him and jumped into

his arms. He caught me, and my legs wrapped around his waist as I tried to kiss him.

"Oh, someone had a very good time tonight," David said.

"I did! I think I'm buzzed. Being buzzed is fun. Do you guys want to dance with us? Let's dance."

"Finley," Aidan warned, but I'd had lots of tequila, so I pretended I didn't hear the warning.

"Please, Sir. Please dance with me. I want to dance with you. I want to do everything with you." I slid down his body and went for his mouth again. Aidan pulled back and didn't let me take it. "Please?" I asked again. I wanted this, God, I wanted it badly, and I didn't know why, but I thought maybe Aidan did because he knew everything.

Something changed in his expression, and he nodded. This was Aidan always giving me what I needed.

"You may."

Then I was kissing him, kissing him like my life depended on it. When I pulled away, I backed my ass against his groin the way Ian had done to me. He was hard, and I whimpered. He felt so good against me. Aidan's hands were on my hips, his blunt nails and fingers digging in enough that I knew he would leave marks. I couldn't wait to see them, wished I could get them tattooed into my skin so they were always there.

Jordan began to drunkenly cheer, and David let out a hoarse, "Jesus Christ."

My eyes caught David's, and I saw how turned on he was, how much he liked what he saw, and damned if that didn't do something to me. It made me soar. Not the way Aidan made me fly, of course, but it made me feel sexy and wanted, and yeah, I was digging that.

Aidan growled into my neck and bit me. I cried out, not embarrassed at all because Aidan was making me feel this way, and whether he was hurting me or pleasuring me, everything Aidan did to me was beautiful.

"I don't know who I am when I'm with you," he said into my ear before nipping it. He was right. This wasn't him, dancing and grinding on me in front of others as Lady Gaga played in the background.

"Feels so good."

"This is what you want?" Aidan asked.

My buzz was beginning to fade, my mind clear enough to know this was what I wanted. "Yes."

As always, Aidan knew what I meant. He lifted his hand under my shirt and rubbed my chest, then slid it down to cup my aching cock. "Ian...if you're not comfortable, now might be the time to go into the other room," Aidan said. It meant a lot to me that he considered Ian's feelings about my lifestyle, making sure my friend was okay.

"No…um…I wanna stay," Ian said, surprising me. Maybe he was a little more curious about things than I'd thought. Either that, or he was just horny.

"He's magnificent, isn't he, David?" Aidan said, continuing.

I blushed, but there was something else there too, this giddy feeling, and my cock throbbed harder.

"Fuck yes. I've always told you he's a pretty boy, but seeing him like this…he's got my dick aching."

"You can look but can't touch," Aidan said. "He's mine."

"Yours," I said breathlessly. My eyes darted to Jordan and Ian. They were looking at us too, both riveted, and I could see the bulge in Jordan's pants.

Aidan spit in his hand and shoved it down the back of my shorts. He rubbed my hole, then pushed his finger in.

"Oh fuck," I gasped. I couldn't believe this was happening, couldn't believe we were doing this, but I wanted it, wanted it like crazy.

"Tell him, David. Tell him how gorgeous he is, how very well he yields to me."

There was a quiet voice in my head telling me I

should be embarrassed about this, but I wasn't. Later, maybe, but right then I couldn't be.

"Such a pretty, pretty boy. He's riding your fingers like a little slut," David said, and damned if I didn't smile.

"He *is* a slut…he's a slut for me, getting off in front of his friends this way. He's also a naughty, naughty boy, and I hope he doesn't think he's not getting punished."

Oh…oops.

I couldn't find it in myself to care, though. Aidan's punishments made me feel cared for.

I pushed against his hand, let Aidan finger-fuck me even though it was a bit dry and rough. "Please…please, Sir," I begged, not really knowing what I was begging for.

"Fuck, this is hot," Jordan groaned. "Can I jerk?"

"Yes," David answered him, which surprised me. Hell, it surprised me that Jordan had asked too.

Jordan shoved his hand into his shorts and started jacking himself. Ian watched, eyes wide, then sat on the couch and began doing the same.

"Suck," Aidan said, pushing the fingers of his free hand into my mouth.

I did as told, sucked them like they were his cock, and then he pulled them from my mouth and the others from my hole before pushing the wet fingers in roughly.

"Oh God!" I cried out.

"Tell him, David. Tell him how much you want him, and then you can come, Finley. Oh, and I'd enjoy it, because it'll be the last time you do for a while."

"I want to share him with you. Fuck his pretty little mouth while you take his tight hole. He's gorgeous, Aidan. Such a sweet, horny boy dying for cock," David said, and then Aidan massaged my prostate.

My vision went blurry, and the room spun. I heard Jordan cry out in the background, but I couldn't see him, couldn't see anyone as my balls drew tight and I shot my load in my shorts. My knees went weak, but Aidan held me up. He pulled his fingers from my hole, and I immediately missed the full feeling he gave me.

With his other hand he rubbed my dick, and I knew he was getting some of my cum. I was embarrassed, so fucking embarrassed, but insanely turned on too. Because this was for Aidan. I was pleasing him. He liked me to eat my load, and I'd do it, even if it was in front of David and my friends.

I sucked my cum from his fingers and heard Jordan say, "Holy fuck," in the background.

I smiled, turning and nuzzling into Aidan. "Thank you, Sir. Thank you, thank you, thank you."

He kissed the tip of my nose.

"I'm sorry."

"Oh, it's too late for that. You're very much going to regret drinking without asking me, but for now, you boys clean up this mess."

"Yes, Sir."

Ian didn't reply, but he began to pick up.

"Um…yes, Sir?" Jordan said as if unsure if he should, but maybe he wanted to.

The three of us, sticky with cum, cleaned up the living room as Aidan and David watched. I couldn't quite catch their eyes, reality sinking in but not enough to make me regret it. Still, I felt completely sober now.

That had been…fuck, it had been *hot*. I liked having eyes on me, liked obeying Aidan where others could see, making sure everyone knew I belonged to him.

When we were finished, Aidan said, "Both of you are to stay. David, can you get them settled into the guest room downstairs?"

"Yeah, no problem," David replied, winking at me. "Someone is definitely in trouble."

My cheeks burned hotter.

Aidan took my hand and began to pull me toward the stairs. I looked over my shoulder at Ian and Jordan. Ian looked confused, and Jordan was hard again.

When we were tucked in our room, Aidan said calmly as ever, "Go to sleep."

"Huh?" That wasn't supposed to be what he said. Somehow I felt…disappointed.

"You heard me. Go to sleep."

"I thought I was going to get punished?" And maybe fucked.

"You are, but that's happening tomorrow, when you haven't been drinking."

"I'm sober now!" It didn't escape my attention that I was arguing *for* a punishment.

"Do as you're told, Finley. I want you to have this night. I'm not upset you had fun with your friends. You deserve that, but you also know you should have told me. Go to sleep."

"I…" Forcing myself to stop, I didn't argue with him. "Yes, Sir."

I took off my clothes and put them in the hamper, then went to bed. Aidan didn't take off his clothes, but he did sit on the bed beside me. He pulled out his laptop and began checking his emails.

"Aidan?"

"Tomorrow," was all he said, so I did as told and went to sleep.

I'D HARDLY WOKEN up the next morning, only having gone to the bathroom and brushed my teeth, when Aidan said, "Lie across the bed and don't come, no matter what I do."

I trembled, pulling out of my clothes, folding them and setting them on the chair. My blood was rushing, my heart thudding, and I already felt like I could cry…or come, or both.

I lay over the bed, and Aidan returned with a belt.

"Oh *God*," I rushed out.

"Did you know you should have told me about your plans last night?"

"Yes, Sir," I admitted, because I had.

"And you chose not to?"

"Yes, Sir. I'm sorry."

"I would have allowed it, Fin."

Fin. I loved it when he called me Fin. He didn't do it often, but I couldn't even appreciate it at the moment because I was filled with disappointment in myself. I'd let him down. I'd known I should tell him, and I hadn't because…because I'd wanted to prove I didn't have to when I really *needed* to, and not just for Aidan, but for myself. "I'm sorry," I said again, and I was.

"I know, but that doesn't change what happened." The belt flew through the air and landed harshly on my ass. Pain burst through me, sharp and intense. "Count."

"One," I replied, and then a second biting *snap* landed against my skin. "Two!"

One after another, Aidan spanked me. The burn was overwhelming, and I lost track of time, even though I knew it wasn't much of it that had passed. Tears blurred my eyes, but I was centered too, grounded in him and in this moment, in myself and the world in a way only Aidan could give me…and I still continued to count.

My dick was hard again. I didn't think twice about the fact that getting whipped with a belt did that to me. It was just who I was. And I wouldn't allow myself to come and disappoint him again.

Suddenly the belt dropped to the floor. I knew in the back of my mind that Aidan was grabbing the lube, and then his wet cock pushed inside me, and yes, oh God yes, I loved it when he filled me, when he made me real. That's what it felt like—Aidan making me *real*.

My hands fisted into the blanket as he fucked into me.

"Don't come."

"I won't, Sir," I managed to reply.

My dick was aching, and I worried it might kill me

not to have an orgasm.

His body slapped against mine as he took me roughly and completely and…beautifully. Then his teeth bit into my shoulder and his dick spasmed inside me as he shot, filling me with his load.

Then I was empty, unbearably empty. Aidan's arms were around me, and he was lifting me, situating me in the bed, rubbing cream into my ass, then holding me. Kissing me and wiping my tears.

"I'm sorry."

"Shh. It's okay. It's over now." He kissed my head.

"I love you."

"I love you too."

We lay there together for who knew how long, Aidan holding me. Eventually, he said, "You liked that…performing for them."

"I did. It made me feel…even more owned by you. Like I was this treasure other people wanted but couldn't have because I so fully belong to you."

Aidan was quiet for a moment. "We'll go to the next party. You'll be on my leash. Others can look but can't touch. They'll see you and want you, but they'll know you're mine."

"Thank you!" I kissed his chest, because oh yes, I wanted that. I hadn't known it until last night, but I did.

"You have nothing to thank me for," he replied, then chuckled. "I think Jordan is curious."

"I think so too." I snuggled into him, licked the sweat on his arm.

"I hope you have a hangover, you naughty boy," Aidan teased, and I laughed. God, he was perfect. He was everything.

"I love you."

Aidan replied with a kiss that stole my breath, that I felt in every part of my body.

CHAPTER THIRTY-EIGHT
Aidan

I COULDN'T STOP staring at the information in front of me.

Finley had given me everything he could on his family—mom's full name, date of birth, where she'd been born.

They were from a small town outside of Houston, where they loved God and football over everything else—his own family even more than their daughter or her son, apparently.

I hated this, hated not knowing what would happen and having no control over it. This could very easily devastate him, but it could also give him a piece of himself that he'd always felt was missing. It could give him family.

But I had hope too. Years changed people sometimes, and sometimes things just weren't what they seemed. The aunt, whom I'd been able to find after discovering his grandparents passed, had only been ten when Finley was born. Who knew how the woman would feel about him?

Maybe she would turn him away.

Maybe she would welcome him with open arms.

Maybe she would take him away from me.

I rubbed a hand over my face and sighed. Fuck, this was hard, but it needed to be done. I was glad he hadn't wanted anything to do with it until he knew that any relatives I might have found wanted to get to know him. I would carry the burden, any burden, if it lightened the load for my boy.

Not wanting to risk the possibility of him coming home early from his afternoon out with Jordan and Ian, I picked up the phone and dialed.

"Hello?" a woman answered a couple of moments later.

"Hi, is this Jennifer Douglas?"

"Speaking. May I ask who's calling?" There was a slight twang to her words. "Jeff, can you get the girls? Oh, no, sweetie, don't climb on that," she said to her kids and her husband, whom she'd married at twenty.

"My name is Aidan Kingsley. I'm from Los Angeles, and I... There's no easy way to say this, but your nephew, Finley, he's my partner. We've been researching his family and came upon your name."

"Nephew?" she asked, the confusion in her voice palpable.

"Your sister, was she Amanda Moss?"

"Oh God...just a second. Jeff, I'm going to go to the other room for a minute. I'll be right back." A shuffling followed, and then a door closed. "Mandy had a son?" There was no hint of deception, nothing but sincerity and the soft sound of surprise.

Her parents never told her? "Yes, she did. From what Finley had gotten from his mother, she got pregnant with him at sixteen. We're not sure who his father is. She tried to hide it for as long as she could, but of course your parents found out. Your mother took her to California. There was an arranged adoption, but Amanda changed her mind. She couldn't give him up, and they wouldn't allow her home with him. She and Finley stayed in California, and your mother went back to Texas."

There was a long pause on the line. If I couldn't hear her breathing, I would have thought she was gone. "I... They told me she ran away. I never knew about the baby. They said she ran away with a man... I remember my mom leaving with her beforehand, though, but I just... How could I ever have thought something like that happened? They were my parents, and I believed them—oh God, where has he been since her death?"

"He was in foster care and then on his own. He ran away from the last one. He's been in my home since he was nineteen."

"He was alone all this time… He's been out there, and I didn't even know he existed. He has me and my girls. He was *alone*."

"Yes, he was, but he's not alone anymore, nor will he ever be if I have anything to say about it."

And then…then she started crying, loud, aching cries, and my heart went out to her. For the time lost, for the lies and betrayal. The minutes stretched on as she mourned—maybe her sister, maybe her parents and who she thought they were compared to the truth, and for the boy, my boy, who had grown up without the love of family because of it.

"I'm sorry, I just…"

"You don't need to apologize to me."

"Who are you to him again?"

"I'm his life partner. Boyfriend, for lack of a better word," I added to ensure she knew and understood. I wouldn't have him hurt by her if she was ignorant.

"I'm not my parents. If they were alive, I…I can't even think of them. It makes me too angry, but I'm not surprised they behaved the way they did. Mandy was young. My father was a beloved Baptist minister, very deeply rooted in his faith. We had our own issues as I got older. I don't care that he's gay. I love him. I don't even know him and I love him. Poor Mandy…poor…"

"Finley," I supplied.

"I like it. Is he there with you? Can I speak to him?"

"He's not home right now. He knows I was looking for his family, but he wanted me to deal with it. He only wanted to know if there were people out there who would accept him. He can't take any more heartache."

"I do. I would love nothing more than to get to know him. I missed my sister so much over the years. I was so angry with her because I thought she left me, but she didn't…they forced her to go, her and Finley."

"She did her best by him. From everything he's told me, his mother loved him very much."

"That was Mandy. She had the biggest heart."

"He does too." He'd had enough heart to break mine free from the chains I'd locked it in.

"I'd like to call him."

"I'll speak with him when he gets home, and when he's up for it, he'll call you."

She breathed through the line before saying, "I understand."

"I won't have him hurt. What's best for him will always come first."

"You sound like you love him very much."

"I do."

"I don't want to hurt him either. I just want to know him. He has twin nieces—"

"Twins?" I asked, a heavy ache in my chest.

"Yes. Melody and Harmony. And Jeff and myself."

"I'll speak to him," I managed to get out around the boulder in my throat. "Either he or I will be in touch."

"Thank you. What did you say your name is?"

"Aidan Kingsley."

"Thank you, Aidan."

"I just want him happy." No matter what it took, that was what I wanted for him.

A LITTLE OVER an hour later he came in, that familiar smile on his face.

"We had the best day." Finley pushed up on his toes and pressed his lips to mine. It was a quick, chaste kiss, but I felt it in my chest as I did every one of his touches. "I'll go cook our dinner. And just so you know, my legs are a little sore from our workout this morning. It's always more work when I have to exercise with you." He cocked his head a little and frowned. "Hey, what's wrong?"

"Nothing. Come with me." He followed me to the living room. "Kneel."

"Yes, Sir." Finley's knees kissed the carpet. I sat on the couch, with him between my legs, looking up at me expectantly. "You're scaring me, Aidan."

"Shh. I don't mean to scare you. Everything is fine. I have good news, actually." I cupped his cheek, brushed my fingers along the skin there, knowing that good news or not, he would need my touch, my presence and support, because it was a lot to take in. "Head on my thigh, please, and wrap your arms around me."

"Yes, Sir." There was a small twinge of trepidation to his voice. His arms locked around my waist, our gazes still holding one another's. I ran my fingers through his hair, scratched his scalp, trailed them down to his nape.

"I found some information on your family."

"Is it good?" he asked cautiously.

"Your grandparents are gone, but...did your mom ever tell you about her sister?"

"No...she has a sister?"

"Yes. Her name is Jennifer. She's only ten years older than you."

"Jennifer? She mentioned her…she would cry for her sometimes. She said she was her best friend back home, but she never told me she was her sister. Why wouldn't she have told me that?"

"I don't know, precious boy. Are you fine there, or do you want on my lap?"

"I like it here." He nuzzled in close, the way he so often did.

"I spoke with her on the phone today. She didn't know about you. She had been told that her sister ran away. You have an uncle—her husband—and twin nieces. Your aunt would very much like to speak to you and get to know you."

His chin trembled as tears flooded his eyes. "She would? Like really would?"

My heart shattered for him, that he had been expecting to be shunned, that he didn't feel himself lovable by his own family. "Yes. She was devastated at the time lost, at what happened to you and your mother. I'm quite sure she would have jumped on a plane today if I would have allowed it."

"She wants to know me?" he said again, as if he still couldn't believe it.

"She's the lucky one, my little warrior. Tell me you know that."

"She's the lucky one—oh, *Aidan*. I have an aunt? And nieces? Twins? Oh…I didn't think. I'm sorry."

"Stop." I pressed a hand to his mouth. "Don't apologize. Not for that."

"Thank you!" His hold on me tightened. "I wouldn't have this without you. I want to call her right now! Can I call her now?"

"If that's what you want, yes. The number is in my office. I called her from the landline, so it's not in my cell."

"Will you stay with me while I do?"

"I'll do whatever you need. Always."

"I can't believe I have family." He stood. "I'm kind of scared. Like I don't know if I believe this is true. Like I'm going to wake up and find out it was all a dream. Do you promise this is real?"

I chuckled. "Yes, it's real. Now come on so you can do this."

We went to my office, and I grabbed the number from my desk. Finley was pacing the room, and I could see his nerves getting the better of him.

"Hey. Stop." He did so immediately. "You're okay. I'm here, and no matter what happens, I'll always be here. You can do this."

He wrapped his arms around me, his face in my

chest. "Because of you."

"You give me too much credit. Now sit down, please."

"Yes, Sir." He went to the couch, and I sat beside him. Using my cell phone, I called the number and handed it to him. "Is this Jennifer?" he asked a moment later. "This is Finley…your, um…nephew?"

They spoke for hours, and I didn't leave his side. There were tears and laughs and getting-to-know-yous. When he was finished, he hung up, climbed into my lap, and wrapped his arms around me. "I'm so happy. I can't wait to get to know her more, but I realized something. I said I had family when you told me, but even before Jennifer, I had family. I have you. No matter what, you're my family, Aidan."

I kissed the top of his head, felt myself getting choked up. "I'll always give you what you need."

CHAPTER THIRTY-NINE

Finley

I SPOKE TO my aunt every day for the next couple of weeks. Sometimes it was just texting, other times it was chatting. She was able to share so much about my mom with me, all these funny stories I'd never heard. She emailed me photos, and we talked about her girls and things we had in common, and it was...incredible.

It was perfect—my life was beyond perfect, really. It was summertime, so classes were out, but I was excited to go back in the fall. I got to serve Aidan every day, take care of his home, cook his meals, and follow his schedules. I still didn't love the workouts every morning, but I did it because he said I should, and I wanted to do what Aidan said.

And every night I slept in his bed. He fucked me and hurt me and bound me, and it was... Jesus, it was as close to complete as I'd ever felt. Like I was where I belonged and fulfilled in the very best of ways. There was nothing like giving myself to him. There was such power in that, in the *giving* of power to him. It made me strong and settled in my skin and as if there was nothing I couldn't do.

When I cried for him, I was free.

When he pushed his cock down my throat until I couldn't breathe, I felt possessed.

When he punished me, well, it hurt like hell, but I needed it and wanted it, and there was so much love in that, in Aidan giving me what I needed. He'd told me once that it was his job as my Dominant to help me become the best version of myself in every way, to help me reach my fullest potential. He did that every day, every second, with his rules, schedules, touches, kisses, spankings, and in the way he fucked me.

Feeling owned by him made me feel loved by him. Being used by him made me feel important, and there was nothing like serving Aidan. My Sir.

We had plans to see my aunt the following week. I couldn't believe it—I would see her, my mother's sister. My thoughts were racing, but like always, Aidan saw. Aidan knew and made it better.

When we woke this morning, Aidan fucked me, then plugged me, then let me hold his cock while he pissed. I served him breakfast, and we worked out together, and there was a chance, maybe, that I was beginning to enjoy this kind of physical activity more.

We spent the day together, just being, watching shows I knew he had no interest in, and swimming together, and talking.

It was early evening when Aidan instructed me to go to our room, strip, and kneel for him.

"Yes, Sir." The familiar zip of excitement and hunger shot through me.

A couple of minutes later he came into the room, carrying a small box, and sat on the edge of the bed. "Come," he said, and I crawled to him, curious and confused but eager for whatever he would give me. Aidan opened the box. "Do you know what this is?"

My chest got tight, and I began to shake. "A collar." Oh God. Aidan was collaring me? *Please let him be collaring me.*

It was soft leather, obviously very expensive. There was a dainty gold lock on it, the key sitting beside it. Engrained into the leather was the word *Aidan's*, and on the inside it said *Precious Boy*. "Can I wear it? Please put it on me. I'll never take it off."

It was silly, maybe. I already felt completely owned by Aidan, but this, this made me feel even more possessed by him. I would wear it proudly so everyone knew I was his.

"We'll have to see about the never-taking-it-off part. If you take it, there may be times when it's not appropriate, which we'll discuss together. But I would very much like to give this to you. I would like you to wear it tonight so everyone knows you're mine."

I didn't care about appropriate. I wanted everyone to know I was his, all the time. Still, I asked, "Tonight?"

"It's the party. Would you still like to go?"

My stomach swooped slightly, but my skin buzzed in the best way. My answer came easily, and truthfully. "I'm nervous, but I want it…so much. You won't let anyone touch me?"

"No. They can look. They'll be envious, but they'll all know you belong to me."

I trembled, my body flushed with heat. I felt a bit slutty, but *God*, did I want that. I wanted to be flaunted and desired but completely under Aidan's command. "When can we go? I want to go now."

Aidan chuckled. "Such an eager little slut, aren't you? Lean in. I'd like to see this on that pretty neck of yours."

He plucked the collar from the box and set the packaging aside. I held my breath as he wrapped it around my neck, fastening the lock with a *click*.

"Beautiful," he said, running his fingers along it.

"I feel beautiful," I admitted.

"Come on. Let's get you cleaned out."

I groaned. Doing this was another thing that wasn't my favorite, especially in front of him. "Well, I *did* feel beautiful," I teased.

He smacked my cheek, not hard, but definitely letting me know he was there and he hadn't liked what I said.

"Sorry, Aidan."

"Even what we're about to do is beautiful, Finley, because it is what I want to do to you. It is another way I take care of you and prepare you for me."

Well…when he said it like that… "You're right."

I crawled behind him to the bathroom. He got the enema kit out, attached it to the shower, then got the water going and told me to get in. He lubed the end of the nozzle, and I stood with my back to him, my ass out, my hands on the wall. I winced when he put it in, when he began to fill me. Of course, he made me hold it for longer than I wanted. I began to shift uncomfortably, my stomach contracting, before he told me to sit on the toilet and release it.

Afterward, we showered together and he washed me.

"I'm going to fuck you in front of them tonight," he told me as he looked through the closet.

My pulse jumped. "Yes, Sir."

"They'll have permission to praise you and watch us, but that's as far as it'll go. If you decide you want more, we'll consider that for next time." Aidan came out with a pair of my jeans, a black harness I didn't recognize, and a button-up shirt. "Use your colors if you need to. Don't hesitate. If you don't feel comfortable, tell me. If you want to leave, we will, no questions asked. This is supposed to be fun, and if it's not, then we walk out of there together, okay?"

His words made me love him even more. I never realized how much power there was in being a submissive until Aidan allowed me to be his boy. "Yes, Aidan."

"Good. Other than that, I'll push you. I'm going to use you hard and make sure everyone knows what's mine."

My cock began to throb and lengthen.

"Oh, that reminds me. I almost forgot something." Aidan went back into the closet and came back out with a cock cage.

"Aidan!" I whined.

"I know. I'm looking forward to it too," he replied with a wicked grin. He knew that hadn't been what I was thinking.

Once we got my erection down, Aidan put the chastity on me. He cupped me afterward, looking down at me. "They'll know I own every part of you. That you only have what I give you, and tonight, I don't even let you have your cock."

Wow… Why was that so hot? "Can we go now?"

"Christ, I love you."

I gasped. It was still rare that he said the words, even though I felt them every moment of every day. "I love you too."

We dressed after that, Aidan in black jeans and a black T-shirt. He helped me with the harness, then put the shirt on over it and buttoned each button for me.

We were quiet as we drove. He took me to a…fuck, it looked like a mansion, in the Beverly Hills Flats. He parked out front. There were already tons of cars there. My chest ached a bit, and I took in a couple of deep breaths.

"You can do this, Fin," he said, holding my hand.

"I know, Sir. There's nothing I can't do with you by my side."

He nodded, and then we got out of the car.

CHAPTER FORTY

Aidan

HE WAS BREATHTAKING with my collar around his slender neck. He was always breathtaking but even more so tonight.

"Walk behind me," I instructed.

"Yes, Sir."

Finley fell into step behind me as I led him up the porch stairs of the oversize, white house.

I knocked, and a boy wearing a French maid uniform opened it. "Good evening, Sir. What is your name?"

"Aidan Kingsley and Finley Moss."

He checked the list and pulled the door open farther. "The master of the house is happy you could join us."

"Thank you." I nodded and stepped inside. There was a lounge area to the right, which was used as a dressing area for those who needed it. This wasn't the first time I'd been at Micah's home, though this would obviously be different as it was Finley by my side.

"You still with me?" I asked as we slipped into the room.

"Yes, Sir. Very much with you."

I chuckled before taking his shirt off. My fingers went to the button on his pants next. He sucked in a quick breath, and I paused but then continued. He knew what to say if he needed me to slow down or stop.

I stripped him so he wore nothing but my collar, the harness, and a cage, then hooked the leash onto the loop on the back of the harness. "On your knees. I expect you to stay there all night unless I instruct differently."

"Yes, Sir," he replied beautifully.

I led him from the dressing room into the main part of the house. It was extravagant, really, with floor-to-ceiling windows and french doors along the back leading out to a private yard. Inside there were couches, chairs, benches, and other pieces of furniture throughout the space. On the tables were bowls with condoms and lube. I could see people swimming out back, and there were others in the front room, talking, kissing, sucking, fucking, kneeling. There was a man who was a footstool for his Master, and another squeezed between two guys, who were fondling him.

"Wow. Aidan, long time no see!" Micah walked over to us. He was a tall black man with a kind smile that masked his very dominant nature.

"Thanks for having us," I told him.

"And who is this?" he asked, nodding down at Finley.

"This is my boy, Finley. Say hello."

He looked up at Micah. "Hello, Sir." His face was a delicious pink.

"Jesus, he's gorgeous, Aidan. And collared too. That's a surprise."

"I definitely didn't see it coming," I teased, and we laughed. "But he is very much mine."

Finley rubbed his face against my thigh. Reaching down, I threaded my fingers through his hair. Micah and I spoke, not engaging Finley again. He waited patiently, obediently, without interrupting. There was no surprise that he did so well. He was so naturally subservient, so eager to please, that I expected nothing less of him.

"I should go mingle," Micah said after a little while. "David's here. He's watching a demonstration in the back room."

"Thanks, Micah."

I tugged on Finley's leash. He followed, and we went through the room, down a hallway, and into another room, where a man was bound to a cross as a Dom caned him. His ass and thighs were welted, small drops of blood along some of them.

Finley slowed down.

"Are you okay?" I asked. It was a lot. I knew he'd never seen anything so intense.

"Yes, Sir. I just... Do you do that?"

"I have, but it's not something I need. Do you want it?"

I didn't think he did, but it wasn't as if he'd never surprised me. "No. That's not... I think that's too much for me."

"Good boy. Thank you for being honest."

I saw David in the corner, and we joined him. The man being caned was screaming and begging but so obviously in his element.

"Hey, man," David said to me. "And look at you, pretty boy. It's good to see you again, Finley."

"Hello, Sir," Finley said, preening under the praise. I wasn't sure if he even realized it.

"He's flawless," David said.

"He is, isn't he? My pretty, slutty boy."

Finley's body shuddered, and his eyes sort of glowed. Oh yes, he definitely liked this.

"Why don't you show off for me? Show David what's mine."

There was a moment of panic in eyes before he settled into his desires. "Yes, Sir. How should I do it?"

"Turn around." There was no hesitance on my part, no jealousy. There were rules in place, and I knew Finley belonged to me. I quite liked showing him off too.

He turned slowly, giving David a good look at him. Another man approached as Finley showed himself off. When he had his ass toward David, I said, "Stop."

He did so.

"Arch your back."

He did that too, showing off his ass.

"Do you share him?" the other Dom asked.

"No. I show him off, but he's all mine." Finley looked at me, that floating expression on his face that told me he was already finding that space inside him he reveled in. I knelt beside him, dipped my fingers between his ass cheeks, and rubbed his rim. "Whose hole is this?"

"Yours, Sir, always yours."

I pushed my fingers into his mouth, he sucked them, and then my hand was at his ass again. I slid one wet finger inside.

"It's a tight little hole, isn't it?" David asked. We'd spoken before, and he knew I wanted him to help make this fantasy as potent for Finley as I could.

"Fuck yes, so tight and pink. I took his cherry, and I'm still the only cock that's been up there." Finley whimpered, pushed his ass back to meet my finger, so I slapped it with my other hand. "Did I say you could do that?"

"I'm sorry…sorry, Sir. It just feels so good."

I pulled my finger out, and he whimpered again. I patted his full balls over and over.

"Oh God…Sir…"

"Fuck, Aidan," David cursed, and I knew none of it was an act.

"Lucky bastard," the other man said before slipping away.

I pushed to my feet. Finley looked up at me with dopey, needy eyes, and I chuckled.

"You know this night might actually kill me, right? Goddamn, he's gorgeous," David said.

"If I ever share him, you know it'll be with you," I replied, because he was the only one I trusted with him. "Come on. Let's go explore."

CHAPTER FORTY-ONE

Finley

I WAS PRETTY sure I had never been so turned on in my life. Actually, that wasn't true. Everything Aidan did drove me crazy, and just thinking about being with him did more to me than any of these other men ever could, but it was hot. There was so much sex and expression around us. There was this freedom to it that thrilled me. It took complete trust to do what we did, and there was no one I would ever trust like I did Aidan.

David stayed with us as we went into different rooms. I didn't think the man who owned the house lived there. Like maybe he just used it for playing or something.

I was distinctly aware of Aidan all the time, of course, but I was also aware of David. Of his laugh and his voice and the fact that my Sir trusted him. That if Aidan ever shared me, it would be with David, who really was a beautiful man, and who I knew could give me what I craved. Not to the extent Aidan could, of course, but in a way Jordan never could have.

I thought maybe it was something I could like sometime, if the time was right.

Aidan asked me about my knees multiple times. When I told him they were fine, and that I didn't want to stand, he said if we came again, he would bring kneepads to be safe.

We went back into the main room, and there were even more people there than there had been earlier. A guy crawled over to David, who said, "There you are, pup."

"Thank you for allowing me to come late." He had a tail plug in his ass and a thick collar around his neck. He looked like he was maybe twenty-five or so. I hadn't known David had anyone, or that there was anyone there for him.

"Of course." David petted the boy's head. "Kyle, this is Finley, Aidan's boy."

"Oh, wow. You're collared," Kyle said, smiling. "Sorry. That was rude. I just hadn't heard. It's nice to meet you."

"You too," I replied a little lamely. Did he know Aidan? It was silly of me, but I wondered if they'd ever been together.

"Hello, Sir," Kyle said to Aidan, and yep, I could tell by the look in his eyes that he'd been fucked by Aidan. It wasn't fair of me, but a wave of jealousy washed through me.

"Kyle," Aidan said with a nod, then looked down at me. "Come, Fin. I want your mouth."

My thoughts started spinning, and my pulse raced. This was it. It was what we had come for, what we wanted, but now my chest was tight and it felt a little hard to breathe. He seemed to be using *Fin* more often today. Knowing Aidan, it was on purpose, to relax me and remind me what we had.

Aidan walked over to an armchair. I crawled behind him, trying to focus on my breaths—*in, out, in, out*—as I went.

He sat down, and I knelt between his legs. His eyes were intense, this deep stare I felt down to my soul, and I knew he could tell I was scared. I melted a bit when he leaned forward, kissed the tip of my nose, and whispered, "You can do this. It's what I want. You want to please me, right?"

"Yes, Sir," I replied quietly. Pleasing Aidan brought me peace and connected me to the world better than anything else. This had been what I'd desired too, and I still did, but that wasn't as important to me as serving

Aidan well.

"Good boy," he said, then pulled back and smacked me. My eyes rolled back, and my cock strained against the cage, fighting to harden. God, why did that feel so good?

Aidan must have seen the reaction because he smacked me again, making a sharp jolt of pleasure shoot through me, and my thoughts began to slow. "Thank you, Sir," I found myself saying, though I hadn't planned the words. They'd just come because Aidan deserved my thanks for giving me what I needed.

"Take my cock out," he ordered.

"Yes, Sir." My eyes darted around the room, and I noticed a few people watching us. Kyle had David's dick in his mouth. They were only a few feet away from us, David standing and Kyle kneeling.

Aidan's hand fisted in my hair, making me cock my head to ease the pressure, while I was also silently begging, *More, harder, keep going.*

"Take me out," he repeated, then added, "My little warrior."

Those words did something to me. They were like fuel, feeding my thoughts and muscles. I was Aidan's warrior, and there was nothing I couldn't do with him controlling me.

My fingers fumbled as I worked open Aidan's pants. His grip on my hair had loosened, and he was massaging my scalp. He wasn't wearing underwear, and it sounds crazy, but my mouth watered at the sight of him, at his girth and length and that thick vein that ran up the side of his cock.

I wanted to worship him. Wanted to cherish him and submit to him and praise him the way he deserved to be praised. I wanted everyone to see us, to look at us and know I belonged to him. That Aidan owned me, and he always would, and there was nothing I wouldn't do for him.

"Kiss the tip."

"Yes, Sir." A few more people closed in around us as I leaned in and pressed my lips to his slit.

"Lick—root to tip."

My tongue slipped out, and I ran it up and down his salty prick. His balls were full, and I wanted those too, but I also wanted to choke on him, for Aidan to fuck my face until I cried and couldn't breathe.

"Now my balls. Lick them."

"Yes, Sir." I lapped at his sac. I couldn't get enough. I was stronger on my knees than I was any other way. I was more confident and more secure serving him than I ever could be without him.

"Suck," he ordered next.

Yes, yes, yes! I did as told, blowing him. It didn't last long, and then he was fisting my hair again and fucking into my throat. I did everything Aidan had taught me, trusting him and relaxing, opening up for him. He pushed my face down and held it, my mouth full of cock as I inhaled his musky scent through my nose and felt…at peace.

He pulled me off, and I gasped, a long string of spit connecting his dick and my lips.

He shoved his cock into my mouth again, using it like a hole, *his* hole. That's what I felt like, a tool Aidan used to get off, and it was *everything*. It gave me purpose in that moment.

"That's a good slut. You're a good hole for your Sir, aren't you? Such a pretty, pretty cocksucker, isn't he, David?"

"Fuck yes," David replied. "A little cockslut dying for his owner's load. He's incredible."

Their words made me begin to fly, to soar above all the other things in my life, all the shit that was always in my brain. It wasn't subspace, exactly. I'd been much deeper, but still, I was in this gray area where I was all feeling and the world seemed to revolve around me and Aidan, and nothing else mattered.

He pulled my head up and angled it so he could still fuck my mouth but I could see the room. David was riveted on me, fucking into Kyle's face as he watched me. There were more men there, some watching, some jacking off, all of them staring at me, wanting me, desiring me, but I wasn't theirs, was I? I was owned by Aidan and always would be. I'd found where I belonged.

My vision began to blur. My throat hurt, and my eyes watered.

I loved crying for Aidan, loved giving him my tears. He swiped his fingers through them and sucked it off, then pushed a finger into my mouth so I tasted him too.

"Isn't he beautiful when he cries?" Aidan asked.

There were numerous mumbles of agreement. I wanted to keep going, make them all jealous that I belonged to Aidan, for them to see that my Sir was my world and he deserved to be revered.

I cried harder when he pulled me away. I reached for him, fought to get his cock in my throat again.

"Stand up, turn around, and give me your ass."

"Yes, Sir," I managed to say, but I was still crying. I needed him. Wanted to be filled by him.

There was this small place in the back of my mind where I knew I should be embarrassed. I had my ass out, a cock cage dangling between my legs as I cried and pleaded to be filled, but it didn't matter, none of it did. Only Aidan…my Aidan and me.

Wet fingers pushed inside me, fucked me, stretched me. I rode them like the whore I felt like. Then his fingers were gone, and I felt incredibly empty again before Aidan pulled me back to his lap, shoved his cock in deep, and *yes*…this was what I needed. Him inside me. To be connected to him in my body as well as my mind.

He held my hips as he fucked into me. I felt every eye on me, every touch from Aidan, and reveled in them all. He pulled me again so my back was against his chest, his hand around my throat, not squeezing, but letting me know he was there.

"Mine," he gritted out.

"Yours."

"My hole. My boy."

"Always," I replied through panting breaths.

My dick hurt so, so bad, but I didn't care. He was inside me, and I was serving him, and that was all that mattered.

Aidan praised me, told me how good I felt and how beautiful I was, what a good slut I was for him, and I basked in his admiration and all the eyes on me.

His teeth bit into my shoulder, and he thrust up, his

cock spasming as he pulsed his hot load into me, filling my hole in front of all these people. Cum dribbled from my prick, but it wasn't a proper orgasm.

Then Aidan pulled out, and a plug was shoved inside me.

"My little cumdump," he whispered, holding me. I breathed him in and licked the sweat from his skin as he stroked my body. "Christ, you were perfect. So damn incredible, my sweet, precious boy."

It was Aidan who made me feel those things, all of them. I lost himself in him and smiled.

Time passed, but I didn't pay attention to how much. Eventually David was gathering our things and helping Aidan get me dressed. It was like my muscles didn't work and my bones had turned to jelly.

"Thanks for the help," I heard Aidan tell David.

"Of course. Jesus, he's something else. I think I'm half in love with him too—oh look, he likes that. He's smiling."

I was smiling, wasn't I?

"He's a bit of a praise slut," Aidan said and kissed my cheek.

He carried me to the car and buckled me in. As we drove, it all began to settle in, what had happened, what we'd shared. "Thank you," I whispered.

"You were a good boy, Fin. You served me well."

Oh, I was smiling again.

We got home, and he held my hand as we went inside. My ass was full, my dick still straining.

We went upstairs, and Aidan stripped our clothes and removed my cage. My hunger for him, my need, suddenly began to climb and build inside me again. I yearned for...*something*, though I didn't know what it was. I just knew it was there, waiting, wanting. "Will you tell me I'm yours again? Please, Sir, I need to hear it."

"You're mine." He cupped my cheek. "Always mine." Then he slid his hand down, grabbed my ass, and slipped his fingers between my cheeks. He worked the plug out, then pushed two fingers in. I was tender as hell, and it wasn't comfortable, but I needed it. "My hole. My boy."

"Yesssss," I hissed. "More." Though again, I didn't know what I was begging for. Aidan would. He always did.

He led me to the bathroom and ordered me into the shower. No. It wasn't a shower I wanted, it was him.

"On your knees."

I went. This I could handle. At least I could have my mouth filled with him. I reached for his cock, but he didn't let me take it. Aidan grabbed it and pointed it at me. He was hard, and he waited as I tried to work through what he was doing. Once the first splash of his piss hit my chest, I realized he'd been trying to go, but it had been a struggle because of his hard-on. And oh my God, he was *peeing* on me, and I shouldn't want this, but I did, so very much.

"Does this remind you who you belong to? That they can look but not touch unless I say they can? I'll mark my territory so everyone knows you're mine."

It got on my chest, my shoulders, ran down my body, and I'd never felt more possessed, never felt more owned than I did in that moment, and it was everything.

"Yes…thank you. Yours, Sir. Mark me."

Aidan growled and tugged me to my feet. He pushed his fingers in my hole, like he was testing it. They went easy, and I knew I was filled with lube and cum from earlier. He turned me, shoved his cock in, and…oh…*oh fuck*, he was pissing inside me, coating me there too, claiming me. It wasn't much. He hadn't had much left, and then he kept fucking, and he came inside me again.

"Can I come?" I pleaded.

"Yes." Aidan wrapped his hand around my erection and stroked only twice before my body trembled and I shot my load.

Aidan held me to his chest as we breathed together.

"I don't know how I got so lucky. I will always fight to deserve you, to take care of you and do what's best for you, my beautiful, beautiful boy."

I clawed at him, nearly tried to climb inside his skin. "I love you."

"I love you too."

CHAPTER FORTY-TWO

Aidan

FINLEY COULDN'T KEEP still. When he was sitting down, his leg was bouncing or he was wringing his hands together. Then he would shove to his feet and pace our hotel room from one end to the other, wearing a hole in the carpet. "Finley." When he didn't reply or stop, I said more firmly, "Fin. Stop." He finally did, then walked over to where I sat on the edge of the bed and looked at me.

"I'm sorry, Sir. I'm freaking out a little bit."

"That's understandable." I ran my hands up and down his arms. "You're meeting an aunt you didn't know you had. It's okay to be scared. And if you're not ready, we call and say we'll come tomorrow instead."

They'd tried to get us to stay at the house, but I'd insisted on a hotel room. I believed Jennifer cared about Finley and wanted to get to know him, but I needed to act in his best interests too, and I knew he would need space. This was a lot to take in for anyone.

"I don't want to wait," he replied.

"Then we won't."

"What if they don't like me?"

I stood and cupped his face. "Impossible," I answered, then kissed him. I was more nervous about them not liking me. I was a little gruff, nineteen years older than him, and his Dominant—not that they would know the last part. Not that I cared if they knew, but I figured it was best for Finley. They wouldn't understand, most people didn't, and I knew how much this meant to him. How badly he wanted family. "They'll love you. You're quite addictive."

"Well, yeah, you say that because you fuck me."

I swatted his ass. "Someone will get a spanking when we get back to the room tonight."

Finley grinned. "That helps." He wrapped his arms around me and nuzzled his face into the crease of my arm and chest. "Thank you, Sir. I wouldn't be here without you, and just having you by my side helps."

"That's what I'm here for," I replied, hugging him back.

"Can I wear it?" he asked, and I knew what he was talking about.

"There's a chance they'll see it, and if they do, they

might not understand. I'm going to do everything on my end to make this go well for you, but if you need to wear it, if that'll help you know I'm there, that I'll always be there, that you belong to me, no matter what happens, then yes, you can wear it."

"Please. I need to feel you."

"Then let's go." I dug around in my suitcase. When my fingers wrapped around the leather of his collar, I pulled it out and locked it around his neck. "Change into that blue, short-sleeved, button-up shirt of yours. That will help hide it."

"Yes, Sir."

I had to admit, I loved seeing my collar around his throat.

A few minutes later we went down to the rental car. I entered the address into my phone and began to drive.

"What have you told them about me?" I asked.

"Just that you're my boyfriend. We live together and have for a year and a half."

"They're likely going to be surprised at my age, and they may not approve. You're also naturally subservient to me, in a way that I'm not sure you can hide even if you try. I just want you to remember that there's a possibility these things won't go over well. This is your family, and I know how much that means to you, so you'll have whatever leeway you need while we're with them." It was tricky, as our roles weren't something we slipped in and out of. I controlled all aspects of Finley's life because that was what he needed.

"So don't call you Sir?" he said with a smirk. It felt good to see him grin...but I also gripped the steering wheel tightly. I *was* his Sir, and there was nothing wrong with that. I didn't like hiding it.

"You do what you want, what feels comfortable to you," I said, the words bitter on my tongue. "But keep in mind that you won't be punished. There are ways we can both get what we need without being obvious. And if we are obvious, then I want you to be prepared that it can go badly."

"I know," he replied.

"And it wouldn't be your fault. There's nothing wrong with what we do."

"I know," Finley assured me. "It's all just...a lot. Maybe you should pee on me again." A grin teased his lips, making me laugh. He was so damn special.

"You think you're funny, do you?"

"I make you laugh and smile—more than anyone, according to David."

"David who?" I joked, but the truth was, we all knew he was right. Even the way I was teasing at the moment showed it.

"I still think it was hot, FYI. I hope you do it again."

"Maybe let's not talk about that for now."

Finley crossed his arms. "Yes, Sir."

We were quiet the rest of the drive to their Houston suburb. They lived down a long gravel driveway, and I pulled over on the side of the road before going down it. "Are you okay?"

Finley was fingering his collar, as if it soothed him. "Yes, Sir. I want to get that out of my system now. Sir, Sir, Sir, Sir."

"Christ, I love you." This precious boy had come into my life and blown it all apart. I would never be the same, and I was glad for it. He'd transformed me, made me better, and I would forever be changed because of his strength, bravery, love, and submission.

"I love you too. That's why...that's why this is okay. No matter what happens, I still have *you*."

I nodded once before pulling the car down the driveway. As soon as the large ranch-style house came into view, I noticed a blond woman walking back and forth along the porch. Her eyes darted up and locked on our car.

"I...wow...Aidan, she looks just like my mom," he said softly. I reached over and placed a hand on his thigh before parking and turning off the car.

"You want to leave at any time, you just look at me and I'll know. And if you want to stay all damn night, we'll do that too."

"I know. Thank you." He took a deep breath and got out of the car. His aunt was jogging over, and then Finley was running toward her as I stepped out of the vehicle. They hugged each other and cried. I could see her face and not Finley's, but I knew he was crying as well.

I waited, leaning against the car, giving them time alone.

"I can't believe you're here. You look just like your mom," Jennifer said, still hugging him.

"You look like her too. I guess that means we look like each other?" Finley replied, and damned if I didn't smile.

"Jeff and the girls waited inside. They wanted to give us a moment. I just…Amanda's son. Let me look at you." She pulled away, and that was when her eyes landed on me for the first time. I saw the initial shock, the widening of her eyes, the crease between her brows, but then Finley was pulling away and they were looking at each other.

She touched his face, his hair, studied him, and I

could already see the love there. She wanted a relationship with her nephew, and she hated that they hadn't known about each other.

"Do you go by Fin? Or Finley?"

"Either one."

Then her eyes darted to me again.

"This is Aidan." Finley called me over, and I went. "My *partner*." He grinned, telling me he'd used that word knowing I preferred it to boyfriend. "It's because of him that I'm even here. I never would have had the courage to look for any family without him."

"It's nice to meet you, Aidan. I can't... There are no words to thank you for everything you've done for Finley."

I shook her hand. "You're welcome, but you don't need to thank me. There's nothing I wouldn't do for him."

She shifted a bit uncomfortably but then smiled.

"Mommy! Can we come now?" A small head peeked out the door. Jennifer looked at Finley, who was nearly bursting with excitement.

"Please," he said. "I can't wait to meet them."

"Come and meet your cousin!" she said, and two little girls ran out of the house, followed by a man. His eyes found me first, and again, I saw the surprise, the discomfort, at nothing more than our noticeable age difference, I was sure.

Introductions were made between all of us before they herded us into the house. There were balloons and decorations—flowers and a banner that said "Welcome Home, Finley!"

He wasn't *home* unless he decided he wanted that to be home. Seeing it made white-hot anger stab at me. But then Finley was laughing and so clearly thrilled about it that I shoved my feelings aside. This was for him, and they were his family.

We spent hours there, talking, eating, and getting to know them. The girls loved Finley, and he was great with them. Jennifer was very interested in our relationship—the fact that I was a doctor, and when Finley told them how we met. His aunt had asked, and he'd just blurted out, "I was a waiter, and he came in with his friend. I was sick, and Aidan brought me home with him, and I just…never left."

He grinned, and I bit back a groan. "It was a bit different than that. I gave him a place to get well. He wasn't living in the best circumstances, and when he recovered, I gave him a job. It wasn't until much later that things changed between us." I really hated explaining our relationship to them. It went against every part of myself, but it was for Finley, so I did it.

He felt comfortable with them. That much was evident. As we all spoke, he didn't sit on the couch beside me, automatically going down to the floor between my legs. The girls sat on the carpet too, which could explain it. He was playful with them, but from the looks Jennifer and Jeff exchanged, I was certain they noticed and wondered.

But they were obviously crazy about Finley, and they treated me with respect. When we left that first day, we made plans for the next one.

Finley couldn't stop talking the whole ride back to our hotel, then the whole night. We were back at their house the next day, and it was more of the same—his joy, theirs too, but also their concern about our relationship. It was on the third day that Jennifer spoke to me. Finley, Jeff, and the girls were swimming, and she and I were sitting at a table, not too far away, but far enough to give us privacy.

"I have to admit, I'm a little concerned about the age difference," she said.

"You don't need to be. Finley is an adult. He knows how to take care of himself, and he has me. I love him and would never hurt him." Well...except in ways he wanted to be hurt.

"Yes, but he was nineteen when he moved in with you. I really don't want to be rude. I know it's not my business, but I just... He was vulnerable, and I worry that he's making a big decision."

"Every relationship is a big decision. How old a person is doesn't matter. If Finley wants out, he knows all he has to do is say so."

"He's crazy about you. He looks at you like you're his whole world."

My eyes found him as he played in the water with his cousin on his shoulders. He was laughing and smiling…so damn carefree. "And he's mine."

"He waits on you, yields to you, and—"

"That's quite enough. Our relationship really is no concern of yours."

There was a pause, and then she said, "You're right. I'm sorry." The thing was, I could tell she meant it. She wasn't trying to be hateful; she really did worry about him. She loved him already.

He had that effect on people. They were drawn to him like warm sun on their skin, like he carried your happiness in his chest. I understood it because he'd done the same to me.

CHAPTER FORTY-THREE

Finley

"DO YOU THINK we can extend our trip? Even if it's just a few days?" I asked Aidan two days before we were set to leave. "Jennifer said there's a huge fair coming to town. It's a big deal here, and the girls love to go. They were asking if I could go with them."

"We can't," he replied without looking up from his laptop. "I have to get back to work."

"Oh." My heart sank. I should have known that, obviously. But I was having so much fun there, and I loved getting to know my family.

Aidan looked up at me, because, *duh*, it was Aidan and he always seemed to read me. "I can change your ticket if you'd like. Just because I have to get back home doesn't mean you need to rush."

"What? No. I couldn't stay without you." But really, I could. Why couldn't I hang out with my family without Aidan? "Are you sure you don't mind?"

"Not if it's what you want," he replied, but there was something a little different about his voice. It was…tight.

"Are you sure?"

"Yes, Finley. When have you ever heard me say something I didn't mean?"

I chuckled. "You're right. I don't know what I was thinking."

"Do you want me to keep the room? What about a car?"

"No." I shook my head. "Jennifer said we could stay with her."

Again, he seemed…not like Aidan, and I couldn't put my finger on what it was. But as he said, he didn't say things he didn't mean, and if something was wrong, he would tell me.

"Thank you, Sir." I put my head in his lap, and he played with my hair. "I miss calling you that. It doesn't feel right." But I couldn't imagine what my aunt would say if I walked around calling Aidan my Sir.

"You're happy?" he asked.

"Yes. I never thought I would have this—have family. They're great, and they really care about me. And I have you, so everything is perfect."

"Come," he said and pulled me until I straddled him. He kissed me, then laid me down and pushed his cock deep into my ass, owning me, possessing me. Loving me.

"Mine," he said as he fucked into me.

"Yours," I replied, and nothing would ever change that.

CHAPTER FORTY-FOUR

Aidan

"WHAT'S YOUR PROBLEM?"

"Nothing," I snapped at David as we shared a meal. "Fuck. I'm sorry." I'd been a miserable bastard all day. Hell, I'd been one for a while now, and I knew it. I couldn't seem to stop myself, though.

David sighed. "When does your boy come home?"

I rubbed a hand over my face. It had been two weeks since I got on a plane in Houston, without him. A few days turned into more, and the truth was, I didn't know when he was coming back. We talked every day. He shared what they'd been up to and told me he missed me. He asked permission each time he postponed his trip home, and he asked if I could give him a modified schedule for when he was gone. I hadn't left him with one at all, but he'd missed it, he said, and so he wanted me to decide simple things like when he would wake up, when he would go to bed, and when we spoke each night.

Still, it wasn't enough. I missed him, but I also knew I had no right to ask him to come home. Even as his Dom, I wouldn't do that. Finley needed this. He was getting to know his family, and I would never take that away from him.

"I'm not sure," I replied without looking at David.

"He is coming home, though, right?"

"Yes, of course. I just... He deserves this. I won't be the one to take it away from him. And if he decides that's where he wants to be, I'll have to let him go." I would hate it. Even the thought set my teeth on edge, but I would do it if it was what was best for him. From the beginning, that had always been what I'd wanted. I'd sworn I would never trap him, never hold him back, that all I wanted was to see him grow.

I wouldn't be the one to chop off his wings when he tried to fly.

I wouldn't be my father, no matter how much I wanted nothing more than to demand he come home, and keep him there forever.

"Aidan..."

"I don't want to talk about it," I told David. He must have been able to tell I was serious, because he gave me a sad smile and dropped the subject.

CHAPTER FORTY-FIVE

Finley

I WAS REALLY starting to get homesick.

I loved being with Jenn and the girls. It was... Hell, it was more than I ever thought I would have, but I was starting to feel antsy, edgy, and I missed Aidan. I couldn't wear his collar all the time because I wasn't sure how my family would react. When I could, I kept it on, covered it with a shirt, but I felt off without it, without him.

But I was also scared that if I left, I would lose them. They would realize they didn't care about me or end up forgetting me. That something would happen and I would lose them like I'd lost Mom, or how Aidan had lost his family, and I'd just found them. How could I risk that?

It was a Saturday, and Jenn and I were out together. Jeff had stayed home with the girls, giving us some time to just hang out. We got pedicures and went to lunch, and now we were at a park, walking around.

"I wanted to run something by you," she said as we sat down at a picnic table under the shade of a weeping tree.

"Yeah, sure. What's up?"

"I know this is going to sound crazy, and it's a lot really fast, but I've put quite a bit of thought into this and discussed it with Jeff. We both love you so much, and so do the girls. It's like having a piece of my sister with me again, but even more than that, you're a great kid, and I love spending time with you."

Okay…only I wasn't a kid.

"You're a part of this family, and I hate that you were taken away from us for so long. It's not fair. It wasn't fair to Mandy, and it's not fair to you, and I'd like to make up for that. We wanted to ask if you'd be interested in staying here, in moving to Houston to be with us. You could work with Jeff at his construction company, or if you didn't want to do that, you could go to school. You can stay with us, or you could stay in the small duplex Jeff and I own and have your own place. You've never had your own place, have you? I still have some of the inheritance my parents left us, and Jeff and I both agree that should go to you. You have a right to it as Amanda's son. There will be paperwork and things like that we have to do, but that's not important. I just...yeah, that's it."

I sat there dumbfounded. I had no idea what to say. I was ecstatic they loved me that much, that my mom's sister was there and really wanted me to be in the family, but... "My life is in California. What about Aidan?"

"Oh, sweetie." She reached over and put her hand on my thigh. "I know you care about him a lot, but you're so young. There will be other guys, boys closer to your age, who you'll have more in common with."

"I have plenty in common with Aidan." Maybe not the kind of things she would understand, but we had them. And he made me feel good. Made me laugh and made me want more for myself. I loved him, and that wouldn't change.

"Is it okay to admit I worry about you? He's basically twenty years older than you, and there's something...I don't know, a little controlling about him?"

"Aidan doesn't do anything to me I don't want," I snapped.

"I'm sorry. I really don't mean to attack him. He's a very nice man, and I'll support you whatever you decide. If you love him, you love him. I'll always be here for you. I just... We're your family, and we were robbed of so many years together. Will you promise me you'll at least think about it?"

She *was* my family, and we had lost so much time. I didn't want to lose her again, so I nodded. "Okay. I'll think about it."

It was all I could do for the rest of the day. My mother's sister wanted me move to Houston with them, with my family, but in going, I would lose Aidan. He gave me everything I never thought I could have, everything I'd ever wanted, but he couldn't give me this...my family, and I wanted them too.

Back at the house, I said I wasn't feeling well and excused myself to my room. The girls were disappointed. I'd promised I would play with them, and I loved spending time with them. Kids of my own definitely wasn't something I wanted, but I enjoyed other people's.

When dinner was done, I skipped that too. Jenn gave me a sad smile as she closed my door, and that small thing made me think about Aidan. Oh God, if I'd tried to skip a meal with him, he'd have my ass...and I liked it. He was so particular about being healthy, and regular meals, and blah, blah, blah. Sometimes it drove me crazy, but most of the time it made me feel special, loved.

I texted him when it was time for our nightly phone call and asked if I could call him later. I lied and told him we were watching a movie and I didn't want to miss it, when the truth was, I wanted to talk to Aidan alone, when everyone else was sleeping.

It was after midnight when the house was completely quiet. My hand shook slightly as I picked up my phone to video-call him. He would know something was wrong. All it would take was one look from Aidan to know, and I was nervous to see how he would react.

"Hey," I said, the moment he accepted the call and his handsome face showed up on the screen.

"What's wrong?"

"Nothing."

He sighed. "Try again. What's wrong? I was going to allow you to jack off tonight, but now I won't."

"Aidan," I whined because I really wanted to come. He hadn't let me much since I'd been in Houston without him.

"Don't make me ask again, Finley." His voice was steady, firm, as always, but there was a soft lilt of worry to it.

"I, um…Jenn asked me to stay, to move here with them, in their house or a place they own. And there's money for me too, apparently? She wants to transfer part of her inheritance to me. She said I can work with Jeff or go to school." It was so strange saying those words. A year ago, I wanted nothing to do with school, but now I knew I still wanted to go. I could do that here or in California, obviously, but it was just funny to consider. All I'd ever wanted before was to serve, and while I still wanted that, while I still took joy in being Aidan's houseboy, I wanted more now as well.

"I see," he said, without much emotion. "I can't say I'm surprised. I figured that would be where this would go. I guess the important question is, what do you want, Finley?"

"I don't know." I shook my head. "You're supposed to tell me what to do."

"Not in this, precious boy," he replied softly, sadly.

"What should I do?"

"Again, that's something I can't say. This is your life, Fin. Your choice. I can't tell you what's best for you in this. I'm just a man, like any other."

"What if I make the wrong decision?"

"Then you're human too. Listen to me for a moment—everything we've been doing, all the lessons I've tried to teach you, all the time I tried to show you that you *could* be on your own, that you *can* do anything, it's all been leading up to this moment. When I said I wanted you to be the best you could be, I meant that. When I said I wanted you to be able to stand on your own, I meant that too. Yes, I want you to submit to me, but also to be able to be strong on your own, to feel confident in yourself, and to be able to make important decisions when you *need* to. Like I've said before, I can't always be there. This choice has to be yours."

Logically, Aidan being my Dom didn't mean he knew everything, that he was perfect, but he knew me, knew me like no one else ever could or would. But in the back of my mind, I also knew he was right. He'd been giving me these tools all along. He'd been telling me that I needed to be able to stand on my own, that I could choose to be on my knees for him, to serve him, but I also needed to be able to be my own man.

"I don't want to lose them," I said, because it was easier than thinking about the rest of it.

"They're your family. You won't lose them for this, and if you do, they weren't very good family to begin with."

"I love you."

"I'm not going anywhere."

"I need you. I can't serve you from another state."

"You don't need me, Fin. You never did, precious boy. Want me, yes, but you don't need me. And if you stayed, we could figure it out, but you're looking at this the wrong way. You're afraid of losing me and afraid of losing them, but again, the important question is, what do you *want*?"

"I don't know!" I shouted, tugging at my hair. But really, I did know, didn't I? I was just scared.

"Finley," Aidan said softly. When I didn't answer, he said it again, with a little more meat to it. "*Finley.*"

"Yes, Sir." And oh, did that feel good to say. How could I not spend my days respecting my Sir?

"I love you, but I've told you from the beginning that I would only do what's best for you. This is something I truly can't answer for you. Only you know what's best for you. Trust yourself."

"I'm scared."

"I know, but I believe in you. You're my good boy. You'll make the right decision."

"I...I think I have to go."

He nodded. "Fifteen minutes, and then I want you to go to sleep. Stay in bed at least eight hours. Tomorrow morning eat a healthy breakfast and find somewhere to work out, even if you have to get a temporary pass somewhere. I know you think you hate it, but if you're honest with yourself, you'll admit it clears your head."

A small smile tugged at my lips. He was right. Aidan was always right. "Yes, Sir."

"I'll speak to you soon, little warrior." Then, before I could reply, Aidan ended the call.

CHAPTER FORTY-SIX

Aidan

I WAS LOSING my damn mind.

Finley was in my thoughts all day. I struggled between feeling that I should have ordered him home and knowing I'd done the right thing. I knew what I wanted him to do, but this truly wasn't a decision I could make for him, no matter how much I wanted to.

The hospital was crazy. We had a five-car pileup with multiple trauma victims. I spent four hours in surgery. It was the only time I was able to push thoughts of Finley to the back burner. My patient had come through his operation well and was currently in the ICU.

The house felt empty when I went home, the way it had since he left. I'd spent my life living alone, taking care of myself, but now living without him felt…off. Like my world wasn't on its axis any longer.

He didn't call me that night, and I didn't call him.

I was off the next day. It was a grocery-shopping day,

so I went to the store, marking things off the list the way Finley did, comparing prices with amounts. Not that I needed to, but I liked that he did, and it made me feel closer to him.

I made dinner, got in an extra workout, and then…fuck, I watched television. I *hated* TV, but then, I guess I really didn't. It wasn't something I'd shared with him, but I enjoyed our evenings together, watching whatever silly show he was into.

It was about ten when I went upstairs and showered. I washed my body, my hair, then turned off the faucet. As I stepped out, I grabbed a towel from the rack and began drying myself off. Then, with the towel wrapped around my waist, I went back into the bedroom and—

"Finley? What are you doing here?"

"I just got home."

He was kneeling beside the bed, his head down, his palms on his thighs. He was beautiful sitting there, waiting for me. Beautiful and mine.

"Please," he said, and I stepped closer to him, stopped as I stood right in front of him.

"What do you need?"

"Whatever you wish," he replied. There was nothing like hearing those words from him. "Whatever you want. I just want to serve you." I didn't know if he meant now or always, but whatever it was, I would give it to him. I would give him anything.

He was so incredible, I couldn't help but look at him a moment—this warrior boy who'd stolen my heart. I couldn't believe he was here. Couldn't believe how much I needed him. I knew Finley thought it was him who needed me, but that wasn't true.

"Take your clothes off. Lie on your back."

"Yes, Sir," he replied, then scrambled to get out of his clothes. He folded them and set them aside. My eyes caught on my collar around his neck, making the surge of possessiveness inside me swell until I nearly drowned from it.

I removed my towel and went to the closet. A moment later I came out with a blindfold. "Sit up."

"Yes, Sir."

Finley did as told, a smile on those lips of his, and I couldn't stop myself from leaning in and taking them, savoring his taste and the familiar slide of his mouth against mine.

I couldn't believe my fingers trembled as I tied the cloth around his eyes.

"Colors?"

"Yellow and red."

"Good boy. Lie down again."

I went back to the closet. If he stayed, we would have to expand our collection, maybe turn one of the rooms in the house into a playroom for us.

Finley hissed when I placed the cuffs around his wrists, then lifted his arms over his head so I could clip them onto hooks on the headboard. "Those are new," he said softly.

"I was hopeful I'd get to use them with you."

"Aidan…"

"Shh. Let me give you this." I needed it for myself too.

"Yes, Sir."

From there I added cuffs to his ankles, adjusting the chain and hooking them to the footboard, spreading his legs.

His balls were full and tight, his cock pink and hard. "Christ, you're beautiful." I kissed his chest, his stomach, as Finley writhed beneath me. "This is going to hurt."

I attached the first screw clamp to his right nipple—not too tight since it was his first time, but enough that he could feel it. Finley arched off the bed. "*Ahhh*," he cried out. "Oh *God*, what's that?"

"I don't think I'll tell you, unless you need to know. Just feel, precious boy. Let me know if it's too much." I wanted him helpless, needed him wanting and waiting and never knowing what I would do to him and when. "Are you with me?"

"Yes...yes, Aidan." He took deep breaths, obviously trying to settle himself. He pulled slightly on his arms but couldn't go far.

"Ready for the next one?"

"Yes, Sir." I clamped his other nipple. Finley pulled against the cuffs, his body vibrating beneath me.

"I wish you could see yourself like this, so beautiful, such a good boy, letting me have my way with you."

"Please," he begged. I kissed his chest again, down his stomach, then took his cock into my mouth. "Aidan!" Finley jolted off the mattress, but again, he couldn't go far, just arch and bow and writhe.

"Don't come," I ordered before sucking him again, savoring his cock, this gift he gave me as I tortured him with pleasure.

I tasted his precum on my tongue, blowing him and watching his body's reactions. When he was close to coming, I'd pull off, and he'd cry out and beg for more. I gave it to him, wanting more of those sounds, and his words, anything and everything this boy would give me.

"I can't... I'm going to come." He shook his head, his body fighting against the binds.

"You can and you won't. I'm not done with this cock

yet." I sucked his tight balls before going back to his rod again. My finger slid beneath him, and I teased his rim but didn't push inside. I wanted him mindless with pleasure, delirious with need.

"Aidan...Aidan...Aidan," he said over and over again.

When I pulled off him, he whined.

"Be good, you horny boy," I teased, plucking the crop from the bed. I tapped it lightly against his chest.

"Aidan!" His body jerked again. "It's so much...not knowing what to expect...what I'm going to feel. My whole body is buzzing."

"That's the way I want you." I used the crop on his chest, his thighs, then gave him a smack to his cock.

"Oh *God*." And the way he moved, I could tell his eyes had rolled back. "Please, give me more."

My hits weren't hard, just teasing little stings against his full balls and his cock. Precum dripped from his slit and pooled on his belly. He was babbling words I couldn't understand, tugging and thrashing about as much as he could. My own prick was aching, my balls tight and eager to unload. I needed him, needed inside him, so I dropped the crop just as he begged, "Please, Sir, will you please fuck me?"

I was trembling as I unhooked his legs and arms. I

flipped him to his stomach and pulled him up onto his knees. With impatient fingers, I lubed my cock, using more than usual. I pushed against his rim slowly, but he shoved back against me.

"Settle. I didn't stretch you at all, so I need to take my time."

"Yes…yes, Sir. I'm trying."

The second I pushed the head in, I exhaled. And when I was buried deep, groin against his ass, I knew that if he asked, I would leave for him. I would go to Houston, would follow this precious boy all over the world if it meant he still belonged to me, that he would still serve me, because this, with Finley, was where I belonged.

Where *we* belonged.

I pulled him until he was kneeling with his back against my chest as I fucked into him. I bit his neck and licked it, then sucked his earlobe. "Mine," I whispered. "Whatever you want, just ask, and I'll give it to you."

"You, I only need you."

I removed the first clamp, and he cried out, his body tightening.

"Please."

"Almost. You can hold off for me."

I took the second one off and dropped it. I stroked

his cock and kissed his neck. "Come, Fin. You can come."

And he did. He tensed and shot and cried so, so beautifully for me. My release was there, buzzing at the base of my spine as I fucked into him. I let go and shot, filling him with my load as my own eyes became blurry too.

Finley went limp, and I rolled him to his back, licked his cum from his belly, and kissed him, feeding it to him.

He cried harder. My fingers fumbled with the blindfold as I removed it, and then I pulled him into my arms. Finley buried himself in my armpit, licking and breathing and loving me.

"I love you." I petted his sweaty, slick hair.

And when he cried even harder at that, a brick landed in my gut. I couldn't help wondering if this had been goodbye.

CHAPTER FORTY-SEVEN

Finley

I DIDN'T KNOW how long we lay there, Aidan holding me and kissing my temple, my nose, the top of my head, telling me it was okay, that whatever I felt or wanted was okay.

And I knew it was, because I knew Aidan.

I also knew because…well, because now I knew myself. He was right. It had all been leading up to this moment, to this choice. I'd been forced to grow up too quickly, and in some ways, I'd been slightly immature because of that. I was Aidan's boy, but now I felt more like…well, like a man. Like I *could* be on my own if I wanted.

There also wasn't a doubt in my mind that with him was where I belonged.

When I could form complete thoughts and words, I told him, "I love you."

"I love you too."

Pushing up on my elbows, I looked down at him, at my Sir, who meant everything to me. "I don't want to go. I don't want to leave you. I don't ever want to leave you."

His eyes softened, almost…sad. "If you're afraid to lose me, you won't. As I said, we'll figure it out. You can spend time in both places, or I'll go to Houston. Whatever you need, Fin, because I don't want to lose you either."

I gasped at his admission. I knew Aidan loved me. There was no way I could doubt that because I felt it in everything he did, but to know he would leave for me…that was incredible.

But I also didn't want it.

"This is my home. My mom is buried here. We live our life together here. I love our house and our life and our friends. I don't want to move to Houston. Mom used to tell me that as hard as it was, Los Angeles breathed life into her, showed her a new world, and it's like that for me too. I was just scared and confused."

"Are you sure? This isn't a decision you have to make today."

"It's a truth I've always known and a decision I've already made. I spoke with Jenn about it."

"Such a brave, precious boy." He cupped my cheek

and kissed the tip of my nose.

"She said she understood and that she had a feeling I would say that. I told her that I love you and want to be with you, but that it was more than just you. School, Jordan, Ian, David, this city that can break you but can also build you up."

This time it was me who leaned in, me who kissed the tip of his nose. Aidan rolled his eyes playfully, but I could tell he liked it.

"We can go to Texas often, and you can go as much as you want."

I smiled. "I told her you would say that too. She said she wants to get to know you better, wants to know the man her nephew loves so much."

Aidan grinned, this spark in his eyes I'd never seen before. It hit me then, that this was something else I could give Aidan—family. He was alone just as I was. Jenn, Jeff, and the girls could be... "They're your family too."

"I don't think you know what you do to me," Aidan replied softly.

"I do know. I see it. I feel it in everything you do, in every look you turn toward me, and you give me just as much. You came into my life at three different points, Aidan, all when I needed you. That has to mean something, don't you think? Serving you, being your boy and you being my Sir, it's meant to be."

He shook his head, not in disagreement, but maybe in awe. "I never believed in anything like that before, but I think I agree with you."

"You think?" I teased, then gasped when he flipped me and was suddenly on top of me.

"Be a good boy, Finley."

"I'm always a good boy." His boy. His precious boy, and there was nowhere else I belonged, nowhere I would rather be than here, serving him, being hurt and loved by him. My Sir.

EPILOGUE

Aidan

One Year Later

"MARCO!" MELODY CALLED from on top of my shoulders.

"Polo!" Harmony, Finley, Ian, Jordan, and Jennifer all called from different areas of our pool.

David and Jeff were sitting at the table, talking. We were playing the game a bit differently. Melody had her eyes closed and was directing me which way to go, and so far we weren't doing great, but she was giggling and happy, which I enjoyed.

"Dat way! Go dat way!" she yelled.

"Which way?" I questioned, but then I heard Finley laugh and went for him. My arms went around him and I pulled him close, which made Melody laugh again. "That's it. I'm done. We won," I told her. She cheered, and I helped her off and put her on the cement.

It had been quite the year. Finley spent at least a

three-day weekend in Texas every two months. He'd spent two weeks there at the beginning of summer. Sometimes I went with him, sometimes I didn't, but I'd gotten to know the family more. They were beginning to feel like my family as well, only I wasn't quite as open with it as I could be. I didn't have Finley's ability to open my heart as easily, except with the two little girls who had me wrapped around their fingers.

This was their first time to California. The summer was coming to an end, and we'd wanted to bring the girls to Disneyland. Finley would be starting school again. He'd begun taking a fuller course load the previous fall. He still didn't know what he wanted to do, but that was okay. He had time to figure that out.

His aunt had made good on her promise and given him some of the inheritance. He'd struggled to take it, but they'd insisted. I didn't pay him any longer, something that was his hard limit, but he still served me and took care of our home the same as before because that was who we were and neither of us wanted that to change.

Jordan and Ian spent quite a bit of time at the house, and I still thought Jordan was curious about the lifestyle. Finley had asked him about it, and Jordan said he would let him know if it was something he wanted to try. He teased about having a sugar daddy, but that was the extent of it.

Finley and I had played with David once, in the fall of last year. He'd loved it, and he'd been gorgeous and served us both well, but we also knew it wasn't something we wanted to do again. He was mine, and I didn't want to share him, and Fin said he only needed me. I still believed it had been a good experience for him. He knew there were options, and he chose to be with me because it was where he wanted to be, not where he had to be.

We finished our pool games, and I cooked dinner on the grill. At one point, Finley sneaked up behind me and whispered, "What can I do?"

"Go finish the salad."

"Yes, Sir," he answered softly. We teased the line, not flat out showing the relationship we had in front of the family, but also not totally straying away from it when they were around. We both craved it too much.

While he was gone, Jenn made her way over to me. "Do you need any help?"

"I'm good. Thanks. You're welcome to visit with me, though."

She smiled. "You know, I've wanted to say this for a while—I was wrong about you. I still think the age difference is huge, but…you love him. I know there isn't anything you wouldn't do for Finley, and he loves you too. And he's happy. He has a good life here. That's all we can ever really want for our family."

I smiled, her words settling into my chest. "Thank you, and yes, I love him very much." He was my world. My boy. Owning him, dominating him, belonging to him just as completely as he belonged to me, was more than I could have ever hoped for in life, and I would always be thankful that he chose me.

She nodded, then went back to her husband.

We ate together, and then David left, followed by Jordan and Ian, then Jenn, Jeff, and the girls. They were here for a few more days but were staying at a hotel close by.

The second they were gone, Finley fell to his knees. "God, I missed kneeling for you. It was only a few hours, but it's torture knowing I can't, you know?"

I went into the living room, and he crawled behind me. "I know," I finally replied. "Come."

He climbed onto the couch.

"I think I need my little cock warmer."

"Yes, Sir!" A happy smile split Finley's lips, and his eyes sparked. I was still in awe of how eager he was to please me and how beautifully he did it.

He opened my jeans, lay with his head in my lap, and nursed my dick, while I turned on the new show we had started. He drooled down me and kept nuzzling my balls and inhaling my scent as we watched, and I stroked his hair.

We finished a couple of episodes, and then I ordered him to get me off, which he did, swallowing my load hungrily. He begged me to let him come, but I didn't allow it. I loved torturing him too much.

I patted my lap, and he straddled it and looked at me. "You please me more than you'll ever know," I told him.

"That's not true, Sir. I do know. I feel it."

He had given me so much—his service, his body, his love, a family. In so many ways, the beginning of our journey had been about Finley finding himself, about being able to stand on his own and knowing he had options, but somehow along the way, I'd found myself too. I'd stumbled upon my own happiness, in the finding of Finley. And I was proud of who I was—the man who knew how to love and gave it freely to his precious boy. "I love you."

"I love you too," he replied. "Always."

And this time, I didn't tell him he was too young or that always was a long time. I knew now that we were both where we belonged and forever would be.

Join Riley's Newsletter

Find Riley:

Reader's Group: facebook.com/groups/RileysRebels2.0

Facebook: rileyhartwrites

Twitter: @RileyHart5

Goodreads:
goodreads.com/author/show/7013384.Riley_Hart

THE HAVENWOOD SERIES

Thank you for reading Finding Finley. The first book in my new series will be dropping in March 2020! If you enjoy small-town romances, blue-collar guys, and books with a strong group of friends, then Havenwood might just be what you're looking for! It'll be a three- or four-book series, beginning with Giving Chase.

Acknowledgement

I know my writing is a little all over the place sometimes, so I'd like to thank my readers for sticking with me. Whether it's light and fun like Fever Falls, or something a little heavier and kinkier like Finding Finley, know that every story I write, comes from the heart.

I'd also like to thank Kate, Mia, Christina, Morningstar, Jenn, and Melinda for the beta reads!

Other Books by Riley Hart

Standalone titles with Devon McCormack:
Beautiful Chaos, Weight of the World & Up for the Challenge

Standalone titles with Christina Lee:
Of Sunlight and Stardust.

Boys in Makeup Series with Christina Lee:
Pretty Perfect

Fever Falls
Fired Up
#Burn by Devon McCormack
Whiskey Throttle
#Royal by Devon McCormack
Game On co-authored with Devon McCormack

Saint and Lucky
Something About You
Something About Us

Standalone
His Truth
Looking for Trouble
Endless Stretch of Blue
Love Always

Jared and Kieran
Jared's Evolution
Jared's Fulfillment

Metropolis Series: With Devon McCormack
Faking It
Working It
Owning It
Finding It
Trying It
Hitching It

Last Chance Series:
Depth of Field
Color Me In

Wild Side Series:
Dare You To
Gone For You
Tied to You

Crossroads Series:
Crossroads
Shifting Gears
Test Drive
Jumpstart

Rock Solid Construction Series:
Rock Solid

Broken Pieces Series:
Broken Pieces
Full Circle
Losing Control

Blackcreek Series:
Collide
Stay
Pretend
Return to Blackcreek

Forbidden Love Series with Christina Lee:
Ever After: A Gay Fairy Tale
Forever Moore: A Gay Fairy Tale

About the Author

Riley Hart has always been known as the girl who wears her heart on her sleeve. She won her first writing contest in elementary school, and although she primarily focuses on male/male romance, under her various pen names, she's written a little bit of everything. Regardless of the sub-genre, there's always one common theme and that's…romance! No surprise seeing as she's a hopeless romantic herself. Riley's a lover of character-driven plots, flawed characters, and always tries to write stories and characters people can relate to. She believes everyone deserves to see themselves in the books they read. When she's not writing, you'll find her reading or enjoying time with her awesome family in their home in North Carolina.

Riley Hart is represented by Jane Dystel at Dystel, Goderich & Bourret Literary Management. She's a 2019 Lambda Literary Award Finalist for *Of Sunlight and Stardust*. Under her pen name, her young adult novel, *The History of Us* is an ALA Rainbow Booklist Recommended Read and *Turn the World Upside Down* is a Florida Authors and Publishers President's Book Award Winner.

Find Riley:
Reader's Group: facebook.com/groups/RileysRebels2.0
Facebook: rileyhartwrites
Twitter: @RileyHart5
Goodreads:
goodreads.com/author/show/7013384.Riley_Hart

Printed in the USA
CPSIA information can be obtained
at www.ICGtesting.com
LVHW012140200823
755777LV00023B/361